TOP STOREY MURDER

ANTHONY BERKELEY

HOUSE OF STRATUS

This edition published in 2001 by House of Stratus, an imprint of
House of Stratus Ltd, Thirsk Industrial Park, York Road, Thirsk,
North Yorkshire, YO7 3BX, UK.

www.houseofstratus.com

Typeset, printed and bound by House of Stratus.

A catalogue record for this book is available from the British Library
and the Library of Congress.

ISBN 0–7551–0213–4

chapter one

Roger Sheringham sat on the corner of Chief Inspector Moresby's table at Scotland Yard, prattling of this and that. Occasionally the chief inspector grunted a response, but without looking up from the dossier which he was studying. An onlooker might have feared that few of his companion's words penetrated past the barrier of the chief inspector's ears.

Perhaps some such feeling occurred to Roger himself, for he suddenly thumped the table with his fist. 'Moresby! You told me you'd be ready by one o'clock. It's ten past already, by your official clock. I don't care whether you want your lunch or not; I want mine.'

The chief inspector closed the dossier with a sigh. 'Very well, Mr Sheringham. I was only looking up a point or two in that forgery case you asked me about. I'm ready.' He heaved his burly form out of its chair and walked over to where his hat hung by the door.

Roger jumped alertly off the table, snatching up his own hat and gloves. He had asked the chief inspector out to lunch with him, as he did once or twice a month. He called it 'keeping in touch with Scotland Yard'. Scotland Yard called it 'Mr Sheringham working the pump–handle.'

As the chief inspector's hand touched the door handle the telephone on his table rang sharply.

'Excuse me one moment, sir,' said Moresby.

'Blast,' said Roger

Moresby lifted the receiver and listened. Still listening, he edged round the angle of the table, dropped back again into his chair, reached out for pencil and pad, and began to take notes. Roger noted these actions with disapproval. His lunch receded from him as he watched.

'Yes, sir,' said Moresby briskly, in conclusion. 'And I'll take Sergeant Afford, shall I? At once, sir, yes.' He replaced the receiver, waited a moment, then called another extension number.

'Hell,' observed Roger, in moody valediction to his lunch.

The chief inspector proceeded to call four other extension numbers, making an appointment at the entrance in three minutes' time with each.

'Sorry, Mr Sheringham,' he said perfunctorily, as he hung up the receiver finally. 'That knocks our lunch on the head, I'm afraid. Some other day, perhaps.'

'What's the trouble?'

'Murder. Block of flats up Euston way. Old woman been done in. I've got to get up there at once.'

'Murder?' Roger repeated, brightening. 'No objection to my coming along, I suppose?'

Moresby looked doubtful. 'No objection, perhaps; but I don't think you'd find much to interest you. Just an ordinary case of burglary and murder. No fancy fandangos, like you get in the storybooks. It'll just be a matter of routine, getting our hands on the chap who did it. Dull, you'd find it.'

'I'll come,' Roger said firmly.

'Well, perhaps it wouldn't be a bad thing for you to see what poor old Scotland Yard really can do,' said the chief inspector, in not unmalicious acquiescence. 'This is the sort of case we do know how to handle,' he added, as they passed out into the cement-floored corridor. 'The sort of case we get ninety-nine times out of a hundred. You'll be surprised how quick we get to the bottom of it.'

'Scotland Yard could never surprise me,' said Roger demurely.

In front of the entrance two long-nosed cars were already waiting. Chatting to the driver of one was the detective-sergeant who usually worked with Moresby, Afford; he and Roger exchanged nods of recognition. Making a third in the group was Detective-Inspector Beach, who specialised in this type of crime, burglary in flats. Close on their own heels arrived Detective-Sergeant Andrews, the fingerprint expert, carrying a small case that contained his simple apparatus, and scarcely a minute later the photographer, Detective-Constable Farrar, with his camera. Without a second wasted the cars hurried out of the yard.

Roger was in the first car, in front with the driver. Wedged in the back seat between Sergeant Afford and Inspector Beach, Moresby began at once to pass on to his subordinates the outline of the case which he had received over the telephone from his superintendent. Roger leaned over the back of his own seat to hear it.

The dead woman, it appeared, was a Miss Barnett. An elderly woman, she lived alone in a small flat, No. 8, Monmouth Mansions, in Platts Street, a quiet turning off the Euston Road. At the back of the flats was a well courtyard with access from an alley which ran parallel with Platts Street, to which it was connected by another alley at right angles. From Miss Barnett's kitchen window, which overlooked this courtyard, the inhabitants of the neighbouring flats had noticed this morning a rope hanging to the ground. This, combined with the fact that Miss Barnett had not taken in her milk, and the remembrance of certain strange noises from her flat in the middle of the night, had aroused the neighbours' curiosity; but, with the true Londoner's dislike of interfering in other people's affairs, nobody had done anything about it until half-an-hour ago.

The woman occupying the other flat on the top floor of the building had then gone so far as to knock on Miss Barnett's door. Getting no reply, she had communicated her fears to the caretaker, who had summoned a constable. He, prudent man, knowing the trouble which may await the policeman, however well-intentioned, who breaks forcibly into a Briton's dwelling when he is not wanted, had summoned his sergeant before taking action. Together the two had broken in Miss Barnett's front door, to find its mistress lying dead on the floor in her bedroom and the flat looking as if a herd of cattle had passed through it – contents of the drawers strewing the floor, furniture overturned, cushions ripped up, and general upheaval.

'Ah!' said Inspector Beach sapiently. 'And a rope to the window, eh?' Roger knew that he was conning his well-packed memory for burglars who made a mess of the flats they tackled, and those who used a rope for effecting an entrance or an exit, and those who used violence when surprised. There would be other minor indications of personal peculiarities on the intruder's part to be discovered on the spot, and they too would each suggest a list of names to the inspector's mind. When the same name appeared on each of the half-dozen or so lists which the crime would provide, there was the murderer. So simply are the mysteries solved with which Scotland Yard almost invariably has to deal, as opposed to those invented for them by ingenious novelists.

The rest of the procedure had followed its normal course. Hustling the white-faced caretaker out of the flat, the sergeant had left the constable on guard by the broken door, sent a messenger post-haste for the nearest doctor and himself hurried to an adjacent police-box, where he called up on the telephone his divisional inspector and CID direct, reporting the discovery shortly but with every relevant detail, thereby showing the latter exactly what experts and apparatus were to be rushed at once to the scene. Within twenty minutes from the breaking-in of the door, the full forces of criminal investigation were actually on the spot.

Besides the four of his men (not including Roger) whom Chief Inspector Moresby had brought with him, there were concentrated in addition within that same period in the little flat, having anticipated the arrival of the Scotland Yard contingent by a few minutes, the doctor in private practice brought by the sergeant's messenger, the divisional inspector, and a second constable; the divisional police surgeon arrived two minutes later. Including Roger, twelve men in all. Yet there was no confusion. No large feet fell over other large feet; each man knew exactly his job, and either did it or stood by waiting to do it.

The first constable continued to guard the door, the second was stationed at the street-door, with instructions to admit no one to the building but its residents; the sergeant stood by on the landing for orders, together with the fingerprint man, whose turn had not yet come; Sergeant Afford shepherded Mrs Boyd, the caretaker, down to her own ground-floor flat, there first to soothe her outraged nerves and then to extract from her, with practised skill, every atom of information she possessed concerning the dead woman, her habits, her character and her way of life, and anything else relevant to the case that he could unearth; Detective-Inspector Beach took stock of the sitting-room from the doorway but did not go inside, for the floor had not yet been examined; the two doctors talked in low tones in the passage, whither the first summoned, Dr Akenhead, a tubby, red-faced little man, had retired after an initial hasty and superficial examination of the body, during which the divisional inspector had hung anxiously over him to ensure that he did not disturb its position by an unnecessary fraction; the latter was now in the bedroom with Moresby, who was directing the photographing of the body and the room as the first step of all in this seemingly complicated plan of investigatory action; and Roger, feeling distinctly in the way, very much out of place, and yet exceedingly glad that he had forfeited his lunch and come, was hovering in the bedroom doorway, trying to keep an eye on everything at once.

In a heap on the floor in the middle of the room sprawled the slight body of an old woman, clad in a pink flannel nightdress, with an expression on her dead face at which Roger tried not to keep looking.

As soon as the necessary photographs had been taken, Moresby called the doctors and asked them to make their examination, on which the divisional inspector stayed to keep an official eye, while he himself conducted the photographer on a tour of the other rooms, deciding as he went exactly what views he wished recorded. That done, and the photographer let loose to develop his negatives, the chief inspector made his way to the sitting-room.

'I'll just have a look round here myself,' he remarked genially to Inspector Beach, 'and then you and Andrews can get busy.'

Hovering in the doorway, Roger watched with interest the proceedings of the detective in charge.

Chief Inspector Moresby evidently did not believe in delegating to his subordinates jobs which he considered he could perform more efficiently himself. Down on his chief inspectorial hands and knees he plumped, looking like a benevolent walrus, and proceeded to crawl about the floor, examining rapidly but with close attention every square inch of the none too clean carpet. If the business had not been so serious, Roger would have smiled at the appearance he presented.

Rising at last to his feet he glanced ruefully at his blackened hands and the knees of his trousers. 'And nothing to show for it,' he observed to the two in the doorway. 'Not a footprint, nor even a bit of mud. It's a nice, muddy October, too.'

'Well, I don't wonder that an extra bit of dirt wouldn't show up on this carpet,' Roger remarked.

'It would if it was there,' replied the chief inspector with casual confidence. 'Something for you though, Beach,' he added, with a jerk of his head towards the table in the middle of the room, on which stood a half-empty whisky bottle and a dirtied glass.

'Yes, sir,' the inspector replied with satisfaction. 'So I see.' That is another subdivision of individual idiosyncrasy; those burglars who help themselves to a drink on the house after completing a job, and those who do not; and those who do, do so invariably (when the house can supply a drink), and whose who do not never do; the tendency among burglars appears to be to become set in one's ways.

'All right,' said Moresby. 'I've finished in there. Tell Andrews, will you?'

He moved in the direction of the kitchen, but footsteps from the bedroom halted him in the passage. 'Ah,' he remarked to Roger in satisfied tones. 'Sounds as if the doctors have finished. Now we shall be able to get down to it.'

The doctors came out of the bedroom with the bustling divisional inspector in the rear, reminding Roger of a ferret shooing a couple of rabbits out of a burrow. The tall, cadaverous police-surgeon was their spokesman, and he addressed Moresby as if this was not the first case on which they had been together.

'Not much to tell you, chief inspector. Straightforward case,' he said, in brisk jerks. 'Death evidently caused by strangulation. I suggest the string of beads lying on the floor near her. Age about forty-eight. Decidedly under-nourished – wouldn't put up much of a struggle. No signs of a struggle on the body either, that we can detect as yet. She was attacked from behind, clearly. Line of bruising round the throat of even width, corresponding to the beads, except at the back; big bruise there. I suggest he twisted them into a knot. Condition at present: rigor partial (reached the upper extremities), body cool, post-mortem staining set in. Other words, death occurred no less than twelve hours ago, not more than twenty-four; can't put it closer than that. That enough for you to be going on with? Let you have a fuller report later, of course, after I've had the body.'

'Thank you, doctor. That tells me just what I want to know,' replied the chief inspector with much gratitude.

'And now you want to get rid of us, eh? Yes, yes, I know. Well, we're going. Morning, morning.'

He drove his rotund colleague, who obviously wished to linger, out before him. Their footsteps echoed down the stone staircase.

'Well, he was right enough,' observed Moresby without rancour. 'I did want to get rid of them. No reflections on the medical gentlemen, but I'm always glad when they're finished. Now, Merriman: what've you got to tell me?'

chapter two

The divisional inspector had not very much to report. He had not had time to look round for himself before his Chief's arrival, and the information he was able to impart was more of a general than a particular nature.

Monmouth Mansions, he told Moresby, was a block of small flats, with one bedroom, a sitting-room, and a kitchen to each only; there were four storeys, with two flats opening off each landing. Miss Barnett's was on the top floor. The building was inhabited by persons with claims, genuine or imagined, to gentility, but little beyond the absence (again genuine or imagined) of a Cockney accent to support them. Hardly the sort of place, Roger thought, to merit the attention of a man-killing burglar.

The same notion seemed to have occurred to Moresby. 'What did he expect to get here?' he asked, glancing through the doorway into the sitting-room with its out-of-date furniture, its plush coverings, and its general appearance of faded and impoverished Victorianism. There were even two glass lustres on the mantelpiece; or rather one; the other lay on the threadbare hearthrug. 'Doesn't look as if there was anything to attract even a rag-and-bone man.'

The divisional inspector looked knowing. 'Ah, she was a queer one, sir, Miss Barnett.'

'Queer one,' repeated the chief inspector, glancing into the room again and wrinkling even his unfastidious nose. 'You're right there. That room doesn't look as if it had been cleaned for months. Frowsy...'

Years more like, sir. And that's the best. You saw the bedroom. Regular pigsty. And according to the doctors, she'd been half-starving herself. A real miser, that's what she was. But there were plenty of rumours that might tempt someone to try their luck. I'd heard myself that she was supposed to keep eight hundred pounds sewn up in her mattress; in sovereigns, too.'

'You had, eh?' Moresby approved. 'That's good. You seem to keep in very close touch with the residents in your division.'

The inspector blushed with pleasure, but honesty constrained him to add: 'Well, sir, the truth is that we'd come up against her more than once. Very ready with her complaints always, she was. Come flying round about the least thing. Noisy cars outside this house, chiefly. And I remember she complained three or four times about an organ grinder some years back when I was station-sergeant. Expected us to arrest him for her on the spot. You know, sir; the kind that thinks because they pay rates they've got the whole force at their beck and call.'

'Yes, I know. So she'd been here several years.' The chief inspector did not ask any further about the dead woman's habits; Afford could be relied upon for a full report on those. 'And she had a local reputation as a miser, with a bag of sovereigns sewn up in her mattress. Well, you know as well as I do that there are always these rumours about old people who live alone and don't spend much money; though we may have a bit of a job to find out whether this one had any truth in it or not. Now then, what's all this about noises heard in the night? Where did that come from?'

'Something the caretaker told Sergeant Wakefield, sir, before they broke the door in. She said the folks in the flat below mentioned to her this morning, seeing her on the steps as they went out, that they'd been woke up in the night by the sound of bumps and crashes up here, and they wondered if Miss Barnett was all right.'

'And yet the woman didn't come up to see?'

'The sergeant asked her that. She said Miss Barnett was very particular about not being interfered with. She'd called Mrs Boyd a busybody once for bringing a parcel up to her instead of letting the shop boy do it; said it was an excuse to get her nose inside the flat, and if she had any more of it she'd complain to the landlord. So after that, Mrs Boyd said, she was pretty careful not to go out of her way to seem to be interfering again.'

Roger smiled, thinking of offended dignity and bristling feathers.

'I see,' Moresby said, smiling too. 'Did the people say what time the bumps were?'

'No, sir.'

'Who lives in the flat below?'

'A Mr and Mrs Ennismore Smith. They're both in business. He's a partner in a film-renting office in Wardour Street, and she manages one of those dress shops in Shaftesbury Avenue. I've got the addresses. I thought of sending a man along to find out what they know?' The inspector ended on a query, in case his superior had other views.

'H'm! Both be out at lunch now, won't they? Probably lunch together. Yes, send a man along, but don't tell 'em

12

what the trouble is; ask them if they can come here for a few minutes. Tell him to hurry. I'll have a look round the other rooms now.'

The inspector hurried off to his sergeant, and Moresby strolled into the sitting-room. Roger, with the feeling that at every step he was obliterating vital clues, clung to his side like a climber on a shale slope to a tamarisk bush.

The chief inspector surveyed the activities of his two subordinates with a benevolent eye. 'Well, Andrews? Any luck?'

'None, sir,' replied the fingerprint man disgustedly, looking up from the table top at which he was squinting sideways. 'I've been over most of this room, and there's not a sign of a print anywhere.'

'Ah,' said Moresby, without surprise. It was the usual case of the old hand; and nowadays the old hands wear gloves. 'It's the kitchen window where the rope is, isn't it? Come along and have a look there, Beach.'

The trio went down the passage to the small kitchen, and Roger and Inspector Beach stood in the doorway while the chief inspector, oblivious of his trouser-knees, examined the dirt-encrusted linoleum that covered the floor.

Roger found the scene interesting. The room was as disordered as the sitting-room, crockery lay smashed on the floor, even the gas stove had been moved askew in the frenzied search that had been made, and the kitchen table almost wantonly overturned.

'I should think the people below did hear something,' he remarked to Beach.

'Yes. But there wouldn't be so much noise as you might think. That crockery was probably an accident. The furniture wouldn't be knocked over on to the floor; only turned over, to look at the underneath; though of course soft,

13

light things, like clothes from the drawers, would be thrown about helter-skelter.'

'Do all burglars make such a mess as this?'

'Oh, no. Some of them are most tidy; replace everything. But of course this man would have been in a hurry as well. You don't want to linger if you've just croaked the householder, do you?'

'Got any ideas as to who it was?' Roger asked with interest.

'Several, at present. Too many. I want to get into this room, as soon as the Chief's done the floor, and have a look at the knot in that rope. That may tell me something, and the rope itself.'

Roger marvelled at the minute details in which the Criminal Record Office interests itself.

The rope to which the inspector referred led out of the open kitchen window; its near end was knotted, in what looked like a slip-knot, round the centre of the gas stove. Roger now thought that he had been mistaken in his first impression that the stove had been deliberately displaced; it was the weight of the man on his descent that had probably pulled it out of position. He wondered if the inspector would have deductions to draw from the amount of displacement as to the weight, and hence the size, of the man who used the rope. For once he found himself too diffident to mention this interesting possibility.

'Ha!' said Moresby.

The inspector and Roger craned forward.

With meticulous use of his pocket knife the chief inspector was detaching from the filthy linoleum an object. He laid it on the table, and the other two were able to see that it was a cake of dried mud, bearing the imprint of a man's heel.

14

'Ah!' agreed Inspector Beach.

'And that's all there is,' observed Moresby, regarding his find with much satisfaction. 'All right; I've finished with the floor.'

The two in the doorway advanced into the room, to inspect the little cake of mud which might possibly hang a man.

'Where was it?' Roger asked.

The chief inspector nodded to the corner beyond the stove, where a muddy smudge was visible even on the dirty linoleum.

'Came off when he was trying the weight of the stove to bear him on the rope, I shouldn't wonder,' opined Inspector Beach.

'Uh-huh,' assented Moresby, and went over to the window. 'No prints, of course,' he regretted, squinting at the glass.

With painstaking care he proceeded to scrutinise the woodwork of the window frame, the sill both inside the room and outside it, and, craning out, the wall below and the frame from the outside.

'Well?' said Roger.

Moresby delivered his conclusions. 'He went out this way, but didn't come in. Here's the marks of his feet on the sill, you see, and if you lean out you can see where his toes scraped on the wall before he'd got properly going.'

'And you know he didn't come in that way,' amplified Roger, not to be outdone, 'because we can bank on the window having been shut, and the frame shows no signs of having been forced.'

'That's right, Mr Sheringham,' agreed Moresby kindly. 'And also because it takes a cleverer burglar than this one to tie a rope round a gas stove on the fourth storey through a

15

closed window when he's standing in a courtyard thirty feet below.'

'Yes, of course,' Roger said hastily, with a slight blush. 'But what I want to know is, why the devil did he go out this way, with only two doors between him and the street?'

'Why do burglars burgle?' riposted Moresby laconically.

Inspector Beach, however, took this very reasonable question more seriously. 'Because he carried a rope to use, and because he always had used a rope for his get away before, sir; and that's about as near as you can put it,' he said, looking up from the rope in question. 'You can take it from me that if those two doors had been wide open and he happened to *know* there wasn't a soul in the street, he'd have gone down that rope just the same.'

'What idiots these professional criminals seem to be,' Roger meditated.

'They are, sir,' agreed Chief Inspector Moresby with much heartiness. 'And that's just why we catch 'em. Make anything of the rope, by the way, Beach?'

'Not much, I'm afraid, sir. It's not new, and it's thicker and heavier than usual. Just ordinary rope; not like that thin manilla. Almost impossible to trace, I should think. That bit of mud ought to help us more. I see he wears rubber heels.'

'Yes,' Moresby nodded. 'We must get that analysed as soon as possible.' Within reasonable limits it is possible for the expert to tell from what particular district a sample of mud is drawn.

The divisional inspector appeared in the doorway, with a pleased expression on his face. 'Can you come with me a minute, Mr Moresby?'

'Yes, I've finished in here for the time being. Tell Andrews that, Beach, when he's done with the sitting-room. What is it, inspector?'

'I've been having a bit of a look round, down in the court and on the stairs, and I've found where he waited last night.'

'Good. I'll come and look.'

The divisional inspector led the way down one flight, and indicated a cupboard which had been made by enclosing the space under the flight of stairs they had just descended. He opened the door, and disclosed the usual paraphernalia of brooms, pails and brushes. On the floor was a grey sprinkling of cigarette ash, and the squashed-out butts of nearly a dozen cigarettes.

Moresby picked up one. 'Player's. Not much use. He was here some time.'

'Yes. The bottom door's shut at ten p.m. He must have come in before that. I should say he was in here about four hours.'

The chief inspector counted the stubs. 'Eleven. About three an hour. Yes, that'd be somewhere near it. Or three hours, say.'

'If he smoked from the beginning,' remarked Roger. 'But he probably wouldn't, would he? I mean, not till he was pretty sure the people in the other flats had gone to bed. He wouldn't want the smoke to give him away.'

'Yes, that's likely enough, Mr Sheringham. Anyhow, it doesn't matter so much how long he was here; the point is, he was here. Inspector, get a man posted here, will you, till we've been over it properly; and I think Andrews had better come and look at it at once. If there's going to be a print anywhere, it'll be here.'

He divisional inspector hurried away.

Roger was looking at the cupboard floor. 'Don't seem to be any footprints here either. It was raining last night between nine and ten, too. I know, because I was out in it.'

17

'Oh, one's almost given up hoping for footprints as much as fingerprints with the professionals nowadays,' Moresby answered with resignation. 'They're up to all that sort of thing. You can bet this chap wiped his feet hard enough on the mat downstairs. That is, if he didn't come in before the rain. It was fine up to about eight, if I remember.'

'You think he may have been here by eight, then?'

'Any time after five, if he's one of the patient kind. They'll wait outside a crib for hours, like a cat over a mouse-hole. When Afford makes inquiries about anyone having seen him, you'll find he'll make notes of every stranger noticed in the place from lunch-time onwards.'

'You people certainly don't believe in leaving things to chance,' Roger approved. 'But there's one point in connection with this cupboard that I haven't heard mentioned yet. Know what I mean?'

'No, Mr Sheringham, I can't say I know which one you mean. There are so many.'

'You can't get out of it like that, Moresby,' Roger laughed. 'No, I mean this. Here's the ash of his cigarettes and here are the butts, all turned over and twisted. But where did he grind them out? You can see they've been ground out, not trodden on; besides, there are no burnt or blackened marks on the floor. But where are those round black blodges on the walls that one would expect to find where he did grind them out?' Roger tried, not altogether successfully, to conceal his pride at having remarked a point which had evidently escaped the chief inspector's own vigilant observation.

'It's evident you've only had experience of amachoor criminals, Mr Sheringham, sir,' retorted Moresby with a tolerant smile that reflected nothing of Roger's pride. 'Professionals are different altogether. They don't do things by reason; they do 'em by instinct. And the result is that they do a lot of very clever things, and a few very stupid ones. Now this chap, I wouldn't mind betting, ground out his cigarettes on the toe of one of his shoes just instinctively, because it *is* his instinct to avoid leaving traces. The fact that he flicked the ash on to the floor and dropped the butts there doesn't affect the question; that was habit, and habit's even stronger than instinct. Yes, they're funny cattle, professional criminals.'

'They certainly are,' agreed Roger, marvelling.

'Well,' said Moresby genially, 'let's go and have another look at the body.'

They went upstairs to the flat again.

'No marks of a struggle, so far as one can see at present,' the chief inspector mused, moving slowly round the crumpled form so as to study it from every angle. 'Doesn't look much like a struggle either, from the way she's lying. Of course, as the doctor said, she couldn't put up much of a one in any case; doesn't look to me as if she could weigh much more than six and a half stone. What do you say, Mr Sheringham? Seems to me she's still lying just as he dropped her.'

'I should think so,' Roger grunted.

Moresby dropped on one knee and picked up one of the stiff hands. They were both tightly clenched, and he had considerable difficulty in opening the fingers. Roger noticed that his object was to inspect the nails, which he did minutely.

'Sometimes we find a valuable clue clutched in a clenched hand,' he explained, looking up for a moment, 'but there's nothing here. There's something in these nails though. Bits of skin. But I'm afraid they come from her own neck,' he added regretfully, glancing at the woman's throat,

19

on which several long excoriations were plain above the line of bruising. 'Trying to get the thing loose.'

Roger nodded. 'Would she have been conscious for long?'

'Oh, no. Not a minute. Perhaps only a few seconds. And if the doctor's right and it was done from behind, he wouldn't have given her a chance to mark him.'

'I suppose he must be a hefty, strong fellow?'

'To strangle her so quickly? Not necessarily at all. It wouldn't take much strength to do for her, if he could take her unawares with a sudden, sharp constriction. The ligature was below the larynx, you see, which means that insensibility was very rapid; perhaps almost instantaneous.'

'How do the doctors know for certain that death *was* due to strangulation?' asked Roger, unwilling to take anything for granted. 'Why not hanging?'

'Hanging pointing to the probability of suicide, and strangulation to murder?' Moresby observed, with a slight smile. 'Why, chiefly because of all these abrasions on the neck, which you wouldn't get with hanging; they show the application of violence. Then you can see how livid she is; that's another indication. No, I'm afraid you can't put up a case for suicide, Mr Sheringham.'

'I wasn't trying to. But what I don't understand is why her shrieks weren't heard. People ought to have come rushing up at once. And there must have been a terrible lot of threshing about.'

'A sudden and violent compression of the windpipe,' replied Moresby glibly, 'renders a person powerless to call for assistance and give alarm, and it causes almost immediate insensibility and death without convulsions.'

'Moresby, what a devil of a lot you seem to know about all this,' Roger admired.

'Well, sir, you might almost say that a knowledge of hanging and strangulation was part of my duty,' returned Moresby with great cheerfulness, and proceeded with his examination.

Roger began to moon around the room. Like all the others, it was exceedingly dirty. Dust was everywhere, the tightly-closed windows were grimy, the carpet deplorable. Garments (the garments of female old age, than which nothing is more unprepossessing, not even the male boiled shirt) lay strewn on the floor, on chairs, on every available spot. Miss Barnett evidently undressed on to the floor. Slovenliness was never more graphic. Roger observed as much to Moresby.

'Bit of a pigsty,' the chief inspector agreed, without too much interest. 'But she wasn't as bad as she might have been.'

'Really?' said Roger, who found himself at a loss to imagine anything worse.

'Oh, no. At least she did undress. Now in my experience most of the women of this type only half-undress, and put their nightdresses on over the rest.'

'Then thank goodness I have no experience,' said Roger. 'By the way,' he went on, his eye on something lying on the floor near where Moresby was kneeling, 'that's the string of beads, I suppose? The alleged weapon?'

'Don't touch it, please, sir.'

'Certainly not,' said Roger, offended. 'But I suppose I may look at it.'

He did so, averting his eyes from Moresby, who was parting the dead woman's hair and peering into the result, as if hopeful of finding clues among the roots; which, for all Roger knew, he may have been.

'Have you examined this, Moresby?' he went on with interest. 'It isn't a string of beads. She was a Roman Catholic. It's her rosary.'

'Very ironical, sir,' replied the chief inspector absently, intent on the job in hand.

Finished with the body at last, Moresby gave orders for its removal to the mortuary, there to await the doctor's further examination and the inevitable post-mortem. While the task was in process Roger strolled into the passage, to encounter the divisional inspector, who was doing his best to keep an eye on everything at once and at the same time to do a little detecting on his own account. To him Roger put a question which had been bothering him.

'What I don't understand, inspector,' he complained, 'is how she came to be killed in her bedroom. She evidently was, but how did they get there? There are no marks of forcible entry anywhere, which must mean, I suppose, that Miss Barnett let the man in herself, at her front door. Got out of bed, in fact, to do so. Well, how did they get back into the bedroom?'

'You must remember, sir, that it's a thousand to one that he ever came here with the intention of committing murder. They hardly ever do. Murder, in this sort of case, is usually the result of panic. The victim looks like raising an outcry, or getting dangerous. Then they lose their heads and commit murder. Now, if what we suppose is correct, this man made no attempt to get inside the flat till after midnight, and then he probably rang the front-door bell, as you suggest. Well, you can be sure he wouldn't do that unless he'd got some plausible tale prepared. He's not going to threaten violence the moment she opens the door, and risk her shrieking and giving the alarm. No, his tale is going to carry him, over a couple of minutes at any rate, enough to give him the opportunity to render her powerless.'

'You think he intended violence of some sort, then?'

'Oh, yes. Most probably his intention was to gag and bind her, so that he could prosecute his search unhindered.'

Roger hid a smile; the inspector's choice of words was so admirably suggestive of the witness-box. 'His search for what, though?' he asked quickly.

'For whatever it was he came to look for,' replied the inspector with an expressionless face.

'Then why did he strangle her?'

'For the reason I suggested, sir. That she saw through his story before he was ready, and looked like giving the alarm. Then he just snatched up the first thing that came to hand (didn't I hear you saying it was her rosary?), and – and croaked the poor old girl,' concluded the inspector, leaving the witness-box abruptly.

'I see. Yes, that accounts for the delay all right. But whatever sort of story could he expect to put up to account for his arrival at that hour of the night?'

'Well, Mr Sheringham, suppose he told her something like this,' said a voice behind them. Roger looked round; Inspector Beach had joined them in the passage. 'Supposing he told her he was a detective from Scotland Yard, and having a look round the back of this building in the course of his duties, noticed a man on the roof just above her own kitchen window.'

'Acting suspiciously,' nodded the divisional inspector, entering the witness-box again.

'In fact, tying a rope round a chimney and preparing to descend, obviously with the intention of burgling her flat. Could he therefore come in and make his preparations for catching the intruder?'

'Red-handed,' supplied the divisional inspector with more interest than this simple suggestion seemed to merit. 'Him representing himself to be a member of the force. You've got your ideas then, Mr Beach?'

'I have.'

'Ginger-coloured ones?' inquired the divisional inspector, with cryptic caution.

Inspector Beach laughed, with a glance at Roger.

'Ginger Mack, you mean? No. Flash Bertie.'

'Flash Bertie's down for a stretch.'

'He's not!' cried Beach, chagrined.

'He is. I put him away myself. Couple of months ago. Loitering with intent. Six months he went down for.'

Inspector Beach was obviously puzzled. 'Well, that's funny. This job's got Flash Bertie written all over it.'

'Flash Bertie wouldn't croak,' opined the divisional inspector with confidence. 'I've seen a good deal of Bertie, one way and another. He wouldn't be such a fool as this. Or have the guts, for that matter.'

'Perhaps it was someone copying Flash Bertie's methods,' put in Roger helpfully. 'Hoping you'd think it *was* Flash Bertie, I mean.'

The two detectives exchanged smiles.

'Have I said the wrong thing?' Roger asked.

'Not at all sir,' Beach reassured him. 'Mr Merriman and me were just thinking that you probably read a good many of these detective stories; that was all.'

chapter three

Sergeant Afford had quite a lot to report.

Moresby, Roger and the divisional inspector listened to it as they munched the beef sandwiches which the sergeant had thoughtfully brought up with him. It was now nearly three o'clock.

'Well, I've found the motive,' was his first announcement. 'The old girl was rumoured to have a lot of money, anything between five hundred and five thousand pounds according to preference, hidden away up here.'

'Oho,' said Moresby. 'Figure's gone up, has it?'

'You knew that already, sir?' asked the sergeant.

'We knew she was supposed to have money here. Find out why?'

'Yes, she didn't believe in banks, and all that sort of thing. A small private bank in which she had a few pounds when she was young went smash and she's never banked a penny since. It's believed she had quite a respectable income too, and as she evidently didn't spend much, there may be something in the rumour.'

'We must find out the details. Afford, you'd better take that in hand.'

'Yes, sir. The caretaker couldn't tell me much about it, but I've an idea we may be able to get something from the occupant of the other flat on this landing, Mrs Pilchard. According to Mrs Boyd, she was about the nearest thing to a friend Miss Barnett had, and the only.'

'What about her relatives?'

'Mrs Boyd doesn't think she'd got any. At any rate she's sure no one ever came to see her. But that we may find out from Mrs Pilchard too. And Mrs Boyd says Miss Barnett never had a letter more than once a month, and then only typewritten. At least, by the first post, which Mrs Boyd sorts and distributes; the others, of course, the postman brings up to the different flats himself.'

The sergeant, with many references to his notebook, went on to shed a few sidelights on the dead woman's character, as illuminated by Mrs Boyd. There was, however, little that an inspection of the flat had not already revealed. That Miss Barnett had been unclean in her habits was only too plain, that she was miserly to a degree was equally obvious; a store of empty whisky bottles unearthed by the divisional inspector had shown that she drank; it hardly needed the sergeant's translations of Mrs Boyd's innuendoes to add that she was quarrelsome, suspicious and eccentric. A most unpleasing old person, Roger reflected.

But an important one. She had money. The sum rumoured to be stored in her flat was only the savings from her dividends. Her capital, Mrs Boyd knew, was all in gilt-edged stock; what it amounted to she did not know, but the sum was reputed to be considerable.

'Well, we can soon find that out,' said Moresby comfortably.

'Just asking for it, she was,' was Sergeant Afford's final comment on Miss Barnett's odd fancy for sleeping on her spare cash instead of banking it. 'It's a wonder to me she never copped it before this.'

It was a wonder to Roger too.

The sergeant consulted his notebook afresh and embarked on a list of strangers seen about the place yesterday afternoon and evening, still according to Mrs Boyd; as, however, it was Mrs Boyd's fortunate habit to sit at her front window of an afternoon with a bit of sewing and as Mrs Boyd would certainly keep a proprietary eye on ingoings and outgoings, her evidence was important.

Mrs Boyd had remembered seeing the following persons, strangers to her, enter the building yesterday between dinner-time and dusk: a new postman; a man with a bag of tools (suspected of coming to put a washer on a tap in Flat 3); a boy with the man with the bag of tools; a canvasser for one of the political parties; a travelling salesman seeking orders for a History of the European War in twelve volumes (with Maps and Numerous Illustrations), reduced from eight guineas to forty-eight shillings; a Sister of Mercy collecting subscriptions for some charity (these three had all interviewed Mrs Boyd personally); a large number of other male strangers, estimated by Mrs Boyd at a round dozen, and lastly several persons known by sight or name to Mrs Boyd, a list of whose names or descriptions the industrious sergeant had collected.

His chief inspector grunted. 'H'm! Not much chance there. We can check up on some of them of course, but that isn't likely to help us much. And I suppose she saw no one after dusk?'

The sergeant intimated that this was the case, with the exception of the canvasser and the nun, both of whom had rung Mrs Boyd's own front bell.

'And it's almost certainly after dusk that he came,' Moresby grumbled. 'Yes?' he called, in answer to a knock on the door. 'Come in.'

It was Detective-Sergeant Andrews, of the Fingerprint Bureau. 'I've been over everything now, sir. There's not a print in the place.'

'No, I thought not. You can get back, then; have your lunch first, of course. Has Inspector Beach finished?'

'He's gone down to the courtyard, to see if he can find anything there, sir. I think he wants to examine the scratches on the wall. And I was to tell you that Mr and Mrs Smith are here, sir, in their own flat.'

'Ah, yes. Well, we'll have 'em up. Separately. Him first. Tell the sergeant – the divisional man.' Sergeant Andrews withdrew. Moresby turned to his own sergeant. 'Anything else to tell me, Afford?'

'Nothing of any importance, sir.'

'Well, I'll see Smith in here. You two had better stay. And I suppose you want to, Mr Sheringham?'

'If you don't mind,' replied Roger politely.

'I don't, and I don't suppose Mr Ennisomething Smith will. All right, Afford, if that's him.'

Mr Ennismore Smith was a pleasant-faced man of fifty or so, at present looking somewhat bewildered, but at the same time not unpleasantly excited. He paused in the doorway, looked round, and at once selected Moresby to address. 'Something up, is there?' A person of discrimination Mr Ennismore Smith, decided Roger.

'I'm sorry to say there is, sir,' replied Moresby with the utmost benevolence. Roger noticed with interest how his manner, though never officially curt, seemed to swell and blossom into a larger geniality with the entrance of Mr E Smith. It was Moresby's method when seeking information to envelop his object in a thick and expansive cloud of friendliness, and Roger knew how effective a method it was.

'In fact, not to put too fine a point on it, Miss Barnett here was murdered last night.'

'Murdered!' There was no doubt that Mr Ennismore Smith was genuinely shocked. 'Good God, not really? I say, that's terrible. Rotten! Then those noises we heard – good heavens, we – my wife and I – must have heard them actually at it. Look here, I can give you some jolly valuable information about this. We were woken up –'

'Yes, sir, so I've heard,' interposed Moresby deftly. 'And that's just why I've asked you to be good enough to come back here and give us the information. So if you'll take a seat, we can talk comfortably. Sergeant Afford, just pull a chair up for Mr Ennismore Smith, will you? Now, sir, my name is Moresby, Chief Inspector Moresby, from headquarters – Scotland Yard, you know; and this is Divisional Inspector Merriman, so you can talk quite freely to us, and I'm sure you'll tell us all you know.'

An atmosphere of comfort and confidence having been thus induced, it was intimated that what Mr Ennismore Smith was required to know first of all was his own name, address, and profession or occupation. The last of these, however, Mr Smith did not seem to know quite so well as might have been expected.

'Film-renter, I suppose you'd better put me down,' he said dubiously, 'though it's a long time since I rented a film on my own account. Anyhow, that's what I used to be, when business was better and you could hire a decent film at a reasonable price. What I am now,' added Mr Smith candidly, 'the Lord only knows.'

'Yes, sir,' soothed Moresby. 'Quite so. Film-renter. Now, will you tell us exactly what it was you heard last night?'

'Certainly I will. My wife and I turned in pretty early last night – often do nowadays; get tired more easily than when we were younger. Well, I'm a pretty sound sleeper myself, and so is my wife as a rule. But in the middle of the night she woke me up and said: "What on earth's Miss Barnett up to? Listen. Sounds as if she's throwing her furniture about." Perhaps not those exact words, you know, but near enough. So I listened, and the next minute I'm blessed if there wasn't a great crash as if she'd thrown a couple of washbasins across the room and then a couple of flat-irons after them. "Well, I'll be blowed!" I said. Or something like that. "Do you think she's all right?" asked my wife. "Well, if she wants to smash up the happy home," I said, "who are we to stop her?" Because I don't know if you've heard it, but Miss Barnett was an odd old cuss in some ways. Poor old girl though. If I'd dreamt for one minute that – '

'You didn't happen to notice the time, I suppose, Mr Smith?'

'That's just exactly what I did do,' returned Mr Ennismore Smith with triumph. 'I said to my wife: 'Well, what's the time, anyhow?' And she looked at her bed-clock (she's got one of those clocks with illuminated hands; you know 'em) and said it was just on half-past one.'

'That's good,' Moresby said heartily. 'Thank you, Mr Smith. That may be a most valuable piece of information. Now, did the noises continue?'

'No, that was the end of them; though my wife said there'd been quite a lot before she woke me. So we just turned over and went to sleep again. Good God, though, just fancy it! All the time the poor old girl was being done in, actually over our heads. Her bedroom's right over ours, you know. I say, how perfectly rotten! How was it done, eh?'

The chief inspector satisfied some of Mr Smith's very natural curiosity, and then proceeded with his questions. But nothing further of any importance was brought to light.

Mr Smith had heard no footsteps in the flat above or scrapings on the wall outside, and had seen no suspicious character loitering about the place that evening.

To Roger's surprise Moresby turned to him and said when the examination was obviously concluded: 'Have you any questions you'd like to put to Mr Smith before he goes, Mr Sheringham?'

Roger stared at him before pulling himself together. He was just about to say that he had none, when a thought occurred to him. 'Yes,' he said instead. 'Which was your school, Mr Smith?'

'School? Radley. Why?'

'Oh, nothing,' said Roger, and nodded to Moresby.

Mr Smith was efficiently ejected.

'Why did you ask me if I wanted to put any questions?' Roger demanded, as soon as the door was closed.

'Well, Mr Sheringham, if you want to solve this case before we do,' winked the chief inspector ponderously, 'I'd hate not to have given you every chance.'

'Oh, I'm not in the lists this time,' Roger laughed. 'I like difficult cases.'

'I see, sir. Well, what did you make of Mr Ennismore Smith?'

Roger considered. 'I think he had some difficulty in not calling you "old boy".'

'That just about hits him off,' chuckled the chief inspector. 'Anything else?'

'Well, he's a friendly person, and an impulsive one, and one who has evidently been a good deal better off at one time than he is now. And he's imaginative too. The point that seemed to strike him most was the fact that Miss Barnett was being murdered just over his head while he was actually turning over to go to sleep again.'

'Which certainly wasn't the case,' Moresby remarked carelessly. 'The row that woke them up was made by the murderer looking for the money. The old girl would have been croaked before that, while they were both still asleep. All right, Afford, let's have the wife in.'

Mrs Ennismore Smith, who had been dexterously kept apart from her husband, confirmed what he had been able to tell; the only addition she was able to make to his story was an account of the noise which she had heard before waking her husband – several heavy bumps as if furniture was being frenziedly overturned, not to say thrown about. She was a tall, good-looking woman with greying hair and a quiet manner, and though the news of Miss Barnett's death was obviously a shock to her, it did not seem to distress her as much as it had her husband. Roger decided that she was certainly more practical, and almost certainly more efficient than the perhaps rather happy-go-lucky Mr E Smith. Roger also decided that the 'Ennismore' was her contribution to the family dignity.

'And now for the woman opposite,' said Moresby, when Mrs Ennismore Smith had gone. 'What was her name? Oh, yes; Mrs Roach.'

'Pilchard, sir,' murmured Sergeant Afford respectfully.

'Pilchard, yes. Is she on hand?'

'I should say she is,' replied the divisional inspector, with an unfeeling grin. 'She was screeching round the place when I got here, wanting to get at the body; though what she thought she could do with it I don't know. I persuaded her to go back into her own flat.'

'You have a way with you, Merriman,' remarked Moresby.

'I have, sometimes,' agreed the divisional inspector grimly. 'I had to persuade her by having her pushed through

32

the door of it by a constable. She's still inside – or should be, unless my man's gone to sleep.'

'Then we'll have her out,' proclaimed Moresby. 'See if you can extract her, Afford.'

Sergeant Afford retired, muttering something about winkles and pins.

'You look bored, Mr Sheringham,' Moresby bantered. 'Dull work, isn't it, watching the police on the job?'

'Bored? Good heavens, no. I was thinking. I take it this fellow must have lost his head last night?'

'Not yet, he hasn't; that comes a month after sentence. Why do you say that, sir?'

'I mean, to have made such a noise. When I said something to Beach about not being surprised that the people below heard something, he told me that there wouldn't have been so much noise as one might think to look at the mess. The furniture wouldn't be knocked over; it would be turned over gently. But according to Mrs Smith the furniture *was* knocked over. Therefore I take it that the man must have lost his head.'

'He lost his head to commit murder at all, Mr Sheringham; you're right enough there. And it's probably enough that he didn't recover it until he had made a bit of noise. Probably it was the noise that actually made him pull himself together. That squares with what the Smiths say about hearing no footsteps, although they listened carefully. He was probably standing stock-still, waiting to see whether he'd been fool enough to give the alarm or not.'

'It took a good deal of noise to bring him to his senses then,' Roger said sarcastically. 'Knocking over the furniture wasn't enough. He had to throw a couple of washbasins across the room and a couple of flat-irons after them before he felt really cool. Is that the idea?'

'You like a bit of an argument, Mr Sheringham, don't you?' Moresby replied in tolerant tones.

Roger laughed. He did like a bit of an argument.

The entrance of Mrs Pilchard cut short the possibility of any further developments of this particular one.

Mrs Pilchard proved to be a rather short, rather stout woman, none too neatly dressed. There were traces of recent tears on her face, but grief had not prevented her from being angry; very angry, it seemed, indeed. She spoke with a slight Irish accent, and immediately let loose a flood of words of which the theme was the sheer brutality, the stupid incompetence, and the utter heartlessness of withholding from the dead woman the services of the only friend she had had in the world.

Roger marvelled at the way in which Moresby handled her. Within three minutes Mrs Pilchard was actually apologising to him, with equal exuberance, for having attempted so foolishly to hinder the difficult processes of the investigation that was to avenge her friend. The credit for this remarkable reversal was no doubt mainly due to Moresby, but it was also due in some degree, Roger fancied, to the strange temperament with which the Celts are afflicted.

Harmony being thus established, Mrs Pilchard consented to fulfil her function of imparting information.

According to her own account, Miss Barnett had had few secrets from her. She could give the chief inspector practically a life-history of the dead woman if he wished; or of herself, whichever he preferred; he had only to say.

The chief inspector said that he would like a few particulars of Mrs Pilchard herself first, just for form's sake.

These were rapidly supplied. Mrs Pilchard was a widow. Her maiden name was Kerry. She had been born in Ireland, where her father practised as a solicitor in Cork. On the latter's death, when she was barely twelve, her mother, who was English, had removed to her own native town of Eastbourne, and there existed precariously, helped by such relatives as she still had. There too Miss Kerry had made the acquaintance of Mr Pilchard, a wool merchant from Bradford, who had succumbed to her charms as she to his. Marriage had followed, and a small house on the outskirts of Bradford. Mr Pilchard had done well. The war helped him, and he prudently got out of wool at the height of the boom period after it. He had then set the cap on his virtues as a husband by dying and leaving everything to his wife, with the result that she was able to live at any rate in comfort, if not in luxury, wherever she chose. She had chosen London, six years ago, and Monmouth Mansions at that. Miss Barnett had been occupying her own flat for some years before that, and had seemed to take an immediate fancy to the widow of the late wool merchant. To the undisguised amazement of Mrs Boyd, a close friendship had sprung up between the two at once, developing quickly into intimacy. Miss Barnett must unconsciously have been suffering for lack of a confidant, and had at once set about making up for lost time. For the last two years, so far as Mrs Pilchard knew, the two had had no secrets from each other.

'Ah!' said Chief Inspector Moresby, when all this had been rapidly set out, and switched Mrs Pilchard's ready speech to the subject of her friend.

'Yes; Adelaide – Miss Barnett – was born in Nottingham. She was the daughter of a grocer there. A grocer, yes. I'd better say at once,' observed Mrs Pilchard sadly, 'Adelaide wasn't a lady.'

The chief inspector clicked his sympathy for this shortcoming on the part of Miss Barnett.

ANTHONY BERKELEY

As Mrs Pilchard's narrative proceeded it became apparent that not only was the late Miss Barnett not a lady, but she was very nearly no lady. The trouble dated from Grocer Barnett's death. He had died, in the days before government inspectors with travelling scales and penetrating eyes were sent to vex the souls of grocers, very well off indeed. There were only two children, Miss Barnett and her brother. To his daughter Grocer Barnett left twenty thousand pounds, in Consols and India four per cents; to his son, the business. But – he made no provisions concerning his house and furniture. The brother held in consequence that these naturally went with the business; Miss Barnett considered them an obvious concomitant to India four per cent stock. (Mrs Pilchard made it clear that in her opinion Miss Barnett had been perfectly correct in this opinion.) Neither was inclined to give way. Finally, the brother, who was of a more accommodating disposition, offered to sell the lot and divide the proceeds. This insulting offer Miss Barnett at once rejected, and, waiting till business called her brother to London, sold the lot herself, and retired victorious to Monmouth Mansions with the result. The brother contented himself with writing to her to the effect that he was glad to get rid of her at the price. That had been twenty-eight years ago, and no word had passed between them since.

'I see,' said the chief inspector, stroking his chin. 'We must get in touch with this brother. Do you happen to know if he's still in Nottingham?'

'No, he isn't,' replied Mrs Pilchard promptly. 'He's in hell.'

'I beg your pardon?' said the startled chief inspector.

Mrs Pilchard explained that Mr Barnett junior's soul, though not above insulting a defenceless woman, had proved superior to grocery. He had sold the business soon after the quarrel, and so far as she knew devoted most of the

36

proceeds to experiments in colour photography, a science in which he took considerable interest. The experiments having all proved useless and his money being exhausted, Mr Barnett had given it up and died. 'And' Mrs Pilchard pronounced judgement, 'serve him right.'

'Quite so,' murmured the chief inspector diplomatically. 'Miss Barnett did keep in touch with her brother, then?'

'That she did not, after the way he'd treated her. It was his daughter, Miss Barnett's niece, who wrote and told her when he died. I saw the letter meself. As curt and stiff a little letter as ever you read. "Though she knew that no communication had passed between her father and her aunt for over twenty years, she considered it her duty to inform her that her brother had just died, and the funeral would take place so-and-so." Impertinent little chit! A true daughter of her father, evidently. Of course Miss Barnett took no notice. The girl never wrote again.'

'Ah! Then she has some relatives living?'

'She didn't know she had till she got that letter. Never heard of the girl before. Never even heard her brother had married.'

'Did the girl say whether she had any brothers and sisters, or if she was an only child?'

'Dear me, no. There was nothing of that sort in the letter, though well she might have known that was just what her aunt would like to hear, she not even knowing till that moment that she had a niece at all.'

'Well,' said Moresby cheerfully, 'we know at any rate now that she exists, if she hasn't died since; so she'll be the next-of-kin. Sergeant Afford, you'd better take that in hand. She ought to be easy to trace. Perhaps we'll come across her letter too.'

'That you won't,' snorted Mrs Pilchard, 'because Adelaide threw it in the fire as soon as we'd read it. But I can tell you the girl's name was Stella. Stella Barnett, she signed herself!' said Mrs Pilchard indignantly. 'And her father was to be cremated, if you please, at Golders Green. It was all of a par.'

Moresby caught Roger's eye, and was unofficial enough to ask if Mrs Pilchard did not believe in cremation.

'I do not,' replied that lady with emphasis. 'Isn't it downright against Holy Writ? "Where the worm dieth not," says the Bible. A great chance a worm would have of not dying in a crematorium.'

'But doesn't it go on, "and their fire is not quenched"?' Roger put in gently. 'That seems to me to apply to a crematorium very well.'

Mrs Pilchard contented herself with the usual conclusion of a religious argument, a snort of defiance and contempt.

'Come, come,' said Moresby, 'we're getting a little off the track, aren't we? So Mr Barnett was to be cremated at Golders Green, was he? Well, that ought to give us all we want. About how long ago was all this, madam?'

Mrs Pilchard thought that it was at least five years ago. Moreover, the girl had written from an address in Hertfordshire; something Wood, she believed. Moresby made a note, and went on to question her concerning Miss Barnett's means.

Once more Mrs Pilchard proved herself a treasure trove of information. Miss Barnett had never changed the investments her father left her, but, as Consols went down and down, so had Miss Barnett been forced to be more and more careful. It was this necessary caution which malicious gossip had twisted into parsimony. Not that Miss Barnett had lived up to her income of course, or anywhere near it; but what sensible person did? 'Except us Irish, maybe,' added

Miss Pilchard cheerfully, 'but then everyone knows we're not sensible.'

'What did Miss Barnett do with her savings?' asked Moresby, disregarding the idiosyncrasies of the Irish.

'I'll tell you what she didn't do with them,' replied Mrs Pilchard with energy. 'She didn't bank them. Many and many a time I've said to her, "Adelaide," I've said, "take it from me that –"'

'Did she keep them here?'

'And now me words have come true,' Mrs Pilchard burst into a sudden wail, 'and she's been murdered for them. I knew it, I knew it. But she wouldn't listen to me, never. Yes, she did keep them here. As soon as her dividend warrants came she cashed them, and put the money into a chest under her bed. When she wanted any, she took it out of that; she paid in cash for everything. Sometimes, when she'd got the chest nearly full, she'd buy some more Consols or India stock (never anything else), but not often. She used to say she liked to be able to see her money: then she knew it was safe. Many and many a time I've helped her count what was in the chest, though she always knew beforehand to a shilling what was there. A marvellous head for figures, she had, poor dear. Yes, under her bed the chest was, always. And now it's gone, I suppose?'

'No. It's still there. But it's empty.' Roger raised his eyebrows. This was the first he had heard of a chest. He did not even know that any search had yet been made for the money supposed to have been concealed in the place.

'Have you any idea how much would have been in it?'

Mrs Pilchard thought. 'Let me see. We counted it last about a month ago. So far as I remember it had about six hundred pounds in it then. Yes, I should say somewhere between five and six hundred. Nearly all in one-pound and ten-shilling notes.'

Moresby whistled. 'Well, as you said, sergeant, there's no doubt about the motive. That was enough to tempt any of the regulars. I only wonder she never had a visit before.'

He put a few more questions to Mrs Pilchard, mainly concerned with the disturbances during the night, but without obtaining anything of use. Mrs Pilchard had heard nothing at all. She had not seen the rope dangling from Miss Barnett's window till Mrs Boyd had drawn her attention to it, and just as things had turned out she had had no occasion to visit her friend that morning. They did not, she explained, live in each other's pockets. And not having been outside her own flat at all, she had not noticed that Miss Barnett's milk had not been taken in. When, however, Mrs Boyd had come up just before one o'clock to consult her, she had gone across the landing and knocked on the door; and when no reply had been obtained, it was she who insisted that a policeman must be fetched. As one conscious enough in her own mind of having done the right thing, but anxious that others should recognise the fact too, Mrs Pilchard made quite a point of this.

When the interview was over Moresby allowed her to go into the bedroom, under Sergeant Afford's escort, to say goodbye to her friend before the body was taken to the mortuary.

'And that,' said Moresby, stretching himself mightily, 'is that. Bar searching the place for any other caches we've finished here, though I don't expect anything will turn up; he's got away with it, without a doubt. You'll look after the search party, Merriman, won't you? So there you are, Mr Sheringham. That's how we manage our murders. Dull, isn't it?'

'Not at all. It's extremely interesting. And how long do you reckon it will take you to get the man?'

The chief inspector yawned. 'I shall probably get his name from Beach by the time I get back. And I may say I've got my own opinion on that. He'll be lying low of course, but even we have our methods. What do you say, Merriman? How long before we locate him? Forty-eight hours?'

'At the most,' agreed the divisional inspector. 'So you've got your opinion, Mr Moresby? Beach was thinking it looked like Flash Bertie.'

'Flash Bertie's out of harm's way for the present,' replied Moresby genially. 'But I'll give you three names. Sam Roberts, Alf Jackson, and Jim Watkins, *alias* the Camberwell Kid. Take your choice.'

'Doesn't look to me like Sam Roberts,' doubted Inspector Merriman.

'No, I don't think so either. But – come in! Oh, it's you, Beach. Yes?'

'Just run back to look up a point, sir,' said Inspector Beach. 'I've been up to CRO, and taken out seven cards, but...' He bent over the little cake of dried mud which still lay on a side-table, and began to scrutinise it intently.

'Seven?' said Moresby humorously. 'I've just been putting my money on two.'

'And now it's only one,' said Beach, straightening up. 'This clinches it. I'm not an expert, but I know this mud. Had some of it before. It's a peculiar reddy-brown, with a lot of sandstone grit in it; I'd know it anywhere. It comes from Bracingham, in Kent; about twenty miles out of London. Well, that's very nice.' Inspector Beach looked pleased with himself.

'Let's have it, Beach,' Moresby grinned. 'Who is it?'

'Jim Watkins. He's got a girl in Bracingham.'

41

'I win my money,' said Moresby laconically. 'As you say, Beach, that clinches it. The Camberwell Blessed Kid.'

'Do you mean you identify him on the strength of that bit of mud alone?' asked Roger in surprise.

Inspector Beach looked superior. 'No, sir, I do not. That's only the final proof. There are twenty-two points I've got noted down – burglary at a mansion, methods of effecting entry, method of effecting escape, partaking of spirits, not partaking of food, use of candle for lighting purposes, wilful destruction of furniture, etc, noises heard, and the rest. Four men agree in their methods with over fifteen of those points, two with twenty, one with twenty-one, and Jim Watkins with all twenty-two. That's what we call the *modus operandi*, sir, and that makes it as certain as anything can be. This mud makes it just a bit more certain still.'

'Oh,' said Roger.

'So now all we've got to do, Mr Sheringham,' Moresby took up the tale, 'is to find him and prove he did it to the satisfaction of a thick-headed jury; and we'll do that, however thick-headed they are. Yes, Mr Sheringham, if you've a fancy for it you can be shaking hands with Mr Jim Watkins in his nice little cell within forty-eight hours from now.'

'Thank you,' said Roger without exuberance. 'But as a member of the community I'm glad to hear you so confident.'

'Well, but fancy that,' mourned the divisional inspector.

'Fancy what?'

'Fancy the Kid going and doing a silly thing like that. I thought better of the Kid, Mr Moresby, and that's a fact.' Inspector Merriman spoke as of a close and respected friend gone unaccountably astray.

chapter four

Roger returned to his rooms at the Albany acutely interested but not in the least excited. It had never occurred to him for a moment to attempt to intervene in the case. It was, as Moresby had shown, of precisely the kind with which Scotland Yard is organised to deal: that of the professional criminal. It was therefore of its nature an anomaly, for the professional criminal very rarely murders. Ninety-nine murders out of a hundred are committed by persons of whom the police have no knowledge or records, and whose first and last crime it is. In ninety-nine cases out of a hundred, therefore, the police organisation is working on lines not exactly unfamiliar but without the help of that totalisator of detection, the Criminal Record Office. That in ninety-eight of these cases they are successful speaks its own praise. (It must always be the ninety-ninth which finds its way into detective-story print; most of the ninety-eight are frankly, in Moresby's own word, dull.)

Roger continued, however, to retain enough interest in the case to walk round, two mornings later, to Scotland Yard in order to ask Moresby how things were progressing. The morning papers had reported that no further developments had arisen, and the police were confident of making an early arrest.

Moresby, it seemed, had practically handed the case over to his subordinates. He explained that there was nothing further for him to do; it was now just a matter of routine. There was no reasonable doubt as to the criminal's identity; what further facts had come to light only confirmed his own and Inspector Beach's conclusion. The sample of mud, for instance, had proved on analysis to be exactly as Beach suspected. The other six possibles, whose cards Inspector Beach had taken, had all been examined as to their movements that evening, and had all satisfied the police completely. Moreover, the Camberwell Kid had not been seen for some days in his usual resorts, and none of his intimates appeared to have any knowledge of his present whereabouts; which in itself was almost tantamount to a confession of guilt. It was now only a matter of uncovering the Kid's concealed tracks.

'And that won't take us long, Mr Sheringham,' opined Moresby, inadequately concealing a yawn.

'And there's no other news at all?'

'Oh, yes; I was forgetting; one more piece of evidence has come to hand. Several people saw a man running hard in the reverse direction from Monmouth Mansions, at times estimated variously as betwen 1.20 and 1.38 a.m.'

Roger smiled at the official phraseology which rose automatically to the chief inspector's lips. 'And the description agrees with your Camberwell Kid's?'

'Well enough, sir, well enough. Of course it's impossible to get a really accurate description of a man seen only for a second or two, and you'd be surprised how people vary in what they think they saw. In fact this is a pretty good example of what we have to work on, as often as not.' Moresby pulled a fat dossier towards him, and turned over the pages. 'Here we are. Albert Wiggins, greengrocer,

Euston Road, was returning home along Platts Street; at the Euston Road corner a man passed him running fast, and turned to the left down Euston Road; did not notice him particularly, but saw that he was wearing a cloth cap, pulled well down, and rough clothes; might have been a labourer; was of burly build, and had a savage face; estimated time, 1.20 a.m. (NB – Witness is a small man, and seems to be of nervous disposition.)

'John Cross, chauffeur, was putting his employer's car away in Monmouth Mews (that's on the other side of the alley at the back of the Mansions) when he saw a man scrambling over the wall that separates the alley from the courtyard of the Mansions; he ran off down the alley; witness did not think anything was wrong, so did not follow him; had a good view of him; man was wearing a trilby hat and lounge suit; was of slight build and looked like a gentleman; estimated time, 1.22 a.m.

'Mrs Mabel Jantry, a working housekeeper (that means charwoman), was passing the end of Stone's Alley when she saw a man run out of the entrance and along Platts Street towards the Euston Road; she was on the further side of the street; man was wearing a light raincoat and no hat; she noticed particularly that he had no hat on, which looked funny with the raincoat; witness thinks he was a small man, and had a large, round, white face, and looked frightened; he was gone in a flash; estimated time, 1.38 a.m. (N.B. – Witness's statements as to the reason for her own presence in Platts Street at that time are confused, and it is not improbable that she was under the influence of liquor.)

'Alfred Tanner, bus conductor, saw a man running hard along the Euston Road just past Platts Street, in the direction of Warren Street Station; his bus was travelling fast, but the man kept almost level with it for some distance; witness had a good look at him, because he wondered why he did not jump on the bus if he was in such a hurry; man was wearing no hat, and kept his face turned away from the road; was of slight build, and wearing a blue serge suit, respectable but shabby; certainly was not wearing a raincoat; from what witness could see of his face as the bus got ahead, it was pale and looked distorted from the running; witness put him down as a gentleman on his uppers; was panting and evidently in physical distress; witness kept looking back at him, and finally saw him turn off down Tottenham Court Road; estimated time, 1.32 a.m. (NB – Witness seems intelligent, observant, and reliable.)

'PC XZ 1158 Edward Lofty was on point duty at junction of Euston Road, Tottenham Court Road, and Hampstead Road. There were still plenty of people about. Saw a man running slowly along Euston Road from direction of Euston Station, in obvious distress and panting heavily; he turned into Tottenham Court Road; was of slight build, no hat, blue lounge suit, no raincoat, kept his head turned away; large bulge in right-hand jacket pocket; estimated height, five foot eight inches; was certainly not a labourer, looked like a clerk; was running like a young man, but exhausted; estimated age, thirty or under; time, 1.30 a.m.; witness was in two minds to follow him, but considered there was still too much traffic for him to leave his point safely.

'Curse the idiot!' concluded Moresby, unofficially.

'And you mean to say all those descriptions refer to the same man?' asked Roger. 'The last two agree well, but the others – !'

'It's what we always get,' Moresby replied laconically. 'And generally we don't get anything so good as that bus conductor, to say nothing of one of our own men.'

'So he was seen actually climbing out of the courtyard. That's good. Any traces?'

'Yes; it's plain enough where he got over; but nothing of any use.'

'And you say those descriptions – the reliable ones – fit Jim Watkins, or whatever his name is?'

'Yes, quite well. He's a small man, and always looks neat. You'd take him for a good-class shop assistant.'

'Well, that's all very satisfactory. What about the search of the flat, by the way? Anything interesting come to light?'

'No. Nor a halfpenny, either. He got away with the lot. No, we found nothing more. Not even a will.'

'Oh? So the niece does inherit. Lucky young woman. Or has she an elder brother? I suppose you've found her?'

'Yes, she's got a flat now, off Theobald's Road. Does secretarial work, I gather. No, she's got no brother; she's an only child. But as to inheriting...' Moresby shrugged his shoulders.

'What?'

'Well, she just says she won't. Like that. I don't know whether the lawyers can make her. Says she never saw her aunt, and what she's heard of her makes her glad she never did. Says she's quite sure her aunt never meant her to get the inheritance, and there must be a will somewhere; and even if she'd left it all to her in black and white she wouldn't touch a penny of it; she had no wish to be under any obligation, even a post-mortem one, to anyone who had behaved as disgustingly to her father as her aunt had; and that, she said, was that.'

'And is it?' Roger asked with interest.

'I suppose so. She struck me as a most determined young lady. I managed to persuade her to look after her aunt's affairs for the time being, and see to the flat and all that, after a lot of high-falutin talk about duty and moral obligations and Lord knows what; so she's doing that until, as she says, the rightful heir turns up.'

'Sounds like a Lyceum melodrama,' Roger commented. 'And as for Miss Barnett junior – well, I don't know what she sounds like. If the death of someone I didn't know but whom I disliked by hearsay, presented me with twenty thousand pounds I shouldn't begin talking about Cats' Homes and what not. I should say, 'Ha, ha!' Wouldn't you?'

'I should, sir. But there's no accounting for tastes, as they say. Miss Stella Barnett seems to me a most independent young lady.'

'And an interesting one,' Roger meditated. 'I should like to meet her. A young woman who is prepared to throw twenty thousand pounds to the fishes ought to be useful to me.' With the unscrupulous inhumanity of the novelist Roger was always on the look-out for interesting and original characters to use in his books; it is surprising how rarely he was able to find either an original or even an interesting one.

'Well, that's easy enough, Mr Sheringham,' Moresby pronounced. 'She's round there, so far as I know, at this minute. Sergeant Afford's there too. Now if I were to ask you to take a note from me to the sergeant…?'

'I, having nothing better to do, should reply that I'd be delighted,' Roger smiled.

Moresby picked up some photographs and began putting them into an envelope. 'Perhaps you'd like to have a look at these yourself, Mr Sheringham,' he said, pulling them out again.

Roger took them. They consisted of a few blurred and not particularly interesting smudges. He asked what they were.

'The Kid's prints. We found a few fairly good impressions, on sticky surfaces, and the candle, and so on. No use in evidence, of course, as he wore gloves; but they help our case against him.'

'How can they?'

'Doesn't anything strike you about them, Mr Sheringham?' Moresby mocked. 'Well, fancy that. I should have thought you'd have noticed at once how slim those prints are. Precious few of our friends leave dainty traces like that; but the Kid's got a hand like a girl's; in fact, it's one of his little games to dress up as a girl now and then, and an uncommon convincing one he makes.'

'How awkward for you,' Roger laughed, handing the photographs back. 'You don't know whether you're looking for a man or a woman.'

'That's a fact,' Moresby agreed, putting the prints back into the envelope. 'If he's lying low, it wouldn't surprise me a bit to hear he's doing a bit of female impersonation. Still, that won't help him for long.'

'Forty-eight hours,' Roger murmured. 'You've got about two left, to win your bet.'

'Then it's lucky you didn't take me, Mr Sheringham, isn't it? Here you are, sir. If you'll give those to the sergeant, I'll be much obliged. He'll know what they are.'

Paying off his taxi in front of Monmouth Mansions, Roger glanced up at the top windows. As he glanced, a mop emerged from one of them, was twirled vigorously, and snapped back again. The late Miss Barnett's home appeared to be undergoing a much-needed cleansing.

He did not go upstairs at once, but strolled along till he reached the mouth of the narrow alley, and turned up it. No instinct but mere curiosity prompted him to have a look for the place where the Kid had climbed over the wall. From the alley side he could detect nothing, but opposite the mews was a door in the wall. Roger tried the handle, and the door opened; he noticed then that it had a latch, but no lock. He passed into the courtyard. It may be said at once that he found nothing there of the slightest importance.

The door of No. 8 was opened to him not by Sergeant Afford, but by a young woman in an overall with a blue-and-white check dust-cap on her head. 'Yes?' she said with brief competence.

'I've come from Scotland Yard,' Roger said, raising his hat. This was true enough, but the meaning it conveyed was not quite so true. Roger did not mean it to be. 'Is Sergeant Afford here, please?'

'He's in the bedroom,' returned the young woman. 'You know your way?'

Roger nodded, and walked down the passage. The young woman disappeared back into the sitting-room, whence the next moment came sounds of strenuous labour.

Sergeant Afford jerked his head towards the sounds and grinned. 'I've asked her, why not send for a charwoman; but she says the place is so filthy she'd blush to turn any charwoman on to it.' He became absorbed in the photographs.

Roger strolled to the sitting-room.

Everything was upside down, in more confusion even than when he saw it last. Chairs were piled on top of tables, the carpet was up, pictures were down; dimly to be discerned in a cloud of dust was the young woman.

'I should have thought,' said Roger mildly, from the doorway, 'that a vacuum cleaner would have been more effective.'

'Don't possess one,' replied young Miss Barnett briefly.

'I do.'

'How nice for you.'

'I mean, if you cared to borrow it...'

'Thanks; I'd like to.'

The conversation seemed to be at an end. At any rate the young woman paid no further attention to her guest. Presumably he was now expected to make good his offer by producing the vacuum cleaner. After hovering for a minute or two, without any other result, he went off to do so.

'A refreshingly direct young person,' Roger considered, as he ran down the stone stairs.

And by no means an unpleasing one to look at, he reflected a further half-hour later, as, leaning against the lintel, he watched her wielding the vacuum cleaner in question, observation being thus rendered more easy by removal of the dust cloud. Not at all unpleasing, though perhaps a shade too stocky in the figure for my taste. She doesn't look like a secretary at all; more like a... A what? Roger was not sure. Fishwife sounded rude. Besides, she did not look in the least like a fishwife.

He decided to copy her own direct methods.

'You know, you're wasted as a secretary, Miss Barnett.'

She switched off the mechanism to answer him.

'Why?'

'You handle that machine like a master.'

'Meaning I'd make a better charwoman?'

'Possibly,' Roger laughed. 'But that isn't what I did mean. Merely that you look more like an outdoor than an indoor person.'

'I was trained as a games mistress. Had a job at — ' She mentioned a well-known and large girls' school.

'And you threw it up for secretarial work?'

She nodded. 'Pay was rotten. And I don't care for discipline.'

'Being under it, or inflicting it?'

'Both,' said Miss Barnett, unsmiling. 'So I took a course of shorthand-typing. Now I wish I hadn't.'

'Why?'

'Can't get a job. That's why I've got time to waste cleaning up this gloryhole.'

'Look here, I've got some secretarial work I want doing. If you – '

'Thanks; I'm not in the charity queue yet,' replied Miss Barnett crisply. 'As you seem so interested in my affairs, I may as well tell you I've quite enough private income to live on comfortably; though I should have thought you'd have found that out for yourself by now. My father didn't get rid of quite everything, you know. By the way, I suppose this is an official interview?'

'No, it isn't. You may have misunderstood me. I said I had just come from Scotland Yard; not that I was attached to them. My name's Roger Sheringham; I write novels. The offer was perfectly genuine. I happen to be in need of a secretary. If you want the job you can have it.'

'Roger Sheringham, eh? I've read some of you books. Very sudden decision on your part, wasn't it?'

'It's my job to make quick decisions where character's concerned,' Roger said smugly. 'But really it was your handling of the vacuum cleaner that made up my mind.'

'All right, then, Mr Sheringham; if the offer's genuine, I'd like the job. What salary are you offering?'

Roger was nonplussed. A figure came vaguely into his mind as connected with offices and typing. 'Forty-five shillings a week.'

'Not enough,' returned the young woman promptly. 'Do you want a secretary, or a shorthand-typist?'

'Well, a secretary, I think,' said Roger, not by any means sure of the distinction.

'Then you should offer a proper secretary's salary,' Miss Barnett told him severely.

'What is a proper secretary's salary?' Roger asked humbly.

'I couldn't come to you for less than three pounds.'

'Three pounds it is, then.'

'Very well. I'll be at your address at nine o'clock next Monday morning. Let me have a note of it, please.' Roger gave it to her, and she wrote it down. 'Thank you, Mr Sheringham,' she said, in a tone of dismissal, and switched on the vacuum motor again.

Roger crept down the passage in considerable bewilderment. 'Now why in the name of all that's unholy,' he asked himself, 'did I do that? I don't really want a secretary at all. If I did, I shouldn't want that one. "A proper secretary's salary." Dash it, I don't want a proper secretary. If I wanted a secretary at all it would be an improper one; one I could flirt with. Great author's moments of relaxation, and what not. But could one flirt with Miss Stella Barnett? Sooner with a leg of mutton. And yet that's odd, because she's distinctly good-looking, with those nice hazel eyes and that decidedly moulded chin, firm but not a bit heavy; nice complexion, too. And nice soft hair. Yes, she is good-looking. But attractive, no. Have I ever met a good-looking woman before who was not attractive? The two terms have become practically synonymous. But in Miss Barnett they're not. In fact, an odd young woman altogether is Miss Stella Barnett. Perhaps I'm not so sorry I gave way to that remarkable impulse. She ought to repay a little studying. And after all,' Roger comforted himself, as he turned the handle of the bedroom door, 'there's always the sack.'

But he knew even then that it would need a braver man than himself to employ that useful weapon upon Miss Barnett junior.

He strolled into the bedroom.

There was really no reason at all for Roger to return to the bedroom. Perhaps he turned into it instinctively as one seeks the society of one's own kind after a shattering interview with one of the other sex. Now that he was there, under Sergeant Afford's mildly inquiring glance, he found some difficulty in explaining his return.

'So you people have finished here?' he remarked, more by way of saying some words than with any particular interest in his question.

'Finished, sir?'

'I mean, you're not keeping the place *in statu quo* any longer.'

'Oh, you mean the young lady. Well, we didn't want the sitting-room any more really, so the Chief told me I could hand that over to her.' Sergeant Afford grinned. 'She seemed very anxious to make a start with her cleaning, and wouldn't leave me alone till I'd got on to the Chief and asked.'

Roger returned the grin, understandingly.

'We're still keeping this room and the kitchen locked up, though,' the sergeant went on. 'In fact, I was just going along to the kitchen.'

'I'll come with you,' said Roger.

Chatting, they passed out into the passage, where the sergeant carefully locked up the room they had just left and unlocked the kitchen. He began to busy himself, apparently in checking some measurements, and Roger slouched round the tiny room. By the gas stove he halted, frowning; something looked vaguely wrong about it.

The sergeant, now it seemed in loquacious mood, was retailing the results of the laborious inquiries he had been making as to the possibility of anyone having seen the Kid

54

enter the building; they had taken up a lot of his precious time and led nowhere. 'Not that I ever expected they would,' he remarked fatalistically, 'though they had to be made all the same. It wouldn't have been like the Kid to let anyone see him coming in.'

'Have any difficulty in tracing the people Mrs Boyd told you about?' Roger asked absently. 'Plumbers and so on.' What *was* wrong with that gas stove? It was very small and flimsy; that was one thing wrong.

'Difficulty!' snorted the sergeant. 'But we found 'em all. Or all that mattered. By the way, I don't know if you've heard, Mr Sheringham, but we've got confirmation of our idea that the Kid got into the building before ten o'clock, when the front door was locked. By a bit of luck something went wrong with the lock that night. It jammed, and wouldn't lock. That's the Yale I'm talking about; the one the tenants have keys for. There's a second lock on the door though, a heavy, old-fashioned one that hasn't been used for years, but Mrs Boyd has a key to it, and that night she used it – with the result that she had to come out and open the door herself to everyone who was trying to get in. Lucky for us, because that gives us a complete check on who came in between ten and midnight; no one came in after that. All residents, as it happened. That saved me a bit of work.'

'Has the stove been moved?' Roger asked abruptly. Of course! What an idiot he had been.

The sergeant paused to readjust his ideas to this question.

'Moved? No, sir. None of the furniture in this room has been moved.'

Roger looked at him speculatively. 'It's a very small model, isn't it? I should think you could almost pick it up in your arms, sergeant.'

The sergeant measured its weight with his glance. 'Shouldn't be surprised if I could, sir. Why?'

'Rather odd, isn't it? The rope's tied fair and square round the middle; and the stove stands a good three foot from the wall. I remember wondering when I first saw it the other day if you people would be able to make a guess at the weight of the man on the rope from the amount of the stove's displacement from its usual position. It's only skewed round a few inches, you see.'

'Well, sir?'

'Well, I repeat: the stove stands a good three foot from the window-wall. That doesn't strike you as odd? I didn't realise the other day how light a stove it is. Wouldn't you expect it to have been dragged across the floor right under the window? I should.'

Sergeant Afford had suddenly taken on what seemed to Roger a peculiarly wooden expression. 'The Kid's a small man, Mr Sheringham.'

'Very, I should say,' Roger agreed dryly. 'Almost a miniature one.'

'Then there's the friction over the window-sill, to take some of the strain.'

'Humph!' said Roger, examining the sill in question. 'Yes, there's certainly that. The paint here on the edge looks almost as if it had been rubbed with a bit of sandpaper instead of a rope.'

'He'd swung a bit in the air. There'd naturally be a lot of wear on that edge. But as for the stove...'

'Yes?'

'Why, if you'd looked just a little more carefully, Mr Sheringham, you'd have seen that this front foot, where it's skewed forward here, has caught up against the edge of a floorboard. See, sir? Just off the edge of the linoleum. That'd be quite enough to stop it sliding any further.' The sergeant's wooden expression turned to the odious grin of one who says: 'I told you so.'

But Roger was still not satisfied. 'Yes, I see now. But I shouldn't have said that would stop it sliding any further. I should have thought that resistance there would have caused the stove to tilt right over. I'm sure this rope's just above the centre of gravity, if anything.'

'Perhaps it is, sir,' replied the sergeant patiently. 'But you must remember that the pull wasn't downwards, nor even straight; it was upwards, the way the rope has to pass over the sill. The knot would have to be a good deal higher than it is to tilt the stove over.'

'I'm not at all sure that I agree.'

'No, sir? Well, I heard the Chief remark you were fond of a bit of an argument.'

'Perhaps I am,' Roger laughed. 'And perhaps I'm fond of a bit of an experiment too. I'd like to make one now, with your permission. I'd like to go down to the courtyard and swing for a moment on that rope while you watch how the gas stove behaves.'

'Well, you can do that with pleasure, Mr Sheringham, if you want a bit of exercise,' Sergeant Afford granted affable permission.

Roger ran nimbly down the stairs.

'Ready?' he called up to the window as he reached the bottom of the rope, which hung three or four feet above the ground.

The sergeant's head appeared at the window. 'Ready, sir. Swing away. I'll keep an eye on the stove.' He waited, grinning.

Roger, rather annoyed at being regarded less as one making an interesting scientific experiment than as something in the nature of a monkey on a rope, took a firm hold and pulled himself off his feet. He climbed, hand over hand, till his toes were three or four feet off the ground, and swung gently. Then things happened. There was a thud from the room above. Roger dropped an abrupt twelve inches, and was then jerked back up a couple of them; the next moment he was sprawling on hands and knees on the ground. His first thought was that the jerk had caused him to loosen his hold on the rope; then he realised that he was, in fact, still grasping it. He looked up. The rope had snapped off just above where he had been holding it.

With increasing excitement he examined the end in his hand. The rope was made up of six strands. Two of these showed clean ends; the other four showed dirty.

He hurried back up the stairs.

'Look,' he said briefly, with only a side glance at the gas stove, now lying on its side. 'This rope was frayed.'

'Oh, yes,' nodded the sergeant, annoyingly unperturbed. 'We knew *that*.'

'Then...?'

'And so did the Kid. That's why the fray was down at the bottom. He doesn't weigh as much as you, Mr Sheringham, but he probably wouldn't risk the fray and dropped off when he came to it. It would only mean a fall of half-a-dozen feet, and he falls like a cat. And you notice it held even you all right while it was steady. It was the jerk of the gas stove falling over that broke it, not the deadweight.'

'Ah, yes; the gas stove did fall over after all, I see.'

'Yes, it did, sir,' agreed the sergeant serenely. 'Inspector Beach must have shifted that knot a bit when he was having a look at it. Very careless of him. But then he didn't know you'd be wanting to carry out experiments with it, Mr Sheringham.'

58

'Yes,' said Roger. 'Well, I think that will be all the experiments for this morning. In fact, I must be getting along. Good morning, sergeant.'

'Good morning, sir; and thank you.'

'Thank *you*, sergeant,' Roger returned politely.

He called out a respectful farewell to its occupant, now energetically scrubbing on hands and knees, as he passed the sitting-room, which not being answered he concluded (perhaps a little doubtfully) could not have been heard, and walked, sedately this time because deep in thought, down the stairs. The case was growing interesting; remarkably interesting; extraordinarily interesting. In fact it showed every sign of becoming a very pretty case indeed. Certainly it would not be his fault if it failed to fulfil this promise of beauty, for from now onwards, Roger decided, its prettiness was going to become his own personal concern. As for Scotland Yard he had done all he reasonably could; he had, so to speak, said things very loud and clear; he had, to all purposes, shouted them in the sergeant's ear. It could no longer be considered his fault if officialdom obstinately refused to recognise the one fact in the transformed case which was beyond dispute – that nobody had climbed down that rope the night before last.

chapter five

Roger had hurried away from Monmouth Mansions because he wanted to think, and to think extremely hard. He took a taxi to the British Museum and went into the Reading Room. If one cannot think in the British Museum Reading Room one can think nowhere. Finding a vacant desk, he drew a piece of paper towards him and pulled a pencil out of his pocket.

For a whole hour he sat there, his head on his hand, making a note from time to time on the paper in front of him. Then he jumped to his feet. Every path he tried led to one particular question, which Mrs Boyd alone could answer: the Yale lock on the front door had jammed with the catch back so that Mrs Boyd had had to make use of the large mortice lock, with the result that nobody from outside could get in without her aid, but – *could anyone from the inside get out without it?* That was the really crucial question.

Another taxi hurried him back to Monmouth Mansions.

Mrs Boyd had seen Roger arrive the day before yesterday with the Scotland Yard party; it had never occurred to her that he was not one of them, and Roger saw no reason to disabuse her mind; she answered his questions readily.

'No, sir, I didn't leave the key in the lock. I didn't like to somehow, it being the only one. You'd be surprised how things disappear if one leaves them about, even in a place like this.'

'What time did you lock the door?'

'Half-past ten, same as usual.'

'Then if anyone inside the building wanted to get out after that, you would have had to open the door?'

'I should, sir, and I did.'

'You did? For how many people?'

'For one only, sir. A gentleman who had been visiting Miss Delamere, in No. 5.'

'How do you know he had been visiting Miss Delamere? I mean, was it a man you know?'

'I've seen him here often enough to know where he'd come from,' replied Mrs Boyd, a little offended.

'I don't seem to remember your mentioning this man to the sergeant among the people you knew by sight,' Roger said, searching his memory.

'No, because I never see him come in. The sergeant only asked me about the people I see come in. Still, if he came out it stands to reason he came in, doesn't it?'

Roger agreed that it did, and asked at what time the man came out. Mrs Boyd said that so far as she could remember it was between eleven and half-past. Roger nodded: if that was the case there was no need to bother about him further.

'Now what I really want to know, Mrs Boyd, is this,' he went on suavely. 'Would it have been possible for anyone to have got out of the building after, we'll say, midnight without your knowledge? Take this door first. You left it locked. Was it locked in the morning?'

'It was, sir. On that I'd take my dying oath.'

'May I have a look at the key?'

'Certainly you may.'

Mrs Boyd hurried through her own open front door, and returned with a large Victorian doorkey. Roger thanked her and tried it in the lock. As he expected, the end did not project on the other side; it would have been impossible to turn it from outside with pincers.

'That's all right then. By the way, why are you so sure it was locked in the morning?'

'Because when I came out to open the door as usual first thing, I'd forgotten about the lock having jammed and had to go back for the key. I tried the door, you see, and it wouldn't open. That's how I knew it was locked, because it *was* locked.'

'Well, that's certainly conclusive enough,' Roger laughed. 'Now, what about the other door, into the courtyard?'

'That was locked right enough, and bolted too, same as I do it every night. I'd have noticed quick enough if it hadn't been.'

'Yes, of course you would. Are there any other doors?'

'Not a one. Without he got through a window of one of the flats nobody couldn't have left the building that night, just as it happened, without my noticing something the next morning. But what does that matter, when everyone knows he climbed down the rope, the murdering villain?'

'Yes, of course, Well. I think that's all I wanted to know, Mrs Boyd. I suppose you've got the Yale lock working all right now?'

'Certainly I have. Mr Boyd unscrewed it first thing next morning and took it round to the locksmiths' on his way to work. They sent to put it on again that same afternoon.'

'I see. What had gone wrong with it?'

'That I'm afraid I couldn't tell you, sir. Locks and things is a bit out of my line.'

'Yes, of course. Oh, there's one other thing. I should like a list of the occupants of the flats here, and their professions and so on. If you'll tell me, I'll jot them down. Perhaps we'd better go into your hall, if you don't mind.'

'I gave that sergeant a list, sir,' demurred Mrs Boyd, moving rather reluctantly into her own domain.

'Yes, and now I'd like another,' Roger said pleasantly as he followed her.

In the dark little hall he wrote down in his notebook the names she gave him, with as many details as he could obtain concerning each person. The process was a somewhat lengthy one, and Mrs Boyd grew visibly impatient, but Roger refused to scamp it. He did not leave until he had obtained everything he wanted.

It was now almost one o'clock, and his man, Meadows, looked at him reproachfully as he reached his rooms in the Albany twenty minutes later. Roger usually made a point of extreme punctuality where such a delicate matter as cooking was involved. On this occasion he did not even notice the look, and ate the mushroom omelette that followed it with an absent air which pained the omelette's author considerably. Meadows prided himself on his mushroom omelettes.

Roger pulled his page of notes out from his pocket and laid it beside his plate, occasionally adding something further. His meal over, he took the paper to his study and sat down at his writing-table, still poring over it.

The amount of data he had collected surprised himself. Though not a single one of the points he had noted down was enough in itself to throw the slightest doubt on the police case, their combined effect was, to Roger's mind, disturbingly significant. With the addition of his own observations concerning the rope and the gas stove, he found it irresistible.

His points, and his own reflections on them, ran more or less as follows:

1. No footprints on the floors, and 'a nice, muddy October too,' as Moresby had said. This is naturally accounted for by the assumption that the murderer waited a considerable time inside the building, having already wiped his feet on the front-door mat. But in that case how about the cake of mud that was found? Why one and not the other? Why not the other and yet the one?

2. Why was smashed crockery lying on the kitchen floor? Why smash crockery? Accident? Possibly; but such an easily avoidable accident that one wonders at it. The man's whole object should have been to avoid making noise, yet that crockery looked as if it had been smashed almost wantonly. In any case why bother about crockery at all? A plate cannot contain a sovereign. Odd.

3. Marks on the window-sill and at the top of the wall. Yes, quite to be expected. But why only at the top of the wall? Before he'd got going properly, Moresby had said. But even when he was going properly he'd have bumped against the wall occasionally on that long descent and might have been expected to fend himself off with his feet; after all, the rope hung only a foot at the most from the face of the wall. Yet there is no other sign of scratching; and what is there is all within reach of the window, for a person wielding, let us say, a four-foot scratching-instrument, almost a long poker like the one in the sitting-room. Still, this merely confirms the conclusion that nobody did climb down that rope.

4. As still further confirmation, there is the question why on earth he should have bothered to use the rope at all, with

only two doors between him and the street. Beach explained that, to his own satisfaction and Moresby's, and they if anyone ought to know the strange habits of the professional criminal; but Beach's explanation really does seem a little hard to swallow. A much more feasible one, on the facts that we know now, would be that he went down to the front door and found his way out there cut off. But even then it is difficult to believe that he would have preferred climbing down that rope, with all the possibilities of being observed in the act, than the, to him, comparatively simple matter of forcing the front door.

5. Another point about that mud. It turns out to have come all the way from Kent. How nice and handy of it to have stuck to his heel during all that long journey, to deposit itself as a neat clue just where wanted. Possible? Perhaps; but hardly probable.

6. Another point still. There was a distinct muddy smudge on the linoleum. And the cake had been actually adhering to it. Obviously, therefore, the surface of the mud must have been wet. How was this, when the rest of his feet were dry, as shown by the absence of prints? Did he step into a patch of water with his muddy heel only, causing the surface of the cake to become adhesive and so stick, on pressure, to the linoleum, the part clinging to his heel having become less tenacious through drying? Again possible, but still more improbable

7. The cigarette stubs in the stair-cupboard. No doubt he might have squashed them out on the toe of his boot, as Moresby glibly suggested. But why? Certainly he had not squashed them out on any of the fabric of the cupboard. No, if we are to look at the appearance of that cupboard with a mind unprejudiced by the context of other facts, we should say without hesitation that the appearance it presents is

exactly as if somebody had emptied a very full ashtray on its floor.

8. And if the absence of footprints in the flat itself is noteworthy, still more so is their absence in this cupboard. However carefully he wiped his boots (and he couldn't have wiped them quite so carefully as Moresby thought, or he would have wiped that cake of mud off) they must still have been damp, because it was raining between nine and ten-thirty, at which latter hour the bottom door was shut. Could he have come in before nine? No doubt he could have, but would he? The modern burglar does not operate without careful reconnoitring; he would certainly have known at what time the bottom door was habitually shut; and he would not have wanted to wait longer than was necessary. All the probabilities point to nine-thirty to ten-thirty as the period during which he arrived (though certainly Moresby had said he might have come as early as five; but this is highly improbable, surely.) This leaves the absence of some faint boot-marking on the cupboard floor unexplained.

9. Why was the flat turned upside-down? It is almost inevitable that the chest under the bed was found early in the search, almost certainly before the kitchen, for argument, had been ransacked. The man's object must have been to get away as soon as possible after finding what he was looking for. Why didn't he? Could he really have delayed making his escape, after lifting more than six hundred pounds, on the chance that a little more money might be concealed elsewhere in the flat? It seems in the very highest degree unlikely.

10. There are some odd points about that man running away. In the first place, would a cool hand run at all, and so attract unnecessary attention to himself? He must have lost his head pretty badly to behave so foolishly. Then, except for

the chauffeur's evidence, there is nothing to connect him with Monmouth Mansions at all; and even the chauffeur's does not connect him with No. 8, it connects him merely with the courtyard and the wall. Now the important thing is that there is no lock at all on that door in the wall; anyone can walk in or out of the yard; and yet we have this man, an experienced campaigner, climbing instead over the quite unnecessary wall. Does this tally with the probabilities? It does not. The first thing one would expect Jim Watkins to have discovered in advance is that once in the courtyard his difficulties are at an end (assuming, with the police, that he had gone down, or intended to go down the rope). Is it too much to say (a) that this running man had no connection with the murder at all; (b) that the running man is not the man seen by the chauffeur; or (c) that the chauffeur's memory is not quite accurate and he never saw a man climbing over the wall at all? Yet any one of these possibilities seems more reasonable than that this running and climbing man was Jim Watkins. (NB – It must be borne in mind constantly that the man under consideration is an *experienced* criminal, if an amateur murderer; at any rate his murdering would not be so utterly amateurish as is usual. Yet the police are content to attribute to him blunders which the most amateurish of criminals might be expected to avoid.)

11. One other point about the rope. Beach mentioned that it was not the ordinary type used, thin manilla; it was thicker and heavier. It did not seem to strike the police that with all their repetitions of the fact that the professional criminal never deviates an iota from his accustomed methods, here they were assuming just such a deviation. Why should Jim Watkins, who would naturally want the thinnest and most readily portable rope obtainable, bring with him in this

instance a rope much thicker and heavier than his usual one?

12. The police constantly referred to the absence of fingerprints nowadays from the hands of professional criminals almost as if an absence of fingerprints necessarily indicated a professional criminal. But in these days of detective stories it does nothing of the sort; every man, woman and child in the country knows as much as that.

13. There were no marks of a struggle on the body. Moresby explained this, and took the explanation for granted, by the assumption that Miss Barnett was too frail to put up a struggle. This might well be, *after* the murderer had got his weapon round her throat, having got behind her to do so in order to take her by surprise; but is it captious to suggest that Miss Barnett, a notoriously suspicious woman, would not have allowed a complete stranger to get behind her at all, or take her by surprise, and a male stranger at that? That he did take her by surprise is evident (the absence of markings on the body proves that quite conclusively); an interesting question therefore arises.

14. Again touching this matter of the complete stranger, how *did* Miss Barnett come to be murdered in her bedroom? The divisional inspector put forward an explanation of that, and no doubt a possible one; but *would* she have let a stranger (and a male stranger at that!) into her bedroom? Consult again the balance of probabilities.

15. And she was in her nightdress only. If the suggestion were correct, that Watkins rang the bell of her flat and she got up from bed to answer it, wouldn't she almost certainly put on a wrapper of some kind over her nightdress? And yet she didn't. Why not?

16. And lastly why did Miss Barnett, roused from her bed at one o'clock in the morning to be confronted in the

doorway by a complete stranger, neither slam the door in his face before he could utter a word (which would have been her most probable course) nor give the alarm in any way at all, instead of taking him meekly into her flat, which was about the most unlikely thing that such a woman as Miss Barnett would ever have done?

'It's irresistible!' Roger cried aloud, thumping his desk with his fist. 'Because the man to whom she opened her door at that unusual hour was not a stranger at all. It was an inhabitant of one of the other flats. Every single thing points to it!'

Roger spent the rest of the afternoon jotting these thoughts down upon paper. He also wrote down, while he still remembered it, the information he had obtained from Mrs Boyd that morning.

These latter notes ran as follows:

OCCUPANTS OF MONMOUTH MANSIONS

(With information supplied by Mrs Boyd, caretaker)

No. 1 (Ground Floor) – Mrs Boyd.

No. 2 (Ground Floor) – Mr Augustus Weller; journalist, assistant editor *The London Merryman*, humorous weekly (*soi-disant*); aged about thirty; bachelor; cheerful (perhaps a little too cheerful, in his female friends; a faint note of disapproval in the Boyd tones here), but generous, yes, a *very* generous young gentleman (says Mrs Boyd, who 'does' for him; hence no doubt the faintness of the disapproving note); not a large amount of money, but plenty for a young gentleman like him with no ties (but that depends on the young gentleman's tastes).

No. 3 (First Floor) – Mr and Mrs Kincross. Mr Francis Kincross, a real young gentleman from Oxford College;

aged about thirty-three; employed in an advertising business (name and address surprisingly unknown); a little nervy perhaps, but a *real* young gentleman. Likewise Marjorie Kincross, a real young lady; aged about twenty-eight; daughter of a solicitor in Devonport, maiden name Anderson. Devoted couple. Baby Dora Kincross, aged two; the sweetest little dear you ever saw.

No. 4 (First Floor) – Mr and Mrs Barrington Braybrook. Gentility doubtful. John Barrington Braybrook, manager of the wine department at Harridge's Stores; aged about forty; a very decided gentleman – well, brusque, you might say (or mightn't); but a very clever one; done well for himself, and that's a fact; draws more money than anyone else in the Mansions. Mamie Barrington Braybrook; about same age; rescued by John BB from the provincial revue stage twelve years ago (? And never regretted it); believed to be of American origin, but reticent on this point (the only point, apparently, on which she is so, judging from the mass of detail about her past career which Mrs Boyd has by heart).

No. 5 (Second Floor) – Miss Evadne Delamere. A very decidedly disapproving note here. 'Described as an actress;' but more often out of a job than in one, if you ask Mrs Boyd (as I did). Morals suspected to be doubtful (but more by instinct than evidence, of which there seems to be none at all). Aged thirty-five if a day, but still pretending to be twenty. Far too many men friends, again if you ask Mrs Boyd (which there is no need to do; she is only too willing to volunteer information on this theme). And, surprisingly, far too much money too; the source of which is evidently unknown to Mrs Boyd, but quite plainly, and libellously, hinted.

No. 6 (Second Floor) – The Ennismore Smiths. Further information on this couple suggests that they have had a very hard time for the last half dozen years. From a large house in Hampstead and affluence, they have come down to Monmouth Mansions; and even then Mrs ES has to work (and in Mrs Boyd's opinion it is she who keeps the home going at all). This is a shame, because she was brought up a real lady if anyone was; why, her father was a general in the British army. And Mr ES was at Cambridge College, and is consequently too much of a gentleman to deal adequately with the sharp ones in the film business. A very soft spot in Mrs Boyd's heart for both the Ennismore Smiths.

No. 7 (Third Floor) – Mrs Pilchard. No friend of Mrs Boyd's. Apparent reasons: Mrs Pilchard is (a) Irish; (b) Roman Catholic. She is therefore debarred from being a real lady, and is thus damned.

No. 8 (Third Floor) – Miss Barnett.

(*Note* – The left-hand side of the building contains Nos. 1, 3, 5 and 7, the right-hand side Nos. 2, 4, 6 and 8. The flats are all built on the same plan, so that similar rooms are above similar rooms all the way up, *i.e.* bedrooms above bedrooms, kitchens above kitchens, etc. The noises that wakened Mr and Mrs Ennismore Smith must therefore have come from Miss Barnett's bedroom.)

Roger leaned back in his chair and pushed his hands into his trouser pockets.

'Augustus Weller,' he murmured; 'Francis Kincross; John Barrington Braybrook; Lionel Ennismore Smith. I wonder which of them did it?'

chapter six

Roger sat in his dressing-gown, engulfing a fried sole. A cup of coffee steamed at his elbow. Mr Sheringham was breakfasting. The one real advantage of being an author, in Roger's opinion, is that authors can breakfast in their dressing-gowns, and do so at what hour they jolly well like, and take their time over it too, and (if they are bachelors) there is no one to say them nay. It is the sole remnant of a robust bohemianism, and extremely painful to those strict souls who sit down every morning at the family table, fully clad, at the unpleasing hour of eight-thirty, and are unconscionably pleased with themselves all the rest of the day for thus mortifying their several fleshes.

In deference to habit an open newspaper was propped against the coffee pot, but after a mechanical glance at the headlines, and a hurried study of the short paragraph dealing with 'The Euston Flat Murder,' now relegated to the secondary newspage, Roger paid no further attention to it. When an enthusiasm was occupying him, whether it might be for applied psychopathy, bulbs, or murder, his mind had room for that subject and that only; all else was irrelevant. (Incidentally this was why he achieved results; concentration, though a one-track affair, does reach its destination.) At present the singular business of Monmouth Mansions had ousted every other matter.

It was therefore with dismay bordering on panic that Roger received the news from Meadows that a young lady, announcing herself to be Mr Sheringham's new secretary, had arrived and wished to see him immediately.

'Immediately?' Roger echoed. 'Did she say "immediately"?'

'She did, sir,' replied Meadows, outwardly unperturbed.

'Well, she can't see me immediately.'

'No, sir.'

To Roger's sensitive ear the man's negative did not seem quite so firm as he would have liked. 'She can't see me immediately, can she, Meadows?' he appealed.

'Certainly not, sir,' Meadows soothed him.

The two males looked at each other, the same image in both minds – the image of Miss Barnett junior. Meadows' eyes asked a question which his lips would never have put: 'My good sir and master, why *did* you do this thing?' Roger's eyes echoed it: 'Why *did* I?'

'What have you done with her?' he asked aloud.

'I showed her into the study, sir, and requested her to take a seat.'

'You requested her, eh? And did she?'

'I can't say, sir. I didn't wait to see.'

'No, Well…' Roger considered, desperately. 'Look here, Meadows, just go and tell her that I shan't be able to dictate this morning. I – I'm very busy on other matters, important other matters. Just tell her that, will you?'

'Very good, sir.'

Roger drew a breath of relief as Meadows disappeared.

But the train of his thought was broken, and his breakfast finished. He waited a few minutes, till his new secretary should have had time to make her exit, and then went back to his bedroom to dress.

It was as he was fastening his tie that a budding suspicion in his mind bloomed into certainty: there was a typewriter going somewhere, and it sounded uncommonly as if it was going in his own study. He slipped on his waistcoat and coat and set out to investigate. Cautiously opening his study door a few inches he was gratified by a glimpse of singular devotion to duty: at a small table by the opposite window sat Miss Barnett junior, hatless and coatless, thudding away on his typewriter just as if she had never been dismissed for the morning at all. Roger's spirit moaned within him; it foresaw trouble ahead.

Softly he closed the door; but not, it seemed, softly enough. Before he had taken two surreptitious steps down the passage it was whisked open again and a brisk voice hailed him – the brisk, early-morning voice of the Efficient Secretary.

'Good morning, Mr Sheringham. Will you come in here a moment, please? You won't,' added Miss Barnett kindly, 'be disturbing me.'

'Thank you,' said Roger, and followed her.

'I got your message that you were too busy to dictate this morning, so I thought I'd better get on with some typing. I found these papers lying on your desk. I take it you left them out for me to type?'

'Papers?' Roger echoed vaguely. He looked at the neat pile beside the typewriter. The next moment he snatched it desperately up, as one snatches a half-chewed collar away from a puppy; quite uselessly, for well one knows that collar will never be the same to one again. The pile consisted of the notes for his dossier on 'The Monmouth Mansions Mystery.'

He had been looking through them again the previous evening.

He must have forgotten to put them back in their folder before he went to bed.

'Did you read this?' he asked; as he thought, grimly.

Miss Barnett did not appear to notice the grimness.

'Oh, yes, I managed to make it out all right. I suppose it really is necessary to make so many alterations and interlinear interpolations? It makes it very difficult for me, you know. But, yes, I think I've got it fairly straight.'

Roger swallowed something. 'Up to how far?'

'Up to where?' said Miss Barnett, gently correcting this pleonasm. 'I'm half-way down the third page. The doctor's report on my aunt's body,' she added impersonally.

'I'll dictate,' Roger pronounced.

'Certainly,' Miss Barnett agreed equably. Her manner conveyed that authors must have their little whims and change their little minds; a tactful secretary took such capriciousness for granted. She sat down before the typewriter and inserted a fresh sheet of paper.

'"Ask Mama",' announced Roger, somewhat savagely.

'I beg your pardon?'

'"Ask Mama"!'

'I don't think I quite understand.'

'Title of the story. "Ask Mama", by Roger Sheringham.'

'Oh! I'm sorry.'

A faint deepening of the exquisite damask of her cheek divulged that Miss Barnett actually found herself embarrassed. Heartened, Roger went on to dictate.

He dictated without a break till one o'clock ('If she *wants* to work,' he told himself, 'actually *wants* to work, by Jove, she shall'), forcing his mind along the unwelcome channel; for if ability to concentrate on a congenial theme is one asset, a far greater one is a similar ability when the theme is uncongenial. It was a poor story, however, and he knew it. Only too plainly Miss Barnett knew it too. She said nothing, but her eyebrows were voluble.

At one o'clock she rose, covered the typewriter, and pulled on her hat. Roger held her coat for her. 'I shall be back,' she told him, 'at two-thirty.'

'I shan't want you back today,' Roger said, with what firmness he could. 'I shall be busy on other matters. I can't dictate this afternoon.'

'You haven't finished the story,' accused Miss Barnett.

'No; I'll finish it tomorrow.'

'Very well. I'll carry on with your notes on my aunt's case.' She pulled a powder-puff out of her bag and poised its mirror.

'No,' said Roger, watching the operation with something like fascination. He had frequently seen powder-puffs in use before, but somehow they did not seem fitting with Miss Barnett. Yet the result was wholly admirable.

She paused, to lift her finely drawn eyebrows at him. 'Why not?'

'I don't want them typed,' Roger replied, doggedly.

Miss Barnett thrust this ridiculous idea aside with brisk scorn. 'Nonsense! They're almost unreadable. Of course they must be typed out, if they're to be of any use to you at all.'

This unfortunately was indisputable. Roger took an unexpected decision. 'Very well; type them out this afternoon then. Thank you.' He cast a last puzzled look at Miss Barnett's exquisitely modelled nose, which at the moment was receiving a second coating of rice-powder, and retired from the room.

Over his solitary lunch he examined the reasons, unrecognised at the moment, which must have prompted his decision. He made them out to be more or less as follows:

1. She *said* she hadn't read any further than she'd typed, but I wouldn't put it past her that she had.

2. *If* she had, there will be no harm in her typing the dossier; because undoubtedly it needs typing.

3. If she hadn't, is there really any harm in her learning my opinion about her aunt's case? Was not my reluctance to divulge that opinion just instinctive secrecy? I'm quite certain that if I tell her it's confidential, I can trust her not to let it go any further.

4. Without doubt she is an unusually intelligent girl. And, considering it is her own aunt whose death is in question, a singularly unbiased one. Will not her opinion of my opinion be at any rate interesting and worth obtaining, and quite possibly valuable? I think it might be.

5. Could she not be of real help to me in the inquiries I intend to make in connection with this case? I am sure she could.

6. I realise now that the nebulous idea in my mind was that the typing out of the dossier would be an excellent way of introducing my suspicions to her without inviting comment; I shall therefore say nothing about them and wait to see if she volunteers any comments.

7. Why did my decision coincide with her use of her powder-puff? I recognise, though I deplore the connection. Could it be that I was unwilling to share my confidence with a machine, however efficient, but the powder-puff proved that the machine was after all human underneath the efficiency? I wonder. An interesting point.

8. I'm glad I did take the decision.

Roger spent the rest of his lunch wondering more about his new secretary than about the Monmouth Mansions affair. The three hours he had spent in her company had confirmed his earlier conclusions. The girl was really beautiful, not just pretty, with features of the true classical type, a straight nose, a broad forehead, hazel eyes set wide apart, a perfect mouth, and a firmly modelled chin; and her figure was not really stocky at all, just athletic; to look at, from a safe distance, she was exquisite; the notion of closer acquaintanceship was, to Roger at least, who was nothing if not catholic in his instincts, just impossible. Did she affect every male like that? And if so, how was it that a girl so theoretically attractive could be in fact so repulsive? Less and less did he regret his extraordinary offer of a secretaryship to her. She would be invaluable to him as a novelist. Already he was tentatively sketching out a new book to revolve round her character as he saw it.

After lunch, however, all thought of Miss Barnett junior vanished. There were activities to be performed, inquiries to be made, tedious in themselves and yet not without interest. Leaving a hastily scribbled note on the manuscript of his dossier to the effect that Miss Barnett was to regard the contents as highly confidential and secret, he set out for the neighbourhood of Monmouth Mansions.

A number of matters were ranged in Roger's mind for investigation. First of all, before the Kid could be finally eliminated from the case it must be quite definitely established that an escape could not have been made through a window of any of the lower flats, according to Mrs Boyd's suggestion. Then there was the chauffeur to be interrogated about the man he had seen climbing the wall, and his evidence on this point thoroughly tested. And finally there were the occupants of all the other flats to be interviewed and their circumstances, particularly on the financial side, closely examined. Mrs Pilchard too might possibly have not been drained quite dry of information by Moresby and his officers. And who had been the last person to see the dead woman alive? That point had not been ascertained when Roger was at Monmouth Mansions three days ago, and Moresby had not mentioned it yesterday; but Scotland Yard must have the information by now.

After consideration Roger decided to try the chauffeur first, as of primary importance. It was barely half-past two, and with any luck the man should be at his garage. Paying off his taxi in the street, Roger made his way up the little alley, and turned its left-hand corner. The mews lay exactly opposite the courtyard of the Mansions, overlapping it considerably at each end, for their frontage was more than twice the length of that of the yard. The alley broadened out here, for the buildings that formed the mews were set about twenty-five feet back from the line of the wall that led up to them, the extra space thus made forming a cobbled stableyard which at once raised visions of victorias and broughams. Obviously these were old stables, rented by the well-to-do when Euston was a more fashionable quarter than it has since become, ten or a dozen of them, each with its pair of big, high doors. Now they seemed to be used indiscriminately as garages and stores.

A small boy, playing solitary hop-scotch on the cobbles, the only sign of life about the place, readily gave Roger the information he required. 'Mr Cross? 'Im as is shawver to Lidy Pemmin'ton, djer mean? No. 7, 'e is. No. 7 garridge. Yer'll see the number on the door, No. 7 Seven, it is. 'E's in there nah, if 'e 'asn't gorn aht.'

Roger rewarded him with a sixpence, and the small boy left his hop-scotch abruptly and departed yelling incoherently at the top of his voice. Roger made his way to No. 7. His luck was evidently in, for a cheery hail answered his thump on the door.

John Cross proved, on throwing open one of the big doors, to be a small man with a cheerful, freckled face, whose maroon livery clashed anguishingly with his ginger-coloured hair. 'Wanting summat?' he asked.

'Your name is John Cross, isn't it?'

'Ay, mister, it is that,' replied the little man, in a pronounced Yorkshire accent.

'And from Yorkshire, I imagine?' Roger said, with a knowing smile, for a detective should always detect, and even the plainest deductions sound impressive to the uninitiated.

John Cross, however, seemed rather more amused than impressed. His face split in a large grin. 'Nay, mister, Ah'm fra' Devonsheer mesel. Devon born and bred.'

'That – that's very odd,' stammered Roger, disconcerted. 'I should have sworn... You're quite sure you come from Devonshire?'

'Ay, Ah coom fra' Devonsheer awreet,' replied the chauffeur, still grinning, and in an accent more Yorkist than a Yorkshireman's. 'Maybe it's the way Ah speak? There's bin many thought Ah coom fra' Yorksheer on account of that. But I've worked a lot oop theer, and it's my advice, mister, if you ever have to work for your living in Yorksheer to learn to talk like a Yorksheerman.'

'I see,' Roger laughed. 'Thank you, I'll remember that. But you shouldn't deceive the police to that extent, you know.'

'Are you fra' the police, then?'

'I'm connected with Scotland Yard, yes,' Roger replied, with great dignity but only the merest modicum of truth. 'I

want to ask you one or two more questions about the man
you saw climbing over this wall three nights ago.'

'And welcome,' returned the renegade Devonian with
equanimity. 'But Ah've told your chaps already all I know.'

'Yes, but there are just one or two points... Now let me
see, there's the door into the yard, opposite this next garage,
isn't it? And I gather you saw the man scramble over just on
the left of the door as we stand now; that is to say, on the
further side of the door. Is that right?'

'That's right enough, ay.'

'Now, you've got no doubt at all about what you saw?'

Mr Cross had, emphatically, no doubt at all.

Roger did his best to shake him. What sort of a night was
it? A bit misty, inclined to rain, visibility difficult? Not in the
least; as fine and clear a night as one could wish for;
the moon was that bright Mr Cross could almost have read
a newspaper by it. What was he doing at the moment of
seeing the man, and what had drawn his attention to the
man at all? Mr Cross had just finished putting his car away;
his lady was a rare one for late parties and such-like; half-
past it was as he drove into the garridge, by the clock on the
car, and that doesn't lose above a minute a week; well, he'd
fiddled about a bit, turning off the petrol, putting a rug over
the radiator and so on, but it couldn't have been above six or
seven minutes before he came out. He'd shut and bolted one
door, and was just swinging the other to when he heard a
sort of scrambling noise and a – well, a curious sort of noise
it was, like someone breathing heavy-like; that's what made
him look round, and there was a fellow just popping up over
the wall by the door. Mr Cross stood and watched him, and
the fellow got his leg on the top of the wall, pulled himself
over, and was off down the alley before Mr Cross could have
said 'knife.'

'Did he see you looking at him?' Roger asked.

That Mr Cross couldn't say; but with the moon so bright the fellow couldn't have helped seeing him if he'd so much as glanced that way.

'Then there's no possible room for doubt that he came over the wall?' Roger asked, disappointed, though he had hardly expected to shake the evidence on this point.

Mr Cross showed himself a man of shrewdness. Not only had there been no room for any such doubt, but it had struck Mr Cross as just as funny as it had struck Roger, because everyone round the Mews knew there was no lock on the Mansions' courtyard door; so why did he have to climb over the wall at all?

'Why, indeed?' Roger echoed.

Mr Cross added his own private opinion that the man, not being so conversant with the door as everyone round the Mews, and having just come hot from a murder and so being more or less panic-stricken, had simply jumped to the conclusion on seeing a door that it would naturally be locked and had therefore not wasted time in trying it; because it had looked to Mr Cross, when he came to reconstruct the scene in his own mind later, as if the man must have helped himself up on to the wall by actually using as footholds the projecting parts on the inside of the door; that at least was the impression that remained with him of his first glimpse of the fellow, poised there as if on a solid footrest before scrambling on to the top of the wall; and this action must at least have brought the fact of the door's existence before the man.

'Aye, that must be it,' opined Mr Cross, with a very earnest expression on his freckled face. 'T'chap was in a desperate state, like, and when a chap's feeling that way he goes for to jump over things before he looks to see if he can crawl underneath 'em, don't he, mister?'

Roger agreed readily that he did, with some admiration of Mr Cross' perspicacity. Panic certainly does tend to take obstacles in its stride, and to scramble comes more naturally than to crawl; over rather than under. That undoubtedly must be the explanation. Then he remembered that to fit his new theory the man did not need to be explained; he needed to be expunged. And the chauffeur refused utterly to expunge him. It was a pity.

He went on to question the man about the unknown's appearance. Here Mr Cross was less dogmatic, but still firm. He was quite certain that the man was wearing a hat, because he remembered distinctly wondering if it would fall off during his acrobatics; what is more, he wore it pulled well down over his face. But there was a lamp burning in front of the mews, almost opposite the courtyard door, and in spite of his precautions the intruder had, during his acrobatics, allowed Mr Cross to catch a glimpse or two of his face, but hardly enough to recognise it if he ever saw it again.

'Then you don't think you'll be able to identify him?' Roger asked thoughtfully.

'No, I don't, and that's a fact, sir,' affirmed Mr Cross. 'Your people have been on to me about that, but I keep on telling 'em I won't swear to him. I didn't see him well enough for that. All I can swear to is it's *not* being him, like. I mean if you get the wrong chap I could tell it wasn't him. And I can swear to his appearance all right. Quite a small chap he was, no taller than me, and I'm not a giant. But he was slimmer'n me, by a long way. I'd have made two of him round the chest.'

'And you saw his figure so well because, according to your account, he wasn't wearing a coat?'

'That's right. He wasn't wearing no coat, and that I will swear to. Why, I can see him now, clambering over that wall just like a monkey. Ay, and grinnin' like one too.' Mr Cross, who seemed to have discarded most of his more pronounced Yorkshirisms since the conversation became serious, stared very hard at the place on the wall in question, and screwed up his humorous little eyes as if forcing the clambering man into their vision. 'No, he'd got no coat on him. Dark suit, yes, and not a bad cut either. I know something about suits too, having an uncle who's cutter to a firm of tailors in Exeter, and this chap's suit wasn't nothing off the peg. It was a proper gent's suit: I saw that in a second.'

With some qualms as to whether he might not be divulging official secrets, Roger pointed out that in this matter of the absence of an overcoat, or raincoat, Mr Cross differed from other witnesses. This, however, Mr Cross was unable to help. He knew what he saw and what he didn't see; and most decidedly a coat was numbered in the latter category. The police, it seemed, had been on to him about that too, but they had been unable to shake him.

'Very well,' said Roger, not altogether displeased at this conflict of evidence. The clambering man was a nuisance anyhow, and the running man no less. The more discrepancies there were in the accounts of them, the less likely that the two were identical. 'Now, I take it that you watched him out of sight?' Mr Cross nodded. 'He ran straight down this part of the alley, and rounded the corner to the right, I suppose? In fact, he must have done, because there's no other way out, so far as I know.'

'That's right. That's the only way to street.'

'And he disappeared round that corner at top speed?'

84

Mr Cross was evidently about to nod assent, when a puzzled expression appeared on his face. He looked at once bewildered, surprised and slightly ashamed. 'Well, that's funny,' he said, and scratched his ginger hair very hard.

'What's funny?'

'Why, I'd never given a thought to that before. I just told your chaps he ran off down alley, and disappeared round corner. Well, that's true enough; he did. But your saying what you did puts me in mind of summat else. Well, who'd have thought a thing like that? Clean forgotten it, I had, but now I remember it as plain as anything. He didn't run straight round corner. He stopped first and had a peek round it, and then he ran back a bit towards me, and then – why, lumme, mister. I'll be forgetting whether I was born in Yorksheer or Devonsheer next! – he picked something up from the ground, some sort of a little bundle seemingly, and ran off with it round the corner. Fancy me clean forgetting that, now.'

Roger was interested. The point did not seem to him to have any great significance, but any point was interesting. He asked the chauffeur to show him exactly on the ground where the bundle had lain, according to Mr Cross' refreshed recollection. The spot finally picked out was just about at the end of the courtyard, twenty odd yards before the alley took its turn to the right. Could the bundle have been a raincoat screwed up? Mr Cross thought it could, but was inclined to the opinion that it was just a bit bigger bundle than a single raincoat would make. 'Tell you what it might have been though, mister,' he added excitedly. 'It might have been a raincoat with something inside it.'

'Ah!' said Roger.

A few further questions elicited nothing more of interest. Money passed.

'Lumme!' observed Mr Cross in astonishment and gratitude. It was plain that the real representatives of Scotland Yard had not been free with largesse.

Once more Roger caused himself to be borne, in a taxi, to the British Museum. He wanted to think.

Obviously it was impossible to eliminate this scrambler. Roger was aware of the dangers of the inductive method of forming one's theory first, and then twisting certain awkward facts into confirmation of it and simply ignoring others which refused to be twisted. He was determined not to fall into the trap. The scrambler did definitely exist; he must not be twisted, and he could not be ignored. Either he must fit neatly into place without distortion, or else the whole of Roger's enticiing new theory must collapse. How to go about it?

Well, take as a starting point the fact (Roger felt justified in considering it as a fact) that nobody had climbed down that rope from Miss Barnett's flat. This at least gave the comforting corollary that the scrambler had at any rate not come that way from the flat. This reduced to an even chance the possibility of his having come from the flat at all. An even chance? Less than that. Because if he had come from the flat, down the stairs, why make his escape into the courtyard? That escape must at any rate have been through a window of one of the other flats. Why not make it straight out into the street?

Other points were involved here. *If* the scrambler had come from the flat, *and* via one of the lower flats, he must have broken both into and out of the latter; and this held good whether his escape had been made into the courtyard or into the street. He could hardly have done this without leaving traces (unless he possessed himself in advance of a key to open the lower flat's front door, which was certainly a possibility in the case of a methodical man preparing a minutely careful plan of action). In any case, no such traces had been reported, as they certainly would have been had they existed. The obvious inference was, therefore, that the scrambler had not come from inside the building at all, but only from inside the courtyard. On the balance of probabilities Roger felt quite justified in assuming this. What, then, had been the scrambler's business in the courtyard? Why had he been in a panic? What was the bundle? And – how on earth to find all this out?

Was there a pointer of any sort in the fact that he had been in a panic at all? The police, of course, had taken the obvious conclusion that this man was the murderer because the time at which he had been seen coincided almost exactly with the time at which the Ennismore Smiths had heard the noises in Miss Barnett's flat, and the panic had been put down to a natural terror stricken flight from the scene of the crime; when they learned of the bundle they would almost certainly assume it to be the contents of the strong box fastened up in the man's coat, thrown over the wall, and picked up after he had got over himself. Very right and proper, from their point of view. But according to Roger's notions the panic was not the terror-stricken flight of guilt. On the other hand, it was too much of a coincidence to suppose that a loiterer with felonious intent in the courtyard had suddenly lost his nerve and decided not to be felonious at the time of the murder. No, the murder and the flight must be connected in some way; and in that case flight could only mean guilty knowledge. What did that give? That the scrambler had somehow acquired knowledge of the murder in the very flat he had intended to burgle (that was not too gross an assumption; there was no other flat in the building worth burgling), and had departed in haste so as to avoid any awkward connection with it. That was feasible enough. But how had he acquired the knowledge?

So far as Roger could see, there was only one way: by going up the rope. But if he went up the rope, he must have come down the rope too; and according to everything now, the rope was nothing but a blind, and no one had been either up or down it.

Roger rubbed his nose. This looked like a dead end.

After another half-hour's cogitation he decided that it was a dead end. The man had somehow acquired knowledge of the murder, but how could not yet be decided. Without ignoring the scrambler, he must for the time being be shelved.

Roger proceeded to make meticulous notes of what he had learned from the chauffeur.

When he had finished, he went out of the reading-room and retired to his club for tea. He did not go back to his flat, because Miss Stella Barnett was in charge of that, and Roger did not think he really could face her any more today.

chapter seven

From his club Roger rang up Scotland Yard and demanded Chief Inspector Moresby.

When a little rather heavy badinage had been endured from the chief inspector on the subject of Mr Sheringham's new secretary, Roger asked:

'Well, anyhow, what I wanted to know is, have you caught the Kid yet?'

'Well, no, Mr Sheringham,' Moresby regretted. 'I can't say we have, yet.'

'Any news of him?'

'Well,' said the chief inspector cautiously, 'yes and no, if you know what I mean.'

'I don't. What do you?'

'Why, we haven't found him, you see, but we have found his girl. She's left Bracingham. We found her in London.'

'Oh, yes? So you're going to try a little third degree on the poor wench, are you?'

'Certainly not, Mr Sheringham, sir,' replied Moresby, pained. 'We're not even pulling her in. She's being kept under observation, that's all; and she doesn't know even that. She'll lead us to him sooner or later.'

'I call it disgusting.'

'Do you, sir?' said the chief inspector indifferently. 'Here we call it duty.'

'Moresby, don't be so infernally smug. Oh, by the way,' Roger went on in a very careless voice, approaching at last the question which he had rung up to ask. 'By the way, an odd thing occurred to me the other day. I thought one of the first things you people set out to discover in a murder case was who the last person was to see the victim alive; and yet I remembered afterwards that not a single question was asked on the point. Wasn't that rather slack?'

'Well, really, sir,' Moresby replied indignantly, 'considering the body had only just been found, and you were present only – '

'Oh, I wasn't blaming you, Moresby,' Roger interrupted in an offensively patronising voice, grinning into the telephone as the chief inspector, guileless for once, rose so promptly to his bait. 'Don't think that for a minute. It just struck me as odd; that's all. You have found that out by now, then?'

'I should think we have. It was the fish-woman,' spluttered Moresby, supplying the information Roger wanted in the neatest way. 'Mrs What's-her-name – Dace – no, Pilchard. They had tea together, and quarrelled over it apparently. She shed tears all down Afford's sleeve when she told us. I couldn't quite follow her reasoning, but she seemed to consider the quarrel responsible for her friend's death in some way. Judgement of God on herself, so far as I could gather, for having a hasty tongue.'

'The conceit of the woman!' Roger murmured. 'Did you point out that Heaven would really have been paying her a very great compliment to kill off another human being by way of a hint to her to control her temper a little better? She takes it for granted that in Heaven's regard her temper is of more importance than someone else's life. Well, well.'

'I should point that out to her if I were you, Mr Sheringham.'

'Perhaps I will. Certainly someone should. Well, so long, Moresby. Keep the girl in sight, and good hunting.'

Roger hung up the receiver not ill pleased with himself. But then Roger seldom was ill pleased with himself.

He stood for a moment by the instrument, his hands deep in his pockets, frowning at the floor; what was the next move?

An interview with the fish-woman, he decided, might not be unhelpful.

A taxi carried him to Monmouth Mansions.

Roger's luck held. Mrs Pilchard was at home.

Having seen him present at her very first, and therefore most important interview with the police, Mrs Pilchard had no hesitation in answering Roger's questions; the more readily because there was an air of informality, very different from the stiff, official attitude of the other police, about this gentleman (who must indeed hold a very high position at Scotland Yard, him being so superior and such a gentleman, because clothes never did unmake a gentleman and never would, Mrs Pilchard well knew). Why, it was just like chatting to a friend sitting like this so comfortably beside one's own fireside, with the gentleman's legs sprawling over the hearthrug and wrapped round each other as gentlemen do with their legs. (Mrs Pilchard had never caught his name, but that did not matter; it's the man that counts, not the name.)

They talked comfortably about the case. Roger put no leading questions; he merely encouraged Mrs Pilchard to chatter, in the hope that something significant might drop casually out.

If it had, twenty minutes later, Roger had not recognised it.

He began to put such questions as occurred to him, throwing them out with an air of indifference so that Mrs Pilchard should not recognise that she was being examined. The Irish are a touchy race.

'I suppose it was the fact of both of you being Roman Catholics that drew you and Miss Barnett together first of all?'

Mrs Pilchard crossed herself rapidly. 'Adelaide wasn't one of us, poor lost soul. Many and many's the time I tried to convert her to the faith, but I might as well have tried to convert a stone. And now it's too late.'

'She wasn't?' Roger said in surprise. This was unexpected news. 'But how about the rosary that was lying near her?'

'It was no rosary of hers,' Mrs Pilchard replied with emphasis. 'More's the pity.'

'Had you never seen it before?'

'Never in my life. Your inspectors asked me that, wanting to know where it came from if it wasn't hers and it wasn't mind; but not a bit of help could I give them.'

'That's very strange.' Roger thought rapidly. There ought to be a valuable clue here, but for the moment he could not see its significance.

'And they say it's with the holy beads themselves that the murdering wretch strangled her?'

'So they – so we think. Yes, no doubt he picked them up somewhere and – and thought they might come in useful. Perhaps in this very building. I suppose,' Roger said very casually, 'that several people in the other flats are Catholics?'

Mrs Pilchard shook her head sadly. 'This building's full of the damned. Only a solitary one besides meself there is that acknowledges the true faith – and she,' added Mrs Pilchard with a slight snort, 'doesn't do much more about it than acknowledge it, God save her.'

'Oh! Who is that?'

'Miss Delamere.'

'Indeed? Then in that case I suppose you know her fairly well.'

'I do not, then,' replied Mrs Pilchard firmly. 'Nor wish to.'

Roger reflected that in spite of the hostility between them Mrs Boyd and Mrs Pilchard seemed to have one feeling in common at any rate. He dropped the topic, with the mental note that Miss Delamere would deserve rather more attention than he had considered.

Miss Delamere led easily to the other inhabitants of the Mansions. Roger drew Mrs Pilchard on by gentle degrees to frank gossip. Mrs Pilchard, delighted to find so sympathetic a listener, gossiped freely. Roger listened to her words as well as between them. In a case like this he did not despise gossip in the least, still less the implications of gossip. A woman like Mrs Pilchard, with no real interests of her own, finds a vicarious amusement in the interests of her neighbours. She makes it her hobby, if an unconscious one, to find out everything possible about their daily lives, and still more eagerly about the more uncommon of their tasks; and her information on the whole is generally not inaccurate.

At the end of an hour Roger found himself in possession of a mass of general information about the inhabitants of Monmouth Mansions, most of which was quite irrelevant but with here and there a fact or two that might prove quite useful. On the whole Mrs Pilchard's judgement of her neighbours coincided with Mrs Boyd's. Augustus Weller, the young assistant editor of *The London Merryman*, and

Francis Kincross were plainly her favourites, though she was inclined to shake her head over the former for his rampageous ways and the multitude of his female friends. Roger learnt that the two young men were close friends, and had been at the same school, though Kincross was a year or two older than Weller. Both of them, Roger gathered, always had a cheerful smile for Mrs Pilchard (and would have had too for Miss Barnett had she permitted it) and borrowed her household utensils freely.

Next in favour after them came Mrs Kincross and her baby, for both of whom Mrs Pilchard could not say too many enthusiastic words, and then the Ennismore Smiths, who also appeared to have been as kind to the lonely but sociable widow on the top floor as their circumstances allowed. Mrs Pilchard echoed the caretaker's commiseration of this couple. It was a crying shame that a lady like Mrs Ennismore Smith should have to serve in a shop, fetching and carrying and calling her inferiors 'modom,' like any young miss from Camberwell or Clapham, 'and she brought up with her father a gineral'. About the husband Mrs Pilchard was pitying but a little contemptuous. 'No backbone to the man at arl.' But for his wife he would have broken up altogether, and probably have been carrying a sandwich board through the streets by now. Full of ups and downs too, never the same from one minute to another; now as merry and hopeful as you liked, and the next instant talking about being a drag, and no use in the world, and ending it all one way or another, the quicker the better. But there, their only son had been killed in the war, and that was enough to break anyone up.

Towards Mrs Barrington Braybrook Mrs Pilchard was charitable but cautious. Roger gathered that the former lady's disinclination to enlighten the widow upon her origins, matrimonial adventure and general life-history and had made an unfavourable impression. The only possible inference, which Mrs Pilchard drew with due reluctance, was that there was something extremely discreditable in Mrs Barrington Braybrook's earlier career, into which it were better not to pry too closely. Mr Barrington Braybrook Mrs Pilchard frankly disliked. 'Always laying down the law. A regular know-all. Just because he earns good money, has the impertinence to look down on those better than himself in every way. Not a nice man at arl.'

Concerning Miss Evadne Delamere Mrs Pilchard compressed her lips very tightly and refused to say a single word.

It was nearly seven o'clock before Roger took his leave, and by that time he really did know something about the inhabitants of Monmouth Mansions. The last few minutes of his visit he had devoted to a few desultory questions concerning Miss Barnett, but had brought nothing fresh to light beyond the fact that after a somewhat stormy tea (the cause of the storm was not divulged) Mrs Pilchard had parted from her friend soon after five o'clock, and that was the last time anyone saw her alive.

'Tea and currant buns, we had,' said Mrs Pilchard tearfully. 'Very fond of currant buns was poor Adelaide. Her one extravagance. Two for tea every day, and another at nine o'clock every evening after she'd gone to bed.'

'Oh, yes,' Roger nodded. 'That reminds me. You don't, of course, know what time Miss Barnett went to bed that night?'

'I do. Wasn't I telling you? Every night at nine o'clock as regular as clockwork did she go to bed, poor dear, with a cup of tea and a bun on the chair beside it to sup after she'd got in. "To warm the stomach," she used to say, thinking it easier to sleep on a warm stomach than a cold one. Ah, manny and manny's the toime...' Symptoms of oncoming Celticism reminded Roger that it was high time to go.

He let himself cautiously into his rooms in the Albany, and before seeking his study, tiptoed down the passage to the kitchen and Meadows.

'Ah, Meadows. Yes. Yes. Er – has Miss Barnett gone?'

'Miss Barnett went at six o'clock, sir, promptly.'

'Yes. Of course. Er – yes.' It was not a convincing effort, either to himself or to Meadows, to prove that he was still master of his world and captain of his soul.

But on his study table, nearly typed and bound, with a typed label on the cover, lay his dossier of 'The Monmouth Mansions Mystery'; and undoubtedly it was very much easier to consult in its present form than it had been last night.

It is a sad thing when a male stronghold succumbs to female invasion; but that is not to say that the female is without her uses. Even at Oxford the frail, frog-faced young man of the period must derive some strengthening influence from his sturdy female associates.

During dinner Roger debated his next move. That it was one of the four men who lived in Monmouth Mansions that had strangled Miss Barnett he was more convinced than ever. Obviously the time was ripe to establish personal relations with his suspects.

He decided on Augustus Weller, and set about finding a reasonable excuse for calling on him. Their respective callings formed a bond of a sort, and in his earlier days Roger had contributed occasionally to *The London Merryman*. He determined to invoke the memory of this connection on behalf of a mythical young protégée who desperately needed employment, but could neither type, write nor take down the observation of others in shorthand, not, in fact, do anything of the faintest use to anybody.

Mr Augustus Weller opened the front door of his flat in person. He was a well-built young man, an inch taller than Roger (who was not tall), with a freckled face and sandy hair.

'Cheer terribly ho,' said Mr Weller. 'Step straight in. Topping to see you again. Mind the hole in the carpet.'

Roger stepped straight in, and followed his host into the little sitting-room.

'Well, this is topping,' beamed Mr Weller with the greatest friendliness, switching on another light. 'I was wondering when you'd drop round. You couldn't have chosen a better moment. I was just thinking about a spot of work.'

'If you want to work...' hesitated Roger, rather disconcerted by the warmth of this welcome from a complete stranger.

'Want to? My dear man, who the devil *wants* to work? Of course I don't. Grab a pew. This chair's the safest really. Well, it's topping to see you again. What'll you drink? I've got nothing but beer.'

'Then I'll have a touch of beer. Thank you. But – well, *have* we met before?'

'Haven't we?' said Mr Weller, puzzled.

'Not as far as I know.'

'I thought I didn't recognise you. That explains it. Well, never mind,' said Mr Weller philosophically, dispensing beer. 'We have now, haven't we? So cheer frightfully ho.'

They drank.

'I think really,' Roger remarked, 'that I'd better introduce myself and explain why I'm here, though I do feel it's a charming compliment to my face that you should have taken me on **trust like** that. I knew you lived here, and I wanted to see you; **so as** I was passing the house I thought I might as well **take a** chance of finding you in. My name's Roger Sheringham, and – '

'Roger Sheringham! So you are. That's why I thought I knew you. Seen hundreds of photographs of you, of course. Well, that's marvellous. Great stuff! Topping of you to drop in, in passing. You may not believe it, but I've read quite a lot of your books. Well, well, well. Have some more beer.' Amid another series of ecstatic cries Mr Weller replenished his guest's glass. Roger thought, with warmth, that not only was Mr Weller an admirable young man, but he kept admirable beer; a perfect combination of qualities.

As his host's joy subsided slightly, he went on to explain the object of his visit.

Mr Weller was altruistically enthusiastic on the subject of finding employment for the imaginary protégée. Nor did he seem to imagine that there would be the least difficulty on this head. According to Mr Weller it appeared that the firm which employed himself was simply languishing to employ also large numbers of young women who could not type, take down shorthand, or do anything of the slightest use to anybody; it was precisely this kind of young woman which it seemed that his firm specialised in employing, and found it so strangely difficult to obtain. Mr Weller would make it his business to have a word tomorrow with old So-and-so, sound old This, drop a hint to old That, talk seriously to old Thing, and even penetrate to the sanctum of the great old Sir Isaac Whatnot himself. Good old Sheringham could rest assured that his protégée was as good as working for a large salary already, not to say doing nothing for it. In short, Roger was considerably disconcerted to find that Mr Weller was taking his ridiculous excuse with more exuberant seriousness than he would have thought possible.

With some earnestness Roger began to decry the merits of his protégée, pointing out that not only would she be no asset to the firm, but her very presence under its efficient roof might seriously impair next year's balance sheet; but it was no use; Mr Weller, who had now taken the unknown not only under his wing but to his heart as well, sang her praises with such force and certainty that it was impossible to out-sing him. Roger gave it up and subsided into thanks, reflecting that in any case it was quite impossible for Mr Weller to achieve a tithe of what he was promising with such complete confidence.

But without doubt (Roger told himself) this amiable young man is the most optimistic person I have ever met in my life.

The obstacle of the protégée being thus removed, Roger was free to proceed to the real business of the evening.

To the accompaniment of more beer and yet more beer, which Mr Weller drew from a cask poised conveniently in a corner of the room, he proceeded to do so, introducing his subject without any unnecessary finesse.

'I hear,' said Roger bluntly, 'that you've had a murder here.'

'I bet you do,' retorted Mr Weller. 'And I bet,' he added with quite unexpected shrewdness, 'that that's really why you came here, instead of trotting round to the office in the morning and seeing Sir Isaac. Well, work the good old pump-handle.'

Roger laughed. 'I am interested, of course. And perhaps I did think it would be more interesting to see you when you had a few minutes to talk about it. What's your theory?'

'Well, it's plain enough, isn't it? Somebody broke in, strangled her, and got away with the cash. And I'm pretty sure the police know who. The papers are talking about an early arrest.'

'Oh, the papers.'

'That comes from the horse's mouth, though; the horse in this case being Scotland Yard. Why, don't you expect an early arrest?'

'I don't really know enough about the case to expect anything,' Roger answered cautiously. 'And of course according to the papers Scotland Yard always anticipate an early arrest. What I can't understand is how the man could have got into the flat, strangled her, and, as you say, got away with the cash, without being seen by anyone in the building. I suppose everyone was in bed?' He looked interrogative.

'I wasn't in bed,' Mr Waller replied frankly, 'but I didn't see him, or hear him.'

'Oh? Were you up and about, then?'

'Well, I was up; in this room, reading a pile of manuscripts I'd brought back from the office. But I wasn't about. I mean, I didn't go to bed till after two that night, but I didn't leave this room; and this room, as you see, is on the front, so really I shouldn't have had much chance of seeing or hearing anything that was going on at the back. And anyhow I didn't.'

'No, but you'd have heard what was going on at the front, wouldn't you?' Roger looked as innocent as he could, and put his next question in a careless tone. 'I mean, you didn't hear anything inside the building? No one moving about, or anything like that?'

'Not a cat prowling,' returned Mr Weller cheerfully. 'Not even the bumps and things that woke up the Ennismore Smiths two floors above. I must have had cotton wool in my ears that night.'

In spite of the excellence of his beer, Roger glanced at his host with sorrow. Here was a possible witness who might have been able to give evidence of the highest value, and he could give no evidence at all. Some people would not notice the San Francisco earthquake if they happened to live in the next village. And yet it was reasonable enough that Mr Weller would have heard no footsteps on the stairs that night, however intently he might have been listening. The murderer would not have worn hobnailed boots.

For already Roger had definitely eliminated Mr Weller from his list of suspects. To regard this ingenuous young man as a potential murderer was plainly ludicrous. That much at any rate had been gained by his visit: the issue was now confined to three.

In the conversation that followed Roger had some difficulty in concealing his real interest in the case from his host, who knew all about his criminological activities and asked him repeatedly whether he intended to look into things on his own account. Roger had to pretend a ghoulish attraction to the scene of a murder considered merely as a murder, and an interest simply in persons who found themselves temporarily mixed up with the police.

This last proved not unhelpful, for it brought from Mr Weller a spontaneous suggestion that they should go upstairs and call on some other people who had also been receiving almost daily visits from Scotland Yard, the Kincrosses. Roger, who had been wondering, ever since he found that Mr Weller had nothing of the slightest value to tell him, how to introduce such an idea, fell in with it readily.

'You'll like jolly old Francis,' stated Mr Weller, drawing yet more beer, this time in a jug to take upstairs. 'One of the very best. You may find him a bit heavy in the hand at first, but don't take any notice of that. Though it's true enough,

I'm afraid, that the old lad isn't what he once was. One of the cheeriest souls I ever knew, dear old Francis was once. But marriage,' opined Mr Weller, with resigned philosophy, 'does seem to sober them down a bit. Thank the Lord all the girls I propose to invariably turn me down.'

On this thoughtful note they proceeded upstairs.

chapter eight

Kincross flicked his cigarette toward the carpet. There had been no ash on it; the gesture was a nervous one; Roger had noticed that it occurred several times a minute. His mouth gave a curious little twitch at one corner, which Roger had already learned to recognise as a prelude to speech.

'My dear old man,' he said to Weller, in a high voice of exasperation, 'you're talking through your hat. Simply through your hat, you know. *The Widow in the Bye Street* is the finest thing that's appeared in the English language (of its kind, I mean) since the fifteenth-century Scotch ballads. It's got everything else knocked into a cocked hat. Simply a cocked hat.'

'Don't agree,' Weller replied firmly. 'Too forced. Strains too much after the horror. Now Oscar Wilde, in *A Ballad of Reading Gaol*, does the same thing, exactly the same thing, about ten times better; far more simply, no straining, and consequently twice as much horror.'

'Oscar Wilde!' Kincross flicked his cigarette rapidly several times, looking really upset. He was one of those people who will insist on importing a personal attitude into the most impersonal discussions, in this case the poetry of Mr John Masefield. 'Look here, Sheringham, you agree with me, don't you? Isn't *The Widow in the Bye Street* the finest narrative poem you've ever read?'

'Do you mean, approximating to the ballad type?'

'No,' said Kincross recklessly. 'Narrative, epic, anything you like.'

'Well, I do seem to remember a narrative poem called *The Aenid*,' Weller grinned. 'And wasn't there a chap called Homer who's supposed to have turned out some pretty good stuff?'

Kincross threw him a glance of real anger. 'Sheringham?' he said impatiently, running his long, white fingers through his black hair.

'No. I can't agree,' Roger said, as judicially as he could. 'I should consider Masefield's own *Reynard the Fox* a far better piece of work.'

'Oh, *Reynard the Fox*, yes.' Kincross bore no malice at a disagreement which still kept his favourite poet in the fore, as Roger had tactfully suspected. 'Well, perhaps in some ways it is. Marvellous stuff, isn't it? By Jove, there are one or two stanzas in that... I say, would you mind frightfully if I read a couple aloud?'

'Oh, Lord,' groaned Mr Weller, only too audibly, 'how did we get on to Masefield? We always do somehow, up here.'

'Of course not,' Roger said hastily. 'I'd like it. Do.'

'Marjorie...?'

Mrs Kincross jumped up as if at a cue from the low chair in which she had been sitting, almost silent, for the last half-hour, her eager brown eyes, which would have been beady in their extreme brightness but for their size, darting toward each speaker in turn.

Roger had found some difficulty in summing up Mrs Kincross. She did not fit quite so neatly into type as most. At first he had feared she was going to be gushing, so almost fulsome had been her voluble praise of his work (which was not really good, and Roger, unlike most novelists, knew only too well that it was not, which made him dislike compliments on it all the more). Then he realised that she was not gushing at all but perfectly sincere in every word, that she really did think his books flawless, that he really was her favourite author, and that she was really quite childishly overjoyed at finding him inside her own flat; which, since Roger was only human, at once tipped the scales back heavily in her favour. And when she admitted, blushing, in response to some rather crude pleasantry from her husband, that she herself not only wrote occasional short stories for the cheaper magazines but had them accepted, and that the height of her literary ambition was to write a serial for *The Daily Mail*, then Roger set her down as charming but childlike, not overburdened with brain, and not likely to develop any more than she possessed at present.

But he was still not altogether satisfied with the verdict, and had been surreptitiously watching his young hostess' ingenuous face during the discussion into which the three men had settled, noticing on it at times signs of an intelligence for which he had not been inclined to give her credit, obvious though it was that she took most of her literary opinions machine-made from her husband. Perhaps all, except one. Roger was quite sure that he was not Kincross' favourite novelist. That young man was a good deal more intelligent than that.

And more easy to read too. Roger was sorry for him. He seemed a very likeable fellow, sincere and candid, but from head to foot he was one tangle of nerves. Roger could not guess the immediate cause, though he looked as if he might be inclined to drink rather more than is good for a young husband. But the cause of his nerves was plain: Kincross was one of those most unfortunate creatures who are harassed by the urge to create without the faculty. He should have been a poet, a serious novelist, a thoughtful musician, even a painter; it just happened that he was unable to compose poetry, serious novels, thoughtful music, or even pictures. He wanted to tell the world something, he was not quite sure what it was, he did not know in what medium to express it, and even if he had known he could not have expressed it. Roger understood now his pleasantry when referring to his wife's stories; it was not merely crude, it was almost savage; he was furiously envious of her possession of a gift which was denied to himself. Had he been able to write such futile little things he would have despised them as much as he did hers, but not to be able to write even so much...! That was the prick.

Such men usually take in unconscious self-defence to editing the writings of others, or reviewing, or some such post of vantage whence they can tell the real authors didactically, and not to say peremptorily, how to do their own jobs, secure in the comforting knowledge that the authors cannot hit back. Roger found it an example of the eternal unfitness of things that Francis Kincross, who might have made a really good editor but could hardly be imagined in an advertising office, should be attached to an advertisement firm; while Augustus Weller, who was obviously cut out for an advertising agent, should occupy a sub-editorial chair.

Roger thought he knew *Reynard the Fox* pretty thoroughly. He found he hardly knew it at all. Kincross' reading of it brought out under-meanings and hidden cadences which Roger had never even suspected. He was delighted. Kincross read the poetry better than Roger had ever heard poetry read before, feelingly, with a full appreciation of the beauty of the words as well as their meanings, but without a trace of sentimentalism or the usual solemn over-emphasis. Roger begged his host, at the end of the originally chosen stanzas, to continue, and Kincross did so, blushing with pleasure. When, an hour later, Roger got up to go it was with the registered intention of coming again in the very near future. He said as much, and at once received a sincerely pressing invitation to make that future even nearer.

As he walked round to his club for a final rubber or two of bridge, Roger reflected that seldom had he spent a more pleasant evening; he had had his fill of good beer, and he had heard fine poetry finely read; what more could a man want in one evening? Moreover, it had been a profitable evening too, for from his list of suspects two names had been definitely expunged once and for all; for if it was impossible to conceive Augustus Weller as being capable of murder, it was trebly so to conceive Francis Kincross.

'And Ennismore Smith?' Roger mused. 'I've met him once, and for his type once is enough; I'm quite sure I know Mr Ennismore Smith from his crown to his heels, and I'm just as sure that he simply hasn't the guts to put through any sort of murder at all, let alone one as carefully planned as this. This murder postulates in the murderer both brains and guts. Ennisore may have the brains (which I'm inclined to doubt), but that he hasn't the guts is all the city to one pip of a china orange. There remains Mr John Barrington Braybrook. Well, Mr John Barrington Braybrook must be the man. 'That's all I can say.'

But Mr John Barrington Braybrook was not the man. That became plain within a bare half-hour of Roger's decision on the point.

By one of the coincidences which real life admits and fiction fights shy of, Mr John Barrington Braybrook's name came up at the very bridge table for which Roger had been bound. At the end of the first rubber Roger's partner leaned back in his chair and remarked: 'Sheringham, you're interested in names, aren't you? Let me present you with one for your next novel. I don't know much about such things, but I should think you ought to be able to build up a character out of it alone.'

'Good,' said Roger. 'Yes, I do collect names. What's this specimen?'

'John Barrington Braybrook. And let me tell you he fits it to a T.'

Roger reached for the second pack and began to shuffle it busily. 'Yes, it's rather pleasant. But as a matter of fact I believe I've heard it already, though I don't think I've met him. You know John BB, then?'

'Well, not to say know him. I've met him once; last Tuesday, at the United Empire. I was dining there with a fellow, and John BB helped to make up a four later on. He's manager of the Wines Department at one of the big stores – forget which. If you don't know him I shouldn't bother; you haven't missed much; though you might find him useful to stick in one of your books. Well, shall we cut?'

Roger had pricked up his ears. It was last Tuesday that Miss Barnett had been strangled, or rather in the early hours of last Wednesday.

'They keep it up pretty late at the United Empire, don't they?' he asked with pretended carelessness.

'I should say they do,' the other replied feelingly. 'It must have been nearly two before we broke up the table.'

'And John BB was with you to the end?'

'To the end, yes; but not from the beginning. He didn't cut in till nearly twelve. Why?'

'Oh, nothing.' To himself Roger added a wicked word. All four suspects had now to be considered cleared, and he had no one to substitute in their place. He was where he had been at the beginning, which was extremely annoying.

I wonder, he thought to himself gloomily as he cut for partners in the second rubber, if that girl is going to be any help. I could do with a bit of help at this juncture.

He resolutely put the problem out of his mind from the moment of getting into bed, and so got to sleep without difficulty.

The next morning a deplorable thing happened to Roger; he dressed for breakfast. Feminine influence was having its baleful effect.

Punctually on the stroke of ten he heard the front-door bell ring. He gave the girl three minutes to take off her hat and do the things girls do when they take off their hats, and then strode down the passage like a man.

'Good morning,' said Miss Stella Barnett brightly, looking up from the typewriter at which she was already seated. (It is part of a good secretary's duty to greet her employer brightly in the morning. It is also part of her duty to be ready seated at her typewriter when he enters.)

'Morning,' said Roger gruffly.

He waited. Miss Barnett continued to look efficient, but said nothing.

'Er...' said Roger.

'Yes?' replied Miss Barnett competently.

'Nothing,' said Roger. I will *not* introduce the subject, he told himself. Dash it all, the woman's not human if she doesn't introduce it herself. After all it's her own aunt.

But apparently Miss Stella Barnett was not human. She gave a sharp flick to the keys of the typewriter. 'Are you going on with the story for *The Passer-by* this morning?'

'I suppose so.'

Really this was too bad of the girl. She must be bursting with curiosity to know what his ideas really were about her aunt's case. She ought to know that he was bursting with curiosity to know what her ideas were about his ideas. It was sheer downright cussedness on her part.

Roger's eyes strayed to his writing-table. There, as he had seen it last night, was the dossier, all neatly typed out, tied up, labelled, polished and manicured. Impossible for her to pretend that she had forgotten its very existence. Of all the exasperating, damnable young women...

He would *not* introduce the subject.

Of course Roger did introduce the subject.

'Ah!' he said, with a poor attempt at a casual air. 'Ah, there's that dossier, I see. Er...you got it finished yesterday, then?'

'Oh, certainly. In fact, before half-past four. I waited for you till six, but you hadn't come in by then. And as you had left me nothing else to do,' added the young woman accusingly, 'I was compelled to waste that hour and a half.' Her tone added that Roger could waste his own time as much as he liked, but he would kindly not waste hers in future.

Roger forbore to point out that hers was his, and he would waste it just as much as he darned well pleased. He did indeed think of saying it, for one fleeting moment, and then very quickly thought better of such a preposterous notion. Instead he said, frankly acknowledging defeat: 'And what did you – er – think of it, Miss Barnett?'

Miss Barnett elected to treat this question as an order. It was an order to discuss the matter, to submit, rather, to a discussion on the matter, like the other party in a Socratic duologue, so that Socrates could get off his chest a lot of things that were bothering him and find out whether his own ideas were solids or slops by putting them into words. She switched round in her chair, folded her hands on her neat black lap and replied encouragingly: 'I thought it was very interesting.' Her expression implied kindly that it was very clever of him to have thought it all out by himself, just fancy.

'Yes, yes, yes,' replied Roger, quite testily rejecting the proffered role of Socrates. 'But did you think I was blithering?'

'Certainly not.'

'Then you thought it was good, sound sense?'

'Oh, no doubt.' It did not need a keen ear to detect that doubt was just exactly what was present in Miss Barnett's tone.

'Look here,' said Roger in desperation, 'what *did* you think?'

Miss Barnett looked down her pretty straight nose. 'I am afraid I did not think about it at all, Mr Sheringham. I always take particular care not to pay attention to the subject matter of what I am typing in case I become too interested, which would interfere with my speed.'

'Do you mean to tell me that you typed that whole thing out and don't know what it's all about?' Roger stared at her.

'I should be most interested if you cared to tell me,' said Miss Barnett primly. 'That is, if you don't think we ought to be getting on with your story.'

Roger continued to stare at her. 'Are you trying to tell me,' he said, after a pause, 'that you are one of the

111

unintelligent copyists who copy word by word without any attention to the meaning at all, with the natural result of making the most ludicrous mistakes? Because, if so, I don't believe it.'

Miss Barnett had the grace to colour faintly. 'You're quite right, Mr Sheringham,' she said calmly. 'That was a subterfuge. I did understand your manuscript, of course. I was simply trying to convey that, being so to speak an interested party, I think I should prefer not to discuss my aunt's death with you.'

This was a direct snub, and Roger bridled under it. 'All the more reason why you should be anxious to arrive at the truth concerning it, I should have imagined,' he retorted rather childishly.

His secretary maintained an air of polite detachment. 'Why? The case means nothing more to me than the case of any other complete stranger. My aunt *was* a complete stranger to me, and I neither felt towards her, nor feel, the slightest tie. I don't intend to use the money that has inadvertently come to me through her death, and I am quite content to leave the matter of her death to Scotland Yard, whom I consider perfectly competent to deal with it. If you really wish me to speak plainly, that's quite plain, isn't it?'

'No, it isn't,' Roger replied with exasperation. 'First you say that as an interested party you can't discuss the case, and then you say as an uninterested party you have no wish to find out the truth about it. Which are you, Miss Barnett, and what do you mean?' The flame of battle lit Roger's face. Miss Stella Barnett was no longer an object of unwilling awe. She was an obstructionist in the path of truth, and as such must be handled firmly.

112

Miss Barnett herself must have felt that she was losing her grip. 'I don't know what right you have to speak to me in that way, Mr Sheringham,' she said, but not quite so calmly and without too much conviction.

'Then I'll tell you,' Roger smiled. 'No right at all. Absolutely none. But speak to you like that I certainly shall, if you go on making these silly attempts to stop me when I'm on the trail. Now then, without any slithering and sliding: what did you think of my theory about your aunt's death?'

'Very well,' replied Miss Barnett tartly. 'I thought you were making a mountain out of a molehill.'

'A molehill?' This was the first time that Roger had heard the term applied to murder.

'My simile was unfortunate,' his secretary corrected herself impatiently. 'You know what I mean. You appear to be introducing quite unnecessary tangles into a perfectly straightforward case.'

'Then you don't agree with my ideas?'

'No.'

'The evidence I collected didn't convince you?'

'No.'

'Oh!'

They stared at one another.

'You think the Camberwell Kid did it?'

'Certainly.'

'I see.'

Roger felt sad. This young woman was plainly not so intelligent as he had thought.

The telephone bell rang. Miss Barnett efficiently picked up the receiver before Roger could reach the instrument.

'Yes? No. This is Mr Sheringham's secretary speaking. No, I'm not sure whether he's in. If you'll hold the line I'll inquire.' She covered the mouthpiece with her hand. 'Chief Inspector Moresby of Scotland Yard. Do you wish to speak to him?'

'I do,' said Roger, taking the telephone. 'Hullo, Moresby. Yes?'

'That you, Mr Sheringham? Moresby speaking. I've got a piece of news for you.'

'Oh, yes? Have you found the Camberbell Kid?' Roger asked facetiously.

'Not exactly. He's found us. He arrived here a few minutes ago, cool as you like. Heard we'd been making inquiries about him, and having nothing on his conscience came round to see what it was all about. In other words, he's had time to work out some cock-and-bull story that he thinks will hold water and he's brought it along to throw dust in our eyes.'

Roger was too interested in the news even to notice this strange assortment of metaphors, which no doubt would have brought acute pain to his secretary. 'Oho!' he exclaimed. 'That's very interesting, Moresby.'

'Oh, they often try to swing the lead on us like this, sir. Seem to think that we're ready to be taken in by any piece of bluff. Though I won't say the Kid isn't a bit cuter than most. Anyhow, I thought that as you were in on the case at the beginning you'd like to see the end of it too. I'm keeping the Kid downstairs for half-an-hour to cool his heels a bit, and his head, so if you'd care to slip round you can be present at the interview if you like. It's a bit unofficial perhaps, but you've worked with us often enough to justify it.'

'I should think I should like,' Roger said with gusto. 'So you think this will be the end, do you?'

'I shouldn't be surprised, sir. Why?'

'Well, I mean... Are you expecting him to confess?'

'I fancy we'll have managed to get something out of him by the time I've finished with him, Mr Sheringham,' replied Moresby, with the utmost benevolence.

'A spot of the third degree, eh?'

'Certainly not, sir,' the chief inspector said, pained. 'You know we don't use that sort of method here. I think you'll be able to see that we can get our results without that.'

Roger hung up the receiver. 'I wonder,' he said aloud. 'I wonder. I very much wonder.'

He looked at his secretary. His secretary looked back at him. 'Are you ready, Mr Sheringham?'

'Ready for what?'

'To go on with that story.'

'No, I'm not,' Roger retorted, marvelling at the girl. She wasn't human; simply not a healthy, inquisitive, human female. She was uncanny. She must have known it was her aunt's case which was being discussed; she had heard Roger actually mention the Camberwell Kid; yet she asked no question, not even a hinted one.

Forcing the confidence upon her, Roger recounted Moresby's news. Miss Stella Barnett listened with politeness but certainly not with excitement.

'Really? Then the case is at an end. Well, that will certainly be a relief,' said Miss Barnett.

'The case isn't at an end,' Roger replied violently. 'The man's innocent. This action only proves it all the more. Moresby may talk about bluff, but this is no bluff.'

'No?' said Miss Barnett indifferently. One gathered that the question of bluff among the criminal classes definitely did not interest her.

As her interest diminished Roger felt, to his own annoyance, his own excitement rise. 'Look here,' he said, 'will you have a bet on it? A pair of silk stockings to a hundred cigarettes that the Kid can produce definite proof that he wasn't near Monmouth Mansions after midnight last Tuesday?'

'I don't care for betting,' Miss Barnett returned shortly.

'In order words the odds don't interest you. Very well, will you bet three pairs of silk stockings to a hundred cigarettes?'

'No, thank you, Mr Sheringham.'

'Will you bet a set of underclothes of the very latest fashionable material to a hundred cigarettes?'

'Certainly not.'

'You're not human, Miss Barnett,' Roger groaned. 'If you were I should be calling you Stella by now. I always call human girls by their Christian names after twenty-four hours' acquaintance. It saves time, trouble and inconvenience. Well, will you bet a Paris model hat against a hundred cigarettes?'

'I've not the least objection to your calling me Stella if you wish,' Miss Barnett replied briskly, 'but I won't take your bet.'

'But why not?'

'Well, let us say that a Paris model hat would be no use to me, because I've nothing to go with it.'

'Look here,' said Roger desperately, 'will you bet a Paris model hat, a frock to go with it, a set of underclothes to go with the frock, a pair of shoes to go with the underclothes, three pairs of stockings to go with the shoes, three pairs of gloves to go with the stockings, a – '

'Stop!' Miss Barnett actually laughed, for the first time in Roger's experience. He noticed that she looked prettier than ever when she laughed, but the fact did not seem to interest him. 'Mr Sheringham, why are you so anxious to make this ridiculous bet?'

'I have a reason,' Roger retorted with solemnity.

'Just to prove me mistaken?'

'You can call it that if you like. Anyhow, will you take me? I'm offering long odds.'

'You certainly are.'

'So you won't mind if there's a small condition attached. That the loser buys the goods in the presence of the winner.'

'Why do you want to make that condition?'

'Because without it I should certainly buy all the wrong things,' Roger explained glibly, 'and all that perfectly good money would be wasted. You must see that's reasonable. Well, Stella, will you take me, or are you so utterly unsexed that you won't take a sporting chance of acquiring one Paris model hat, one frock to go with the hat, one set of – '

'All right; you needn't go through the list again. No, I'm not so unsexed as that after all. I suppose you think you're certain to win. Well, I'm convinced you'll lose; and as you're determined to be so exceedingly foolish, I shall certainly take advantage of it. I'll take your absurd bet, Mr Sheringham, but I'll make a condition too; the winner has a completely free choice in the articles specified. After all you may be able to choose Sullivans.'

'I agree to that,' Roger said happily. 'Just make a typewritten note of the bet and the conditions.'

'Very well. And now don't you think you'd better be getting along to Scotland Yard?'

'That,' agreed Roger, 'is about the first sensible thing you've said this morning.'

'But I'm not sure,' mused his secretary aloud as he reached the door, 'whether it isn't really part of my duty to protect you from your own foolishness instead of encouraging it.'

'Oh, don't go and spoil it all,' Roger begged. 'I was just beginning to think that at bottom you really might be human after all.'

Roger's unwonted inferiority complex had already worn thin. Inferiority complexes rarely stood much chance with Roger.

chapter nine

Mr James Watkins carefully peeled off his lemon-yellow gloves, hitched up the knees of his well-creased trousers, and took the seat that the chief inspector offered him. He ran a white, obviously well-manicured hand over his smoothly oiled black hair and smiled pleasantly. Roger, gazing at the slight, youthful, exquisite figure, which needed only a monocle to give the rather vacant face the absolutely last touch, could hardly believe that he was looking at one of the most daring burglars of the day. The fashion in burglars has altered a good deal since the times of Bill Sikes.

'Well, Jim?' asked Moresby paternally. 'And what's on your mind?'

'Now, it's funny you should ask me that, Mr Moresby,' replied Mr Watkins, with a drawl which just did not cover the underlying Cockney accent. 'Really funny, I call that. Because I've come round to ask you what's on *your* mind.'

'There being nothing on yours, I suppose?'

'Why, no,' replied Mr Watkins with dignity. 'I'm on the level nowadays. You know that, Mr Moresby.'

'Humph!' said Moresby sceptically. 'So you're on the level nowadays, are you, Jim? Well, I'm glad to hear it. And what are you doing for a living?'

'What, don't you know?' said Mr Watkins, surprised. 'I've got a little antique shop in Lewes. I thought you knew that, Mr Moresby. All genuine stuff, and honestly come by; no nasty stolen goods, or anything of that kind. Pedigree to every article, if the purchaser wants it. You ought to come and look over my stock, Mr Moresby. Now I've got a pair of Queen Anne brass candlesticks that'd just suit you,' said Mr Watkins with enthusiasm. 'Real beauties. Rather on the heavy side maybe, old-fashioned of course, and a bit dusty, but they'd suit you down to the ground.'

'Thanks, Jim. When I want a present of a pair of heavy old-fashioned dusty brass candlesticks I'll let you know.'

'A present? Oh, come, Mr Moresby, I didn't mean that. You mustn't try to use your position to ask me for presents, you know. There's a nasty word for that sort of thing here, isn't there? Besides, I can't afford it nowadays. But I tell you what I will do: I'll give you ten per cent off the price for 'em.'

Roger smiled. He liked pulling Moresby's leg himself; he liked still more to see a burglar pulling it; he liked also to see the constable in the corner busily taking down in shorthand this irrelevant badinage.

But Moresby was not disconcerted. 'Still the same funny fellow, Jim, aren't you? In spite of the antiques. Well, it's a great pleasure to me to hear you're going straight. What's the address of the shop in Lewes?'

Mr Watkins promptly supplied an address. 'And Rhode's the name they know me under there. James Rhode.

'I see. Well, now you've got that piece of news off your chest, I'd like to know what it is you want to see me about?'

'It's always a pleasure to see you, Mr Moresby,' returned Mr Watkins suavely, touching his tiny black moustache with a delicate finger. 'Very amusing to chat over old times, when you used to think I was one of those bad, wicked burglars you try so hard to catch, isn't it?'

'So you came here to chat over old times, did you?'

'Well, I wouldn't say that exactly,' deprecated Mr Watkins. 'Though I may have hoped we'd have a little chat, and maybe drink a small glass of beer together (I can't afford spirits now, you know). But I did hear from Lil that you'd been making tender inquiries about me, so I thought I'd come round and tell you anything you wanted to know; so long as it didn't mean giving a pal away. I've cut loose from all that crowd of bad, wicked men I used to know, of course, but you mustn't ask me to give any of them away, Mr Moresby; not that.'

'So you heard from Lil, did you?'

'Why, yes, Mr Moresby. And very upset she was.' Mr Watkins shook his head reproachfully. 'You've been trailing that poor girl since she came to London, Mr Moresby. Too bad; too bad.'

The chief inspector ignored this gentle rebuke. 'You haven't been seeing quite so much of Lil lately, have you, Jim?'

'I'm very fond of Lil,' replied Mr Watkins, with an air of virtue, 'but she doesn't like the idea of me going straight, and that's a fact. I'm afraid Lil's a crook, Mr Moresby; I'm afraid so. She says there's more money in it. Now fancy that.'

'Well, Lil always was a bad influence, Jim,' Moresby said, with a return to his paternal manner, 'and there's no getting away from it. I for one shan't be sorry to hear you've broken with her. Now that *would* mean something, that would.'

'Well, stranger things have happened, Mr Moresby,' said the other pleasantly.

'Who's the new girl, Jim?' Moresby asked bluntly.

Mr Watkins waved a deprecating hand. 'Well, really, Mr Moresby, you're so premachoor, you know.'

'Don't tell me you can get along without a girl, Jim. I know that. You're like me: never without a girl till you settle down and marry one of 'em.'

'I never knew you were married, Mr Moresby?'

'Nor I am; but that doesn't alter what I was saying. So who is she?'

'Well, if you're so pressing I will admit I'm interested in a young party at Lewes,' conceded Mr Watkins coyly. 'Name of Parker. A dear, sweet thing she is. Lives with her mother, a widow, in Hillingdon Crescent. Mother keeps a boarding-house there, and Elsie and her sister help with it. Miss Parker's interested in antiques too, which is another bond between us.'

'I see,' said Moresby, in rather dry response to this idyll of a young ex-burglar's love. 'And she knows your record?'

'Oh, come now, Mr Moresby, come,' cried Mr Watkins in high alarm. 'You wouldn't spoil a fellow's chances? Besides, I haven't got a record. You've never been able to hang anything on me, however hard you tried. And why? Because I'm innocent. No conviction, innocent; that's what the law says. But don't tell me, Mr Moresby, that you'd acquaint the poor girl with any of your nasty, low, wrongful suspicions. That wouldn't be playing the game at all.'

'All right, Jim, all right; don't get the wind up; I'll tell her nothing. If her mother's a widow, she'll find out soon enough for herself. Well, it's very nice of you to come and tell us all this; and while you're here I may as well ask you something else.' The chief inspector regarded his visitor benevolently for a moment and then, without altering his expression, shot out suddenly: 'What were you doing last Tuesday evening? A week ago today? Quick, now!'

'Last Tuesday?' repeated Mr Watkins, in high astonishment. 'Why?'

'Never mind that. Come on.'

'Well, give a fellow a chance,' Mr Watkins complained. 'I've got to think. Last Tuesday, now. What was I doing?'

'Last Tuesday evening.'

'Yes, yes.' Mr Watkins wrinkled his brow in thought. 'Well, I came up to London in the afternoon, to see a firm I get some of my stuff from, and – '

'Who?'

'Dear me, Mr Moresby, this is very curious,' said Mr Watkins suspiciously. 'What are you trying to hang on me now?'

'Never mind whether I'm trying to hang anything on you or not. What I'm asking you is what firm did you go to see on Tuesday, and at what time?'

'Well, I don't understand it, but I'll tell you. And for why? Because I've nothing to hide – see? I caught the 2.2 from Lewes, and the first firm I went to see was Copp and Meredith, in Old Street. I suppose I got there about half-past three. Then I went on to Thompson Brothers, in City Road, and on the way back I called in at some shop in the City Road where I saw a pretty little gate-legged table in the window, but they wanted too much for it. I can't tell you their name because I didn't look, not knowing Mr Moresby would want me to tell him all about it afterwards. Then I met Lil for tea at the Popular, and we went on to a cinema in Oxford Street – the Super Palace or something; anyhow it's next door to Sanford's, the toy shop. Nothing wrong in that, I hope?' sneered Mr Watkins.

'You met Lil for tea, did you?'

'Certainly I met Lil for tea. And why not?'

'I thought you said you'd broken with her?'

'You'll pardon me, Mr Moresby, I didn't say nothing of the kind. I said I was breaking with her. And I don't know what *your* methods are in that sort of case, that calls for a bit of delicacy, but *I* do things gradual-like. Probably I'll see Lil off and on for the next twelve months.'

'Yes. Well, and after the cinema?'

'We went back to the Popular and had a bite; and if it's any interest to you, the waitress tried to overcharge us and I had to give her a bit of my mind. Then Lil came down and saw me off on the 8.17. And I hope you're satisfied.'

'The 8.17 from Victoria for Lewes, eh? And after that?'

'Coo, aren't you inquisitive? Well, after that, if you must know, I went round to the Parkers'. I didn't get there till after half-past nine, what with having stayed in London longer than I'd intended, but that didn't matter; there was a regular little party that night, and we kept it up pretty late.'

'Oh, you did, did you? What sort of a party, and how late?'

'Why, Miss Parker's Uncle Ben was just over from America, and they'd asked one or two old friends in to see him, and Miss Parker asked me to come along too. I suppose there was getting on for a dozen of us altogether.'

'Yes, and how long did you stay?'

'Me? I stayed till nearly one meself, or it might have been a few minutes after, and they hadn't all gone then.'

'I see.'

Roger knew Moresby was discomfited, though he did not show it. If the man was telling the truth, his alibi was cast-iron. By no means could he have left a party in Lewes at one o'clock and killed an old lady in the neighbourhood of Euston at twenty minutes past. In correspondence with Moresby's discomfiture, Roger felt satisfaction. He had been perfectly right. The Kid was not the murderer. It had been what the detective-stories call 'an inside job'.

Moresby asked his visitor a few more questions, mostly connected with the party of last Tuesday evening, and then pressed the bell-push on his desk.

As he did so, Mr Watkins uttered an oath, and jumped in his chair. His refinement was jerked off him with the jump. 'Christ! Last Tuesday evening – that was when that job in Euston Road was done. Monmouth Mansions murder. Swelp us, Mr Moresby, you're not tryin' to 'ang *that* on me? Gawd, you know I wouldn't do a thing like that, Mr Moresby.'

Moresby regarded him sourly. 'If you were at a party in Lewes when it was done, you couldn't have done it, could you? So there's no need to get excited.'

'Well, thank Gawd I was at a party in Lewes,' said Mr Watkins soberly. 'That's all.'

A constable entered, and Moresby indicated Mr Watkins. 'Take this man back to the waiting-room, Jamieson, and stay with him. I may want to ask him a few more questions later.'

''Ere, that's the troof, is it, Mr Moresby?' Mr Watkins queried, with anxious suspicion. 'Just a few questions later? No funny business, or frame-ups?'

'No funny business or frame-ups, Jim,' assented Moresby.

The two men disappeared from the room. At a nod from the chief inspector the constable in the corner gathered up his papers and went off to transcribe his report of the conversation.

Before Roger could speak, Moresby had seized his telephone and given a number in Lewes, together with the code word that meant a priority call. Within a remarkably short time the connection was made.

'Is that the Lewes police station? Is that the sergeant in charge? This is Chief Inspector Moresby, speaking from Scotland Yard. Is your superintendent there? Will you ask him to come to the telephone, please? Is that you,

Superintendent? Look here, will you do something for me urgently? Send a man round to some people called Parker in Hillingdon Crescent, and find out whether they had a party there last Tuesday evening, and if so whether there was a man called James Rhode there who runs an antique shop in Queen Street, and if so what time he arrived and what time he left. I'm holding Rhode here till I hear from you, so ring me up as soon as your man reports. Yes, it's in connection with that job at Monmouth Mansions here, burglary and murder. And, Superintendent, for your information James Rhode of Queen Street is Jim Watkins, *alias* the Camberwell Kid. Yes, I thought you'd be interested to hear that. Let me know as soon as possible, won't you?' He rang off.

Roger and the chief inspector looked at one another.

'So that's the cock-and-bull story he's faked up?' said the former mildly.

Moresby growled. For once he was not in the mood for badinage. It is a serious thing for the Criminal Investigation Department when they have put all their money, so to speak, on one horse, and the horse does not even start.

'Well?' Roger tried again. 'Do you believe him?'

'It's lucky for him,' remarked Moresby through his moustache, 'as he said, that there was a party.'

'You do believe him, then?'

'Of course I do, Mr Sheringham,' the chief inspector returned impatiently. 'Jim's no fool. He wouldn't put up a story like that if he couldn't prove it. He knew he'd be held here till we'd checked up on it.'

'Then you think he knew all the time what you wanted him for?'

'He knew all right. Even if he's innocent he'd know. As soon as he read the reports in the papers he'd see how like his own work it was: he'd know we'd be after him for an account of his movements that night.'

'Anyhow, if his story's true that lets him out all right, Moresby.'

'It does, Mr Sheringham.' Moresby gloomed. 'There's no doubt about that. We shall check up on it, of course, apart from the Lewes end, but I'm very much afraid... Anyhow, we'll know definitely in a few minutes whether it was the Kid climbing over that wall or whether it wasn't. I sent a man round to the mews to collect that chauffeur: he's going to take a peek at him in the waiting-room and see if he can identify him.'

'But how can he, if the Kid was in Lewes?'

'Alibis have been known to have holes in them before, Mr Sheringham,' Moresby replied dryly.

'That sounds to me rather too much to hope for in this case,' said Roger. 'The man's innocent, Moresby: take my word for it. There's more in this case than has met your eye yet.'

'But it's met yours, Mr Sheringham, I hear?'

'Oh, you do, do you?' Roger laughed. 'Well, perhaps I have got an idea or two.'

'I should be very interested to hear them, sir.' Remarked the chief inspector politely.

Roger tapped his teeth with his pencil. He was not often troubled by conscience, but his conscience had been a little uneasy during the last twenty-four hours. Was it not his duty, after all, to share with Scotland Yard the contents of his dossier? Or, at least, the evidence and conclusions which had caused him to open the dossier at all? He very much feared that it was. After all, he had been first in the field and had got himself nowhere: the thing was due to be passed into the right hands. Roger sighed. He did not like the idea of shutting himself out from his own ingenious case.

He made his mind up suddenly. He would not shut himself out. If (or rather, when) the report reached Moresby that the chauffeur had been unable to identify the Kid, he would lay before Moresby the real crux of the whole case, his conviction that nobody had descended that rope last Tuesday evening: and with it, its corollary, that the whole stage had been set to point to the fact that someone *had* descended the rope, together with the evidence that supported, if not proved, these conclusions: but of his own theories based on these conclusions he would say nothing. That would salve his conscience, and still leave him a free hand.

He had not long to wait. Almost immediately the telephone bell rang.

'Yes?' said Moresby into the mouthpiece. He listened. 'I see.'

He looked at Roger as he rang off. 'The chauffeur says it's not the man. Quite definite about it.'

'Ah!' said Roger.

They eyed one another.

'Well, Mr Sheringham?' said the chief inspector very blandly. 'Now what is it you're going to tell me?'

Enlightenment came to Roger. 'Moresby, you old fraud. Crook yourself! You got me round here just to pump me. That magnanimous offer to let me in at the death was all my eye. You had your doubts about the Kid yourself, and you thought if you did me a favour I should feel I'd have to reciprocate by telling you all my nice secrets. Moresby, I dislike you.'

'Well, well, now,' said Moresby, unperturbed, 'what could have put a thing like that into your head, Mr Sheringham?

So you were going to tell me that nobody climbed down that rope outside Miss Barnett's kitchen that night?'

'How did you know I was? I mean – what made you think so?'

'Well, you must remember you practically told my sergeant as much.'

'Yes, I did. Yes, Moresby, you're right. I was going to tell you that. And what's more, I'm absolutely convinced it's the case. Certain! Moresby – you hadn't come to the same conclusion yourself?'

'Mr Sheringham, sir,' retorted Moresby, with a wooden expression, 'I never come to any conclusions unless I can prove 'em. But I'll admit that the possibility had crossed my mind, yes. Even mine, sir.'

'That's good,' said Roger. 'And though you may not think it, Moresby, I try not to come to conclusions myself unless I can prove them. And here are my proofs.' He gave the chief inspector the results of his examination of the rope, the gas stove, and the wall.

Moresby nodded. 'I won't say you may not be right, too. Now the Kid's produced his alibi, we've certainly got to look further than we thought. So it's your idea, Mr Sheringham, that not only did nobody go down the rope at all, but the state of the whole flat was a fake too?'

'Yes. Carefully arranged to mislead you.'

'By someone deliberately copying the Kid's methods?'

'Yes!' said Roger defiantly. 'Consciously or unconsciously. I suggested as much to Beach last Tuesday, when he thought it was Flash Bertie: but he was disposed to be scornful.'

'Flash Bertie,' mused the chief inspector. 'Yes, his work is very like the Kid's. But he's out of trouble at present. Still, if we're to admit copying at all, our man might just as well have been copying Flash Bertie's methods as the Kid's, knowing it would lead us to a dead end. But this is all very theoretical.'

'Of course. You seem,' Roger added mildly, 'still sure that it was the work of a professional criminal?'

'Oh, yes,' Moresby replied absently. 'I don't fancy there's much doubt about that.'

'I see.' Roger said no more on that point.

'But we mustn't jump to our conclusions again ' Moresby said more briskly. 'What evidence have we got after all that the stage was set, and the appearance of the flat faked?'

'Plenty,' retorted Roger, and enumerated the points which he considered, in the aggregate, to prove this fact. He did not mention all the sixteen points which he had written down on his first visit to the British Museum. In accordance with his earlier decision, those tending to show that the intruder was no stranger to Miss Barnett were omitted. After all, if he could discover them Moresby could do so too.

The chief inspector nodded approval. 'That's sound reasoning, Mr Sheringham. I think there's a good deal in what you say. These things don't constitute definite proof by any means, but they make up a very strong case; and I'm inclined to agree with you that it's the correct one.'

'Ah!' said Roger, gratified.

'In fact there's only one on which I disagree with you. You seem to want to make out that the man running away had nothing to do with the crime. Now why?'

Roger did not care to explain that this was due to his conviction that the job was an inside one: he had to hedge. 'Not necessarily that he had nothing to do with the crime; just that he might not have had. According to my ideas, you see, the murderer left the building by the front door.' This was quite untrue, Roger felt a little guiltily. He had proved that the murderer could not possibly have left the building by the front door. But, again, it was up to Moresby to cover that ground too – if he had not already done so.

'How does he come to be climbing over the wall from the yard, then?'

'He might have let down the stuff from the kitchen window into the yard, and gone round to collect it. There's no reason why anyone should have seen him getting in. The chauffeur had only just got back, you remember.'

'Yes, that's true enough,' the chief inspector agreed.

Roger was glad to let the point slide.

'It's been nice to talk things over, Mr Sheringham,' remarked Moresby, with a genial eye on his visitor. 'Quite like old times.'

'Well, I'm glad I've been able to help you,' Roger returned offensively.

Once more the telephone bell rang.

Roger, listening to the conversation that ensued, was able to deduce without difficulty (a) that the call was from Lewes, (b) that Mr James Watkins' story had been completely substantiated.

'Well, there ends the second act of the Monmouth Mansions Mystery,' he observed, when Moresby was again free for conversation. 'Exit from the plot the Camberwell Kid.'

'Humph,' said Moresby, with a return to his former gloom.

chapter ten

Roger soothed his easy-going conscience with the reflection that it is quite necessary for a detective occasionally to be deceitful. Besides, he did not actually lie.

'Well, Stella,' he said, entering his study with an air of gloom that might have matched Moresby's. 'Well, what *is* the latest fashionable under-material?'

'You've lost the bet?' said Miss Barnett with satisfaction. 'I knew you would, of course. These things, I should imagine,' she added kindly, 'are much better left to the police. But I warned you, I'm not going to let you off a stocking of it.'

'I'm not asking you to do so,' Roger replied with dignity. 'More, I'll add a ribbon to tie up your pretty brown hair. You have got very pretty hair, you know, Stella.'

'I don't care for compliments, Mr Sheringham, please,' said Miss Barnett, quite indifferently. Roger reflected that most woman bridle when they make that hackneyed remark. Miss Stella Barnett sounded as if she really meant it.

''No? That'll save a lot of trouble. One has to offer them, you know,' Roger said maliciously.

This time Miss Barnett did bridle. 'Thank you, Mr Sheringham, but I am not that kind of girl.'

'It's my experience,' Roger meditated, 'that any girl who says she is not that kind of girl invariably gives away the fact that she is, whatever kind is under implication.'

'I'm not at all interested in your experience, Mr Sheringham,' retorted Miss Barnett, colouring slightly.

'You're in a very negative mood altogether, Stella,' Roger smiled, with the comfortable feeling that for the first time since his acquaintance with Miss Barnett he was scoring all along the line.

'You won't find me so in Papillon's, I can tell you,' Miss Barnett said, quite vindictively.

'Why Papillon's?'

'Because it's the most expensive place I can think of.'

'Then we won't go there. You have choice of article, but I have choice of shop.'

'I don't think that's fair.'

'Fair or not, that's how it is. Add a note to the memorandum of the bet, and then put your hat on. It's nearly one o'clock, and I'm going to take you out to lunch.'

'I prefer to lunch by myself, thank you.'

'Stella Barnett, I don't care a hang whether you prefer to lunch by yourself or not. You're on duty during the lunch-hour today, and if you insist on overtime I'll pay you for it.'

'Please don't be absurd, Mr Sheringham.'

'You don't insist on overtime? Good; that comes cheaper. Now I'll explain. You remember I was held up yesterday for the conversation at the bottle-party, and you couldn't help me (which I may say is what you're really here for). Now I know a restaurant in Soho where the frog-faced young modern man congregates in all his frail preciousness, and the robust young women who bear-lead him too. You will bring pencil and notepad, we shall occupy a table next to a typical party, and you will take down in shorthand selected passages of their conversation as I indicate to you. And in case you don't know it, this is quite in accordance with the best literary traditions. I need cite only Synge: who certainly did it through a hole in the floor, which may be more picturesque, but the principle is the same. Now then, have you any more impertinent objections to eating your lunch in my presence?'

'Certainly not, Mr Sheringham,' said Roger's secretary coldly, 'if that is why you require me.'

'The trouble with you women,' Roger told her, 'is that you will import a personal aspect into the most impersonal matters. You're all the same. It's conceit, of course. As a sex your conceit is intolerable.'

But Miss Barnett had vanished.

Roger felt more pleased with himself than usual. There is nothing like the vanquishing of an inferiority complex to produce complacency.

Lunch proceeded as he had planned. He had been speaking nothing less than the truth in that he did really want notes of the conversation that took place at the next table among a party who seemed to lunch there regularly; Roger had listened to it with fascination before, but had been unable afterwards to remember the choicer fragments: but really he wanted, now that she no longer alarmed him, to get to know the girl better. She interested him as a type no less than the frog-faced young men at the next table, although he felt no more inspired to make love to her (as indeed he did to nearly any pretty girl, almost automatically) than to them.

Conversation, however, was difficult, with an ear kept necessarily and constantly on their neighbours.

'Do hats nowadays match shoes or gloves or what?' Roger would ask. 'And what do stockings match? No, I'm quite serious. I want the information. A conscientious novelist always describes in some detail the clothes of his female characters, because he knows that his female readers will be more interested in them than in the characters themselves; but that's where I'm hampered, without a wife; I don't know the difference between triple ninon and sarsenet, or even if there is any, or which is used for what; it will be part of your duties to keep me informed of such important matters. Now – '

'Where *is* Cricklewood?' would ask a plaintive frog-voice from the next table.

'Take this down, please,' Roger would say hastily, and Stella would get busy with the pad concealed on her knee.

But it was not an unsuccessful lunch, especially after the frog-party had been led away by their Amazons, and at the end of it Roger did feel that he had made progress; that is to say, his secretary did at least reach the stage of conversing with him as if he were a rational person and not some strange new brand of nitwit, as her manner before had seemed to imply.

But she still refused completely to divulge willingly any single thing about herself, in response to Roger's by no means subtle leads.

'Have you ever been in love, Stella?' he asked finally, after being rebuffed on every other topic he could think of.

To his surprise Miss Barnett did not snub him out of hand. Instead she smiled at him sweetly. 'I've been in love ever since I can remember, Mr Sheringham.'

'What!' exclaimed Roger, taken aback by this most unexpected revelation. 'But – not with the same person.'

'Oh, yes; the same person.'

'Great Scot!'

'Yes,' amplified Miss Barnett briskly. 'Myself. I think it's quite time we went.'

They went.

They went to Shaftesbury Avenue, in a taxicab. In the same taxicab Roger drew from his pocket, and affixed to his face, a small black moustache and a pair of enormous horn-spectacles. He also produced a small brush, with which he proceeded to brush his eyebrows up the wrong way, giving himself an aspect of wild ferocity.

'Mr Sheringham,' cried Miss Barnett, astonished for once into a question, 'what *are* you doing?'

Roger beamed at her through the spectacles. 'I always disguise myself before buying clothes for young women. Then I can't be brought up in evidence later.'

Miss Barnett shrugged her charming shoulders.

'No; it's this way. We're going to get your things at the shop run by Mrs Ennismore Smith, of Monmouth Mansions; she's seen me before, and I don't want her to recognise me. Has she seen you?'

'Not that I know of; at least, I don't think I've seen her. But why are we?'

'Well, let's say because I want an opportunity of studying her at her work.'

'But why?'

'Oh, I think she might be useful to me,' Roger said evasively. 'Her history is curious, you see. I don't know if you've heard it. She was brought up in comfort, not to say luxury, and now she finds herself serving in a shop. That's piquant, after all, isn't it?'

'I suppose so. Though it sounds to me rather tragic.'

'Oh, tragic, yes; that's the piquancy. And I dare say it sounds to you very unfair on my part to be wanting to study her, but I can't help that; it's my job. And I want to do more than study her. I want to see if she has spirit; if she has a devil, in fact, and if we can rouse it.'

'Really, Mr Sheringham...'

'Yes, yes. And this is what I want you to do: insist on being served by her in person, and then find fault with everything; not merely the clothes, but what she does. I want you, if you can, to make yourself distinctly common, not to say vulgar, but giving yourself tremendous airs. Treat her like dirt, order her about and grumble at her all the time. In fact, behave just like the kind of person I want you to represent. Can you do that?'

'This seems very mysterious.'

'It may; but it's a matter of considerable importance to me. *Can* you do it?'

'I suppose I could,' said Miss Barnett slowly, 'if I saw the necessity. And what about you?'

'I shall be a rich American, and you've got me in tow.'

'You really want me,' asked Miss Barnett calmly, 'to represent a girl of the streets?'

'I do. Well? Can you? Dare you?'

'There's more behind this than you've told me; that's quite plain. You intend to give me no chance of judging for myself the necessity for this extraordinary imposture?'

'I do not. I'm the sole judge of that. I'd do it alone if it were possible, but it isn't; I must have female help. I can get it elsewhere if you funk it, but as my confidential secretary I'd prefer you. But there's no sort of obligation, and I don't put it forward as part of your duty to your employer. What about it?'

'I don't understand in the least, and it seems quite incomprehensible; but you evidently consider it important, so I'm prepared to accept it as part of my duty to help you.'

'That's fine,' said Roger with enthusiasm. 'It's a pity you're so quietly dressed, but that can't be helped. Of course, by the way, if you can't get what you really want here, we'll go somewhere else. That's understood.'

He sat back and crossed his arms, thinking. He had not really expected for a moment that Stella Barnett would consent. She really was a most unexpected person. Her acquiescence would make things very much easier.

For since the previous evening a thought had been crystallising in Roger's mind. If it was either a moral or a physical impossibility that any of the men directly implicated in the case could be the murderer of Miss Barnett, then a wider net must be cast. And what after all was there inherently impossible, or even improbable, in the idea that the criminal was a woman? There was really only the question of the amount of strength required to effect strangulation, and Moresby himself had said, when they were examining the body, that not very much was needed. A normally strong woman could have lifted that slight figure off its feet almost as easily as a normal man.

Given the possibility then, where was one to look for this woman? Again, among the inhabitants of the building. And what sort of a woman was one to look for? Obviously a woman of determination and quick brain; a desperate woman; a woman at the end of her resources. And among all the women in Monmouth Mansions, Mrs Ennismore Smith seemed to stand out in Roger's mind for character, for determination, for desperate resource. But was she capable of murder? That was the point, and that was just what Roger, on the glimpse he had already had of her, was not prepared to say. But one thing was certain: Mrs Ennismore Smith was a secret woman. Very much more went on behind that quiet manner of hers than she would ever show. The problem was to make her show it; to make her show what hidden potentialities she possessed for rage, for patience, for determination, for self-control, for submission to circumstances or for rebellion against them; and in Roger's opinion the plan he had devised could not fail to force Mrs Ennismore Smith into the open.

It was not a nice plan, and Roger could hardly feel proud of it. On the other hand, it should be a most effective plan in more ways than one. Roger felt that he would be most interested, for a minor thing, to see whether Miss Stella Barnett could act a part.

Miss Barnett herself only spoke once more before they reached the shop. 'Do you wish me to speak with a Cockney accent?' she asked, in her usual efficient way.

'A slight accent would perhaps be advisable,' Roger replied gravely.

From the very way in which she entered the doorway, with a defiant swagger and a slight swinging of the hips, it was plain at once that Miss Barnett could act a part.

A young woman in a black dress, with extremely pale hair, came towards them.

'What can I do for you, madam?'

'Ay want to see some afternoon dresses,' replied Miss Barnett, in correctly refined tones.

'OK,' added Roger, in what he hoped was American. 'Trot out the dandiest you've got, sister, and never mind the price tickets. That's all right with me.'

The girl smiled tolerantly and turned away, but Miss Barnett made sounds as of further speech.

'Perhaps you'd better send us the manageress, Ay think.'

'Certainly, madam.' The girl disappeared into hidden regions at the back.

'Attaboy, Stella!' Roger whispered. 'You're marvellous. Where did you learn it?'

'I once had a part not unlike this in some amateur theatricals,' explained Miss Barnett. 'Is this what you want?'

'Exactly. In fact, you might put it on a little bit more. Decidedly more, in fact. Not to put too fine a point on it, I want you to goad the woman.'

'Goad her?'

'Goad her,' said Roger firmly; he did not add, into showing what she really was.

'Ay see,' responded Miss Barnett.

Roger turned round. Mrs Ennismore Smith was coming towards them, a professional smile on her lips. She too wore a black dress, and with her tall figure and erect carriage looked really distinguished. 'You wish to see some afternoon dresses?' she said. Roger noticed that she did not add the customary 'modom'; nor did she offer him more than a fleeting glance; quite evidently she did not recognise him, though Roger had had small fear on that score.

'Ay shall want a dress, and a hat to wear with it, yes.'

'Say, don't forget the other trimmings too, baby,' Roger put in. 'I guess we'll want some stockings for the lady too, miss, and some gloves, and – '

'That will do, Hannibal,' said Miss Barnett.

Mrs Ennismore Smith turned to the pale-haired assistant who had followed her. 'Miss Hall, run upstairs and get that beige lace and the jade *peau de soie*, please.'

Miss Barnett waited until the girl had gone. 'Jade! Well, reely. Ay should have thought anyone could see jade doesn't suit *me*, not with my colouring. I must ask you to take a little more trouble than that with *me*.'

'That's right,' Roger nodded. 'It'll pay you to take some trouble with us.'

'I'm sorry,' replied Mrs Ennismore Smith gently. 'I should have said myself that jade would suit you very well; but of course if you don't care for the colour... However, I can judge better what would suit you if you would allow me to see you without your hat.'

'Certainly, Ay'm sure.' Stella removed her hat and showed her soft, light brown hair. She held the hat out to the older woman. 'Put this somewhere for me.'

This time Mrs Ennismore Smith's eyebrows did rise a little, but she took the hat and laid it on a side table. 'If you don't care for jade, I have a very nice little model in midnight blue.'

'Ay'll see it.'

'Or if you would prefer turquoise blue, which is the newest shade, I've got a chic little day frock just over from Paris in turquoise marocain.'

'Reely, Ay don't know yet which colour Ay want,' Stella returned impolitely. 'You'd better bring everything you've got. Ay can't tell till Ay've tried them, can Ay?'

'That's right, baby,' put in her supporter. 'You try the whole boiling.'

The assistant returned with the frocks, and the three women disappeared into a curtained cubicle. Roger could hear Stella keeping up a refined grumbling, and a few minutes later she emerged in the beige lace, speaking back over her shoulder. 'Well, I'll just show it to my friend, but Ay'm afraid it won't suit.' To Roger she said, indignantly: 'It's too tate under the arms.'

'That's too bad,' said Roger.

'It would be very easy to put that right, I assure you,' said Mrs Ennismore Smith, also appearing.

'Ay've told you once, and Ay'll tell you again, that Ay won't have anything that needs altering.'

'I understand. And you don't wish to try on the jade?'

'No. Ay said Ay didn't care for jade.'

'Miss Hall...' Mrs Ennismore Smith gave further instructions.

'Yes, madam. The midnight blue is down here, I think.'

The midnight blue was produced. Miss Hall disappeared.

'Ay'd like to see this on a model,' said Stella. 'You have a model of mai build, Ay suppose?'

'I'm sorry,' Mrs Ennismore Smith said quietly, 'I have only the one assistant here.'

'Well, reely! Ay'm accustomed to shopping to places where Ay can see anything Ay want on a model.'

'I'm sorry.'

'Say, this is a one-horse place,' sneered Roger. 'Let's try Reville's.'

'I'm sure I have what you want, if you will only wait just another moment. My assistant will be back directly, if you'd care to try on this model. It's extremely chic.'

'Oh, Ay can't wait about all day for your assistant. Ay'll try it on, and you can help me.'

Mrs Ennismore Smith's eyebrows rose definitely at this. Roger gathered that the function of the manageress was merely to stand and admire while her assistant did the trying on. However, she merely answered quietly: 'Certainly, if you'll come into the cubicle.'

The game went on. Frock after frock was produced and tried on, only to be pronounced too tight in the hips, unsuitable, not a model, even downright ugly. Mrs Ennismore Smith's patience must have been wearing thin, but she did not show it. Finally, a frock was chosen; but then no hat could be found to go with it. Miss Barnettt said so at last, rudely, and Miss Hall was despatched in a taxi to the wholesaler's for a fresh supply.

'Now Ay want a set of underclothes.'

'Yes. What colour would you prefer?'

The colour was decided, and sets were produced. They did not satisfy, and the manageress was peremptorily sent for more.

Stella turned to Roger and shrugged her shoulders. 'I've been as rude as I can be, but apparently she isn't to be goaded. I don't see what more I can do.'

'She must have a breaking-point. You've got to try and find it, Stella.'

'But *why*?'

Roger hesitated. 'I want to see what she's like in a rage; that's the truth. I'm afraid you must take it from me that I do consider it important whether she goes into a cold or a hot rage. I can't explain any more.'

'Well, if you really say it's important I suppose there's one thing more I can do; but I don't care about it.'

'Never mind that; do it. What is it?'

'Hush!'

Mrs Ennismore Smith was approaching them with more garments on her arm. Her air of pleasant attention was a little worn, but not unduly so.

Stella turned them over. 'This isn't quite so bad as the others.'

'It's a charming set,' Mrs Ennismore Smith agreed mechanically. 'Won't you try it on?'

'No, Ay won't. Ay'm sick and tired of traying things on that don't fit. Ay must see it on a model.'

'But I have no model to display it.'

Stella looked at her insolently. 'Well, you'd better display it yourself then. Yes, you'll do. Your build isn't near enough to mane for frocks, but it'll do for these.'

Mrs Ennismore Smith coloured slightly, and bit her lip.

'If you don't mind me saying so, it's a – a very unusual request.'

'Ay don't agree at all. If you don't keep a model you must expect to do the work yourself. Hurry up, please; Ay've wasted enough taime here already.'

Mrs Ennismore Smith hesitated, and for the first time looked at Stella as if she would like to throw the things in her face. Then she picked them up, and walked into the back of the shop without a word.

The two exchanged glances. The manageress' self-control seemed unbreakable.

Roger glared at a hat on a stand, thinking hard. He had learned a good deal about Mrs Ennismore Smith already.

'If you will come in here…' The manageress, in a wrapper, was standing at the entrance to the cubicle.

Stella went inside with her.

Roger listened. Stella was comparing Mrs Ennismore Smith's figure with her own, to the decided disadvantage of the former.

'But they will fit you much better than me,' he heard the manageress say patiently. 'You must remember I am at least an inch taller than you.'

'Well, I'll hear what my friend thinks,' Stella said. 'After all, he's paying.'

'Please,' Mrs Ennismore Smith said in agitated tones, 'I would much rather you didn't. I displayed them for you, as a special concession, but…'

'Nonsense!' Stella cut her short. 'Hannibal, come here. I want your opinion.'

'Coming right now,' Roger called back. But he did not go into the cubicle.

'Do you like these? I don't think much of them meself, but…'

'Good afternoon,' said Mrs Ennismore Smith calmly, reappearing in her wrapper.

'Eh?' Stella followed her out of the cubicle.

'I said, good afternoon. I'm sorry we have nothing here that suits you.'

'Eh? But I'm taking that dress I chose, and – '

'I'm sorry, I've just remembered that dress was reserved for another customer. *Good afternoon.*'

'Oh, well, if you put it like that...' said Stella with hauteur.

'I do,' agreed Mrs Ennismore Smith pleasantly.

They left the shop.

'I feel all the cads in London rolled into one,' said Roger outside. 'But I've found out what I wanted. Good heavens, it's past four. We'll have some tea.'

'Tea is what I want,' said Stella gratefully. 'I feel like all the other cads outside London. But what a look she gave us at the end. If looks could kill...'

Roger glanced at her quickly.

'You disliked that performance?' he asked, curiously, as they walked down towards Piccadilly Circus.

'I detested it.'

'Indeed? I thought you were rather enjoying it.' Was it his fancy? *Had* Stella begun by rather enjoying baiting the older woman?

'I can assure you I wasn't. It was a beastly thing to have to do.'

'Well, I must congratulate you on your acting.'

'Oh, that,' said Stella indifferently.

'And you've certainly earned the articles specified in the bet. Did you really like best the frock you chose?'

'Yes, I think I did. Why?'

'Because directly after tea I'm going to slink back to that shop, buy the frock, and a hat, and the set of unders, and

145

some stockings, and try to persuade her to allow me to pay double for each. You see, what I was hating so much was the fact that she certainly gets a commission on what she sells, and that's why she was so inhumanly patient; because they're very hard up.'

'Well, it's the least you can do; and I shall occupy myself in getting the gloves and shoes you still owe me.'

'Do!' said Roger with enthusiasm. 'I should love to give you some gloves and shoes, Stella.'

'Though what my young man will say to the idea, I don't know,' remarked Miss Barnett calmly. 'Nor, probably, will he.'

'Your young man?'

'My fiancé.'

'I – I didn't know you were engaged.'

'I saw no reason to tell you.'

Roger reflected that he had certainly learned a surprising numbers of things today.

Among others he had learned that Mrs Ennismore Smith, alone so far among all the inhabitants of Monmouth Mansions, was almost certainly capable of committing murder.

chapter eleven

'She could have done it,' Roger muttered to himself as he once more emerged on to the pavement in Shaftesbury Avenue. 'I'm certain she *could* have done it: but I hope she didn't, because I like her. But if she did do it, it's a certainty her husband knows nothing about it. *He* couldn't keep a good thing like that under his hat without showing it. She could. So then the question arises, Could she have done it without his knowledge? While he was asleep? Risky, to say the least. Besides, there's evidence that she was in bed when the crashes were going on. And if we decide that he's not privy to it, that looks like a sound alibi. I suppose it *is* a sound alibi?' He became aware that he was standing in the middle of the pavement, muttering with a large cardboard box under each arm.

He had bought the frock, and he had bought the midnight blue velvet too: he had crawled on his tummy before Mrs Ennismore Smith and bought two sets of unders instead of the one: he had bought stockings, scarves, handbags, and a number of other articles seen mistily as in a dream: he had bought three hats. It was lucky Roger was making more money just then than he could conveniently spend.

He called a taxi, put the boxes inside, gave the man his card and told him to give them to the porter at the Albany and have them sent up to his rooms. Having paid the man and tipped him, he walked rapidly down the street towards Cambridge Circus. He had no objective in view: it was just that one's brain seems stimulated by fast walking, and he wanted to think about Mrs Ennismore Smith. Roger found himself perturbed about her.

He walked aimlessly but rapidly for a considerable distance, but his brain this time remained uninspired. He could not get beyond the idea that Mrs Ennismore Smith's alibi might possibly be upset, and it would be a great pity if it were so. Roger would much rather have upset Mr Barrington Braybrook's, but that seemed cast-iron.

He looked up vaguely at a street name, and realised that he was within a few hundred yards of Monmouth Mansions.

'Mrs Barrington Braybrook,' he told himself. 'She has no alibi at any rate (or so far as we know). And then the Delamere woman. It's no good going on with the Ennismore Smith possibility until we've had at any rate a look at the others. And after all, if it does come down to a question of strength in women, what about Mrs Boyd? There was bad blood at least between them. Dash this case! There are too many possibilities about it. And not one of them is really a probability, not even (thank goodness!) Mrs Ennismore Smith.'

He remembered as he was climbing the stairs that he was still wearing his American disguise. He retained it. There had been some mention of Mrs Barrington Braybrook being of transatlantic birth.

A maidservant opened the door to him, and on his request to see Mrs Barrington Braybrook allowed him to wait in the hall while she went in search of her mistress. Roger had refused to give a name, merely saying he wished to speak to Mrs Barrington Braybrook on a matter of importance.

Mrs Barrington Braybrook was apparently willing, for Roger found himself ushered into the usual-sized sitting-room of Monmouth Mansions, which in this case seemed smaller than the others owing to the amount of furniture that was crammed into it. Roger steered a careful course between two small tables and round a pouffe cushion towards the young woman who had risen on his entrance.

She was a young woman of not unpleasing aspect, if a cow may be said to be of not unpleasing aspect: that is, she had large, mild ox-eyes, a broad white forehead, plumply indefinite cheeks, and an amiably indeterminate expression which faded through an uncertain smile into a weak but pretty chin.

'Type,' Roger thought to himself, 'bovine; potentiality for tears, infinite; potentiality for passion, five per cent; potentiality for cold-blooded murder, minus one million; exit Mrs Barrington Braybrook from the list of suspects. Why waste time?' Aloud he said: '*Ex*-cuse me, Mrs Barrington Braybrook, I'm mighty anxious to get hold of the address of a man who lived in this building fourteen years ago, by the name of Smith. Now I wonder if you have in your records any trace of this guy Smith and can put me wise to his present domicile?'

'Why, no,' regretted Mrs Barrington Braybrook, 'I guess I never heard of him. But gee, you're American, aren't you?'

'Queen, you said a mouthful,' agreed Roger.

'From Borston, I reckon? Well, isn't that just too cute. I can't tell you what it means to me to hear a little good American spoken in this room, why, yes, and to speak it too, instead of everlastingly pretending to speak like these English. Say, you must certainly stop and have some tea, Mr – why, there now, I don't believe you mentioned your name?'

'Jones. I'm sawry, madam. I can't stop now. I'm trailing this guy Smith, and I must get round before he beats it. I'd be mighty pleased to come and drink a cup of tea with you another day.' He made a hasty exit, with the feeling that he had mixed up irretrievably the Boston accent with the Chicagoan: a conclusion which the puzzled expression in Mrs Barrington Braybrook's ox-eyes confirmed.

'Humour,' Roger continued his category outside, 'nil; capacity for swallowing confidence stories, one hundred per cent; transatlantic birth confirmed; rumoured experience in musical comedy, highly probable; interests, none; hobbies, none; intelligence, none; well, well, well. Now for Miss Delamere. Rather more subtle methods here, I think. Now come; let us be very subtle indeed.'

Roger's idea of being very subtle indeed when Miss Delamere opened her door to him in person was to say: 'Miss Evadne Delamere? How do you do? My name is Winterbottom. Dick told me if ever I was round this way to call in and remember him to you.'

Rather to his own surprise, Roger found this subtlety worked on all cylinders. 'Dick told you?' said Miss Delamere, pleased. 'That's fine. Come on in.'

Roger went on in.

'I'm afraid the sitting-room's in a simply terrible muddle,' simpered Miss Delamere over a slim shoulder.

'Good,' said Roger. 'I like muddles.'

The sitting-room was, in fact, extremely tidy. So far as could be seen the only symptoms of muddle were on the couch, in the form of Miss Delamere's sewing, which appeared, in the glimpse that Roger had of it, to be of an intimate nature. Miss Delamere pounced on it with arch little cries of dismay and embarrassment, stuffed its flimsiness under the cushion, and then spoilt the effect by saying; 'I make *all* my own things myself.'

'Do you?' said Roger heartily. 'Wonderful. I never do.'

'Oh, but then you're a man,' pouted Miss Delamere.

'So I've been credibly informed,' Roger replied cautiously.

Miss Delamere looked a little nonplussed for a moment and then burst into another small series of cries. 'Oh, do sit down, Mr Winterbottom. I am terrible, aren't I? I *always* forget to ask people to sit down. Here I am sitting down myself, and I never asked you to. Of course people usually do nowadays without being asked, don't they? But I can see you're different. I *am* so sorry. Well, fancy you knowing Dick. Do you know, I haven't seen him for *ages*. How is he?'

'Oh, about the same,' Roger said, pulling up a chair.

'Oh, don't sit on *that*. All these chairs are quite impossible, I'm afraid. There's plenty of room here.' Miss Delamere patted the couch beside her.

'Thank you.' Roger sat down on the rest of the couch. 'But look here, you were sewing, weren't you? Please don't let me stop you.'

'Oh, I couldn't, with you here,' said Miss Delamere coyly, glancing at him out of the corners of her eyes.

'Why not?'

'Well, you're rather a stranger, aren't you? And a man.'

'Has some gypsy been warning you against strange men?'

Miss Delamere laughed.

After a little further badinage of the same description she assented to go on with her sewing, which she did, now that the conventions had been observed, without a hint of embarrassment.

Meanwhile Roger and she observed each other covertly, in swift side-glances.

Roger saw an extremely small person who, he thought, was really the daintiest human creature he had ever seen. She could not have been quite five feet in height, and she was perfectly built and proportioned: her figure, the lines of which were plain enough through her very becoming little frock of black velvet, was really exquisite. She was pretty too, up to a point; but a nose just a little too large robbed her face of the perfection of her body; her eyes were enormous and dark velvety brown, her hair jet-black; her complexion was the worst thing about her, being distinctly sallow. She spoke with a faint Cockney twang, and from the lines about her eyes and throat, Roger put her age at thirty-five, though otherwise she did not look it.

'Really, if you don't mind me being personal,' said Roger, knowing well that personalities, so long as they were flattering, were just what would please the small lady best, 'really, I think you have the smallest feet I've ever seen.'

'I dare say I have,' replied Miss Delamere complacently. 'I take twos in shoes, and so far as I know I'm the only woman in London who does. They have to get them for me from Paris specially.'

'I can well believe it. And what size do you take in gloves?'

'Fours.'

'Miraculous! You must let me send you a pair as a tribute.'

'You'll have some difficulty in getting them. Hardly any shops keep them so small.'

'Where do y*ou* get them?'

'Rossiter's, in Bond Street,' replied Miss Delamere promptly.

Roger reflected that Miss Delamere was not above accepting tributes from strange men, in spite of the gypsy.

'But I'm Australian, of course,' she went on, as if that explained everything. 'I expect Dick told you.'

'No, I don't think he did. That's very interesting.' It also explained the Cockney twang. The Australians have the misfortune to use the same way of mispronouncing English as the less meticulous Londoners. 'When did you come over?'

'Oh, years and years ago. When I was fifteen. I used to be on the stage, you know.'

'Indeed? Aren't you now?'

'Oh, no. I left it soon after the w— I left it years ago.'

'And what do you do now?' Roger asked, wondering as soon as he had spoken whether this might not be a tactless question.

But apparently it was a highly tactful one. 'I write,' replied Miss Delamere with pride.

'Oh! You write, do you?' Roger said tolerantly.

'Yes, but you needn't pretend you've heard of me,' Miss Delamere said, with one of her arch glances. 'I don't write under my own name.'

Roger reflected that this sounded almost as if she got published. 'What name do you write under?'

But on this point Miss Delamere proved most coy. It was, apparently, a very great secret. Not a single person in Monmouth Mansions knew it. Really, she couldn't tell Roger: oh, really, no.

'"Madeleine Griffiths,"' said Miss Delamere shyly.

Roger stared at her. Madeleine Griffiths' name was perfectly familiar to him. He had never read a word she had written because he did not care for newspaper serials; but to any reader of *The Daily Wail*, *The Daily Distress*, or *The Daily Blues*, Madeleine Griffiths represented the last word in the literature of the day. She knew what her public wanted, and she gave it them, tepid and as strong as her editors would permit.

Roger's brain was working quickly. This was no arch little nincompoop, as Miss Delamere had elected to represent herself (no doubt mistaking the result for charm), but a shrewd woman. How would this effect his plans – or how could it be made to do so?

It did not take him more than fifteen seconds to decide. Stella Barnett was not the right type; quite definitely not, in spite of her ability to act a part. Besides, she had shown herself unwilling to help in his inquiries, even uninterested; he had only obtained her aid by a ruse, so that she did not know she was affording it. And if Stella had a footing in the building, this woman was wholly inside it. Besides, not the remotest suspicion could rest on her now; as Madeleine Griffiths she must be making all of a couple of thousand a year, even had she not been far too tiny almost to lift a terrier off its feet and strangle it.

'Well,' said Roger, 'that's great. I'd better introduce myself again. My name's Sheringham – Roger Sheringham. So we're birds of a feather, after all. And if you'll keep my secret, I'll keep yours.'

'Roger Sheringham! Well, how extraordinary! Are you really? Yes, I thought I'd seen you before as soon as you came in. But didn't you say your name was Winterbottom?'

'I did, but I was mistaken. At least, I've as much right to call myself Winterbottom as you have to call yourself Griffiths. Or say it's my maiden name if you like. Anyhow, I'll confess. I obtained entrance to your flat on entirely false pretences.'

'Then you don't know Dick Myers at all? At least, I supposed it was Dick Myers you meant?'

'I don't; nor any other Dick. The truth is that I got in here as I've got into every other flat in this building, because I wanted to discuss the murder with you.'

'The murder! Oh, I see. And I thought you wanted to discuss poor little me. This is a terrible blow. Are you going to use our murder for a novel, then?'

'I thought of doing so. The old woman seems to have been an interesting character, and after all she did come to an interesting end. And some of the other people in this building might be worked in too. But I didn't know you lived in this place, and I'll admit you have the first claim to the story.'

'Oh, I couldn't use it. Murders are no good to me. Sobs and strong men and pew-erity are my line,' said Miss Delamere candidly.

'Good. Then tell me all about it,' said Roger, settling himself more comfortably in the corner of the couch. He noticed that since he had declared himself, and the gloves were presumably off, Miss Delamere had discarded nine-tenths of the archness, her coyness, and her simpers. But one-tenth did still remain. Roger gathered that affectation had been worn by her so long that it had become like an eighth skin on her, unremovable.

She had embarked on an account of Miss Barnett (whom she had hardly ever seen) and the murder. Roger learned nothing new. The story was really an account of the murder as it had affected Miss Delamere. His hostess had evidently not learned to apply to fact what she applied so successfully to fiction, perspective. Roger was a little disappointed.

However, as personalities were evidently Miss Delamere's strong point, he led the discussion quickly round to Mrs Ennismore Smith, and canvassed his hostess' ideas upon the subject, without, of course, giving any hint of his own.

'Well, she's not my sort,' responded Miss Delamere frankly. 'Really I hardly know her. Him, yes; and if I did know her I'd still like him a good deal better than her; in fact I might once have liked him quite a lot; but he can thank his lucky stars he married a woman like her, and not one like me.'

'Yes,' said Roger thoughtfully, 'that does about sum her up. And him.'

There was a little silence.

Roger rubbed his chin. In spite of the work he had put in he seemed no nearer the solution; and if Mrs Ennismore Smith really was the solution (which in his heart he had difficulty in believing), he had nothing but a balance of probabilities to show for it; and of what use to a jury is a balance of probabilities?

'Do you know Barrington Braybrook, Miss Delamere?' he asked suddenly.

Her arch expression flitted across Miss Delamere's face. 'How do you know that wouldn't be telling? Why?'

'Oh, he sounds as if he had something to him,' Roger replied carelessly. 'Besides yourself, he seems about the only person in this building who has made a success of things.'

Miss Delamere nodded slowly. 'That's just what I feel about him. Yes, I do know him. Slightly. Well, fairly well, perhaps. He's the only person here who knows what I do. He comes up here occasionally in the evening for a drink and a chat, when his wife's been boring him worse than usual. Oh!' One tiny hand flew to her mouth. 'Perhaps I oughtn't to have said that.'

'Why not?' Roger said easily, reflecting that tininess usually suggested helplessness; in Miss Delamere's case it did nothing of the sort; there was always the feeling of hardness in her diminutiveness; the mechanical toy, not the wax doll. 'Why not? I've talked with the lady. She evidently hasn't more than one idea in her head.'

'Not that,' replied Miss Delamere, almost fiercely. 'It's very hard on him, being tied up to a roly-poly pudding like that. John – Mr Barrington Braybrook is a very able man. With the right wife he might have gone a long way.' There was plainly little doubt in Miss Delamere's mind as to the identity of Mr Barrington Braybrook's right wife. 'Yes, if Mr Ennismore Smith married the right woman for him, Mr Barrington Braybrook didn't.'

It was on the tip of Roger's tongue to point out that at least both ladies had provided their husbands with double names, but a doubt of this being true in the second case stopped him. 'Well, it takes all sorts to make a Mansions,' he said feebly. His mind played round this new light on the interior of Monmouth Mansions. Did it throw any light on the mystery? Not the least, so far as he could see. Evidence was the only thing that would do that. Real, solid, definite witness-box evidence; and just that was what he could not unearth.

He pondered his next move for a minute or two, while Miss Delamere sewed silent hatred of the wrong wife into her nether garments.

'You say you heard nothing at all on the night of the murder?' It was very fortunate that his profession allowed him to ask any kind of question he chose without exciting any surprise in his hostess as to the interest he found in this apparently very ordinary murder.

'Not a thing. For once I'd gone to bed early. I do most of my work at night, as I expect you do too, but I was rather tired last Tuesday and got to bed before twelve for once.' Roger noticed that she did not mention her visitor.

'Not even the crashes and bumps that woke up the Ennismore Smiths?'

'No, nothing.'

Roger reflected that nobody but the Ennismore Smiths had heard these noises; neither Miss Pilchard nor Miss Delamere; yet both of them might have been reasonably expected to do so. Was it significant that Mr and Mrs Ennismore Smith were the sole witnesses to the fact that there had been crashes and bumps at all? But they were not the sole witnesses after all. Furniture may be overturned without bumping, but china cannot be smashed on the floor without crashing. If not bumps, at any rate crashes had most certainly occurred.

Wait though. Roger jerked himself into a new position as a fresh thought occurred to him. There was a good deal more in the Ennismore Smiths' evidence than that bumps and crashes had occurred. There was the time at which they had occurred. And on that the whole case depended, for the time of the bumps had been accepted without question as the time of the murder. Now an interesting point occurred to Roger. It was Mrs Ennismore Smith, and she alone, who was responsible for this mention of 1.20 a.m. Her husband had asked her the time, and she had answered that it was 1.20 a.m. If he had not asked her, would she have volunteered the same information? And what check was there on its accuracy? None.

Moreover (another point), Mrs Ennismore Smith had woken her husband up to hear the noises. And she had said that there had been a lot of noises before she did so. But Augustus Weller had heard nothing. Might not all this be considered significant? Undoubtedly, if one suspected Mrs Smith enough, it might.

There was, however, risk in a deliberate misstatement about the time. Ennismore Smith might so easily have verified it for himself. Suppose, therefore, just for the sake of argument, that the crashes *had* occurred at approximately 1.20 a.m., as both the Ennismore Smiths agreed, but that the murder had not; would it have been outside possibility for Mrs Ennismore Smith to have arranged things so that the crashes *would* occur then, and so provide her with an alibi that would be hardly likely to be questioned (for, of course, she would hope that at least Mrs Pilchard and Miss Delamere would hear them too), while having already a little earlier...?

No, it would surely not be outside possibility for an ingenious as well as a determined woman. Matter can be set to move matter. Clocks can be made to do surprisingly ingenious things. An alarm clock could be made to break a tightly stretched piece of cotton; the breaking of the cotton could drop a tiny weight; the tiny weight could upset a heavier object balanced delicately; and so on, until china crashed on the ground and light furniture bumped on a floor like a sounding board. It *could* have been done. For of course a duplicate latch key to the flat might be postulated, so that the simple apparatus, alarm clock, cotton, weight, what you like, could be removed an hour or two later, while one's husband soundly slept.

And dash it, thought Roger gloomily, she's capable of it. If the need was desperate enough, she's psychologically capable of it. I only wish she weren't. But that cold rage of hers was too illuminating. And her patience. Substitute desperation as the spur instead of rage, and with that grim patience of hers... I suppose it all hangs on how hard up they are just now, or how badly they need ready money. I wonder how I can find out that?

'Getting the plot?' asked Miss Delamere, with the sympathy of a fellow-artist.

'I believe I'm getting *a* plot,' Roger replied, with a touch of grimness.

'Have a drink?' suggested Miss Delamere, failing to perceive the grimness.

'That,' said Roger, 'is an exceedingly sound idea.'

His hostess jumped up nimbly and went to a cupboard on the other side of the room. Roger thought that, seen from behind, she really was the daintiest creature on two legs; it was a pity her front view did not quite come up to the same standard.

Miss Delamere produced a variety of bottles and began, with nonchalant skill, to shake up a cocktail.

Roger tasted it, and lo! it was good. He accepted another. Persiflage superseded murder in the conversation.

Under the frothy stream of badinage that issued from him Roger was thinking in this way: 'If I go now, the odds are she won't tell me what I want to know, because I have a feeling that there's an inhibition of morality somewhere connected with it, and two cocktails are not enough to break down this small lady's inhibition so far as giving herself away is concerned (I don't fancy she has any others); on the other hand, if I stay much longer I shall certainly be expected to make love for my information. Is it possible to insert my question into the split second that must elapse between the ending of the one period and the beginning of the other? We can but see. I shall put my money on the fifth minute after the serving of the third cocktail.'

At the fifth minute after the serving of the third cocktail, Roger accordingly asked: 'You know Ennismore Smith pretty well, you said?'

'Pretty well.'

Miss Delamere had not sounded quite so guarded and Roger was encouraged to proceed. 'I've only met him once or twice, but I liked him enormously. Not a business man of course; he ought to have been born with a silver spoon in his mouth; but a most likeable fellow.'

'That's exactly what he is,' agreed Miss Delamere at once, perching herself like a dear little bird on the back of the couch. 'One can't take him seriously, of course. I mean, not like Mr Barrington Braybrook. But he really is so sweet and helpless one would do simply anything for him. Women are funny that way, as you probably know.'

'I do,' Roger nodded gravely.

'It is funny, too,' mused Miss Delamere, now not at all guardedly. 'Because I'm really much fonder of John than Lionel (they both drop in here to see me off and on), and yet Lionel can get things out of me without any trouble at all that John can – could ask and ask for, and I wouldn't. I suppose really it's because one simply can't take him seriously. Still,' said Miss Delamere more brightly, looking on the profit side of the ledger, 'Lionel *is* useful to me. Well, so is John for that matter. I've used them both a dozen times, under different names. That's the best of my kind of work, you know; stick a new name on, and you get a different person; no bother about character, or anything like that. Nobody worries, so why should I?'

'Precisely. Yes, Ennismore Smith *is* the sort of person who gets things out of one,' said Roger, resolutely treading back to the main path. 'You've put it exactly. Money, for instance.'

'Oh, has Lionel been borrowing from *you*?' cried Miss Delamere, like a parent who deplores an offspring's act but

ANTHONY BERKELEY

cannot evade a feeling of responsibility for it. 'Now that's too
bad. You hardly know him.'

'Oh, that's all right,' Roger said hastily, reflecting that this
case seemed to have led him into the implication of more
untruths than ever before in his life. 'That's perfectly all
right. Somehow one rather expects it, you know. He borrows
from you, of course?'

'Oh, well, from me, yes, of course. He knows I've got
plenty, though he doesn't know where it comes from. But I
do wish he wouldn't borrow from John. John takes that sort
of thing so seriously. I don't know what's come over Lionel
lately. This time last year he wouldn't borrow even from me,
though I offered to lend to him several times; but just lately
he plucked up his courage and asked John too for ten
pounds. John let him have it of course, though he didn't like
it, and Lionel told me afterwards it was the bravest thing
he'd ever done in his life. I was terribly cross with him,
because I could easily have lent it to him myself. You see,
I'm so afraid John will expect the poor darling to pay him
back.'

'Doesn't the poor darling pay you back, then?'

'Oh, he will one day,' said Miss Delamere cheerfully. 'If
he's got it.'

A few minutes later Roger took his leave, with gratitude.

He had received the twin answers to the double-barrelled
question that had been in his mind. He knew now that not
only were the Ennismore Smiths hard up, but they were
desperately hard up.

The solitary question he had put to Ennismore Smith last
Tuesday had not proved irrelevant after all. It was a large
point that Ennismore Smith had been to a public school. For
the kind of thing one really learns at a public school is not
the capes of Africa (when one is never in one's life going to

162

Africa), but far more practical things, such as that one must never borrow money from a woman (because one certainly is going to be hard up earlier or, more unfortunately, later); and that even if one does sink to that, there is still one thing that remains simply impossible even to contemplate, and that is to borrow money from a woman whom one knows intimately.

Contrary to the general idea, one does *not* forget the things one really learns at school.

Roger knew now that, somehow or other, the Ennismore Smiths had got themselves into a situation that could be nothing short of desperate.

chapter twelve

Roger had not after all followed up the first impulse that had
occurred to him on learning Miss Evadne Delamere's
identity with Madeleine Griffiths, namely to make her his
full confidante in the unofficial investigation he was
pursuing. He was glad now that he had refrained. Miss
Delamere was a shrewd woman; she had imagination and
ideas; her assistance and her views might have proved of
real use to him, far more so than those of Stella Barnett, for
instance, even had the latter been willing to give them. But
Evadne Delamere was too closely mixed up with the people
concerned. When the idea of telling her of his suspicions had
jumped at him, Roger had not gathered how well she knew
Ennismore Smith. Now he did know that, he was sure Miss
Delamere would not make a correctly impartial assistant.

Roger wondered, incidentally, just how much Mrs
Ennismore Smith knew of her husband's friendship. Either
nothing, in Roger's opinion, or everything. It all depended
how far Mrs Ennismore Smith went in agreement with Miss
Delamere, that one could not take Lionel seriously. But it
makes a difference when Lionel is one's husband, of course.

Meditating gently by his fireside that evening, Roger had
decided his new line. He was going to work inductively,
on the assumption that Mrs Ennismore Smith was the

murderess. Not that he was by any means convinced on this point even now, but he felt that such a method might lead to interesting results which, even though the assumption should prove to be a mistaken one, might still be of value. And at least it did give one a starting point in all this shapelessness.

One interesting possibility had already emerged: the conception, shattering to the whole case as it had stood till now, that 1.20 a.m. might after all not be the time at which Miss Barnett had met her death. That must be examined at once.

Roger crossed his legs and stared into the fire. What was it that the doctor had said? He was not definite about the time of death of course; he had to put it within two limits. So far as Roger could remember, the limits had been not less than twelve hours, and not more than twenty-four. But that could easily be confirmed from Moresby in the morning.

At that stage, of course, the doctor would only have had three indications on which to base his opinion – the respective extents of the rigor, the temperature, and the post-mortem staining, and the second of these did not help in the least to fix the period more definitely within those limits, for the body was already cold. But the autopsy might have added something; there is always the condition of the stomach, the stage of digestion of the last meal and so on, to give a further pointer or two. It occurred to Roger that he had not seen a copy of the divisional surgeon's report on the post-mortem. He must get on to Moresby about that in the morning too.

But of course the trouble was that after a body has been dead for twelve hours at least, it is practically impossible to say how long it has been dead under the twenty-four. Rigor is responsible for that. It does not work nice and tidily, with

fixed stages at fixed times. In the case of the violent death of
a healthy person it may set in within ten hours, and it may
not set in for a whole twenty-four. Most annoying of it, Roger
considered. In Miss Barnett's case he remembered the
doctor saying that it was partial. That was at about 1.30 p.m.
Miss Barnett might have been killed, therefore, so far as the
indications of her body went, as early as half-past one on the
previous day. It was too wide a gap; far too wide.

Mrs Pilchard had been the last person to see her alive, at
a few minutes past five. The gap was still far too wide. For
all the evidence to the contrary, excepting only and always
(perhaps) the midnight bumps, Mrs Pilchard might have
strangled her friend over the tea table and decamped.
Mrs Pilchard!...

Now one came to think of it, Mrs Pilchard had been
excluded mechanically from the list of suspects simply
owing to her friendship with the dead woman. Was not this
most unprofessional? Friends have been known to murder
friends. And Mrs Pilchard though short was stocky. And
there had been that emphasis of hers about it having been
herself who had insisted on a policeman being fetched: it
had not struck one as suspicious at the time, but now
perhaps... Had it been overdone, even allowing for the Irish
in her? And after all Mrs Pilchard was the only person who
knew all about Miss Barnett's financial possibilities. And
that anxiety of hers to get at the body...

'I'm getting confused,' Roger muttered. 'That's impossible.
The woman was in her nightdress, and the bed had been
occupied. But what was there to stop Mrs Pilchard
undressing her friend as well as murdering her, and rumpling
the bed?' Roger rumpled his own hair. 'This must stop. I'm
letting my infernal imagination run away with me.' And yet
it did not seem really any more wildly imaginative to see Mrs

Pilchard strangling over the tea table than to see Mrs Ennismore Smith creeping murderously up the stairs round about midnight.

What time did the Ennismore Smiths go to bed that evening? What were they doing in the evening? Were they together? How was Mrs Ennismore Smith occupied from the time she came home from work to the time she went to bed?

Roger made a mental memorandum of the fact that an interview with Ennismore Smith was very much needed, and the sooner the better. If he was not privy to the crime, Roger thought there would be little difficulty in making him talk.

But wait a moment. When Roger had decided that Ennismore Smith was as incapable of murder as his wife was capable of it, he had not known that the man was in a desperate position. Could that affect the question? Did a man who in a normal condition was psychologically incapable of committing murder remain incapable when the conditions were abnormal? Not of the hot murder of a mad moment, when the reason goes numb and brute instinct takes charge of the body; this murder was not of that kind. Ennismore Smith might perhaps be capable of the former, but that is no pure murder at all; murder to be pure must be planned. Could Ennismore Smith possibly have planned and executed such a painstakingly contrived murder as this, complete down to the last detail – complete even to the cake of mud from the supposed murderer's heel? Roger hardly needed to deliberate the question. He was practically convinced that Mr Ennismore Smith could not, however abnormal the conditions, have brought himself to the execution of such a murder; he was quite convinced that such a muddler could never have planned so perfect a crime.

Once more Mr Ennismore Smith must be wiped off the slate.

And yet somehow Mrs Ennismore Smith... She must have been very desperate.

Roger shifted uncomfortably. There was simply no escaping the parallel between that cool, efficient, determined patience she had shown in the shop, and the cool, efficient, determined patience that had planned this crime. No one without an eye for the most meticulous detail could have done it. The detail, in the aggregate, was tremendous. The rope, the scratches on the window-sill, the scratches on the wall, the displacement of the gas stove, the evidence of search (but rather overdone that, considering that the chest was in one of the first places that would have been examined; was there a psychological pointer here? Feminine overemphasis?), the cake of mud, the cigarette ends and ash in the cupboard (but not altogether convincing; that, either), the use of a candle, the professionally gloved fingertips...

A point occurred to Roger. His choice of Mrs Ennismore Smith had been simply a case of residue after elimination; everyone else in the building had been rejected on one ground or another; Mrs Ennismore Smith alone remained as the sole possessor of both the mental and the physical attributes with which the murderer must be credited. Yet so far there had been not the slightest evidence to suggest that the criminal might be a woman at all. Now Roger realised that such a piece of evidence did in fact exist: the gloved fingerprints. Moresby had cited their smallness and slimness as an additional pointer towards Jim Watkins, whose hands, as Roger had noticed, undoubtedly were small. Yet was it not just as reasonable, and more reasonable, to consider their smallness rather as due to their having been made by a woman? Roger was quite sure that it was.

That was a line worth pursuing for a moment or two. Did the crime afford any other indications of a female perpetrator? How was this inductive case against Mrs Ennismore Smith to be bolstered up?

In its meticulousness? Attention to detail is sometimes considered a feminine rather than a masculine attribute; and this affair was all detail; there were no broad, sweeping, typically male effects; it was pre-Raphaelite, not post-Georgian. But the pre-Raphaelites were male. No, that was really too fine an argument in a case of murder.

Yet there was something cat-like about the affair; something prowling rather than prancing, slinking rather than striding. But there are male cats, and male cat-burglars too. No, apart from the fingerprints there was nothing more definitely in favour of a murderess rather than a murderer except a mere feeling, and Roger knew that the best detectives take no account at all of mere feelings.

But there was, though. Something quite definite. Miss Barnett had been in her nightdress. That was almost certain evidence that her visitor had been a woman.

Well, that was very interesting.

Roger passed on to more tangible evidence.

There was, however, very little tangible evidence. Even the rosary with which it was supposed that the crime had been committed had not yet spoken up. Or had it? Moresby had said nothing about its having been traced, but that did not necessarily mean that it had not been. Moresby seldom volunteered information unless he wanted something in return. Moresby must be asked about the rosary tomorrow.

This rosary now...

Why a rosary? They had all jumped to the obvious conclusion that Miss Barnett had been a Roman Catholic and the rosary her own. But Mrs Pilchard had said definitely that Miss Barnett had not been a Roman Catholic. It is true that the use of rosaries is not confined to the Roman Church; many Anglo-Catholics use them too. But Mrs Pilchard had said that Miss Barnett possessed no rosary at all; and Roger was sure that if she had Mrs Pilchard would have known. There was only one possible conclusion: the rosary had been left by the murderer.

The more he thought about it, the more significant did this rosary seem. Even if it could not be traced, it ought to provide valuable information by its mere existence, if one could only read the puzzle right. There seemed to be two main questions: (a) why a rosary at all? and (b) had the murderer left it accidentally or intentionally?

Roger got up and helped himself to a glass of beer from the barrel in the larder. There were possibilities about this rosary.

Taking the second of the two questions first, if the murderer had left it accidentally its value as a clue was obviously much increased. The criminal would have made a mistake, and the rosary's message, if only it could be induced to deliver it, would be easier to read. But if the rosary was a plant, all sorts of complications arose. What is the immediate conclusion on finding a rosary lying beside a corpse, dropped there by the murderer? That the latter is a Roman Catholic. If the leaving had been an accident, the odds certainly were that the murderer was a Catholic of some sort, whether Roman or Anglo, with a preference for the former. But if the thing had been left with intention, that could only mean that the murderer wished to be thought a Catholic, whereas in reality he (or she) would probably be

170

most rigidly C of E. The secondary question at once arose, therefore, *why* this anxiety on the part of the murderer to be identified with the Catholic faith?

This seemed to lead back to the first main question, why a rosary at all?

Well, why a rosary at all?

By assumption, the murder was a premeditated one. Why, then, come armed with a rosary of all things when a piece of cord would have done just as well, and better? (And why, for that matter, strangulation as the means? Well, a woman would shrink from a blow on the head with a poker or anything of that nature. She would distrust her own arm. That hung together.) It was impossible to avoid the conclusion that the answer had something to do with Catholicism; but apart from the notion attributable to the murderer of inaugurating a second Popish Plot, which was at least unlikely, Roger could think of nothing at all.

The rosary problem must be temporarily shelved. He wished now he had mentioned it to Miss Delamere. She was a Catholic, it seemed. She might have been able to throw a little light on the intricacy. She might even have been able to identify the rosary. What if she had dropped her own on the stairs, and the murderer had picked it up? That would explain its choice as a weapon. But Moresby would be able to answer those questions tomorrow.

He passed on to a consideration of the mysterious running man – the running man who was now quite definitely *not* Mr James Watkins.

This running man was nothing short of a nuisance. He was the only piece of the jigsaw which could not be fitted into the interior of Monmouth Mansions; he was the only flaw that Roger could see in his own private theory of the murder. And though for the last few days Roger had been ignoring him altogether, he could not be ignored forever. The running man must be tackled, pulled down and explained.

There was another awkwardness about this running man. Not only did he not fit into the otherwise impregnable (or so it seemed to Roger) theory that Miss Barnett had been murdered by one of the other inhabitants of Monmouth Mansions, but he also upset the ingenious idea based upon the alarm clock, the thread of cotton, and the like. The running man confirmed entirely the Ennismore Smith story; the times agreed. And his appearance did seem to knock the alarm clock theory on the head. It was really too much of a coincidence that just at the time when the alarm clock went off, an entirely fortuitous running man should go off too.

But – need he have been an entirely fortuitous running man?

Roger's reason gave an uneasy twitch, but he ignored it. He was *not* arguing soberly from fact to fact; he was deliberately encouraging his imagination to the wildest leaps it could make. The very take-off that he had given it, the assumption of Mrs Ennismore Smith's guilt, was quite probably mistaken; the alarm clock bound (and by alarm clock Roger meant any mechanical device for producing crashes at a given time) was no doubt utterly aimless; but, if one leaps about a meadow long enough and assiduously enough, however much at random, one is just as likely as not to alight on a four-leafed clover in time, assuming that a four-leafed clover exists in the meadow. And in this meadow four-leafed clovers were rife, though exceedingly difficult to recognise. Let the agility therefore continue.

Very well then. That could be granted; that the only way of reconciling the running man with the alarm-clock theory was the bounding assumption that his appearance was not fortuitous in the least; it was deliberate.

That meant that the running man was an accomplice. Well, why not? Stranger things have happened than that a murderer should have an accomplice. And at least it was no more odd that the running man should be an accessory to a murder instead, as had first been thought, the murderer himself. Moreover, the fact of him being a mere accomplice might explain his climbing over the wall instead of going through the doorway. The criminal himself would naturally have spied out the land better for himself; a mere accomplice might not.

But that did not fit. Mrs Ennismore Smith – and by Mrs Ennismore Smith, Roger meant the murderous inhabitant of Monmouth Mansions whom the probabilities so far seemed to indicate – Mrs Ennismore Smith would know all about the door in the wall. With her care for detail it was incredible that she should not have told her accomplice about it, so that he should not make himself needlessly conspicuous by climbing over the wall. So that –

Roger's reason gave him a sharp kick. This time he did not ignore it. He had been a fool, his reason told him, and Roger agreed. The whole point about the accomplice was that he was there to *make* himself conspicuous, and nothing else. Roger had already proved, to his own complete satisfaction, that nobody could have got out of Monmouth Mansions that night unobserved, murderer or accomplice. Monmouth Mansions last Tuesday night was faster than a mediaeval fortress. The accomplice had therefore never been inside the fortress. The sole thing he had to do, and the sole thing that there was any need for him to do (granted that Mrs Ennismore Smith had the nerve to perform the main job herself), was to be seen scrambling over the wall into the alley and then running madly away from the neighbourhood at precisely 1.20 a.m. on the Wednesday morning. Who then would have the wit, the super-wit, to realise that murder had not taken place at 1.20 a.m. at all, that the running man had not perpetrated it, and that the alibi for his wife to which the unknowing Mr Ennismore Smith would swear with such completely convincing conviction was utterly demolished?

No one, Roger Sheringham told himself with pleasure, except apparently Roger Sheringham.

He finished his beer and went back to the larder to draw some more. He was making more progress this evening than he had made since the case began, and he modestly put it all down to the beer.

Of all the flies he had cast so far, the running man had proved the most remunerative. Settling down again, Roger thought he would try a few more casts with him.

The position at the moment, then, was that the function of the running man had been to make a conspicuous getaway from the yard at 1.20 a.m., climbing the wall instead of going through the door in order to draw the chauffeur's attention, and then –

Roger pulled himself up. How on earth were the two to know in advance that the chauffeur would just have returned at 1.20 a.m.? His return had been completely haphazard. Not even his employer could have foretold it three hours before.

This needed a readjustment. That the man had climbed the wall in order to attract the chauffeur's attention seemed obvious; there was simply no other explanation of the act, if one disregarded ignorance of the doorway. It must follow, therefore, that the moment of his climbing was dependent on the chauffeur's time of return, and not on a prearranged time with Mrs Ennismore Smith. How then to account for the time of the crashes coinciding so neatly?

'Well, hang it!' Roger exclaimed aloud, after a moment's thought. 'It was the accomplice, not a mechanical device at all, that produced the crashes!'

This was progress.

The more he examined this notion, the more feasible it seemed. The accomplice's part had been not merely to be seen running away, but to make the noises which (it must have been hoped) were to waken half the inhabitants of the Mansions at the moment of running away. And he would make no move at all until the chauffeur, for whom he would have been waiting for hours and watching through a crack of the door, was on the point of emerging from the garage. Then swift action.

And that gave the problem of how in the world an accomplice waiting in the yard below could possibly have produced crashes in a flat four storeys above his head.

Roger was in particularly good form that evening. It took him exactly five minutes' thought to find the answer to that riddle, and as he was convinced, the only possible answer to it too.

Having found it he went to bed and resolutely read *Punch* from cover to cover, to induce sleep.

chapter thirteen

Miss Barnett whisked the cover off her typewriter and sat down in front of it. If she had felt at all disconcerted at finding her employer actually waiting for her in his study, in his dressing-gown and pyjamas, she certainly did not show it.

'"Ask Mama"?' she queried efficiently.

'Certainly not. And you needn't sit there. Sit at the desk. I'm going to dictate some notes for you to take down in shorthand.'

'I can take them down quite well here,' replied Miss Barnett, producing her pad and pencil like magic.

'Sit at the desk,' repeated Roger, preoccupied.

Miss Barnett sat at the desk.

'Oh, by the way,' Roger said perfunctorily, 'you'll excuse my dressing-gown, won't you?'

'Certainly – if you prefer it.'

'I do. Ready? This is for the Monmouth Mansions dossier. I'll give you rough notes. I want you to arrange them into some sort of order, type them out, with a fresh sheet for each heading, take a carbon copy, and put the original in the file. And as quickly as possible. Understand?'

'Perfectly.'

Roger swiftly dictated his conclusions of the evening before, with such proofs as he had been able to collect in support of them; where no proof was available, he indicated baldly the arguments in their favour. His conclusions were three in number, and they fell under the following headings: (1) the murder was not committed at 1.20 a.m., but earlier; (2) the crashes heard at 1.20 a.m. were caused not by the murderer but by an accomplice; (3) the man seen by the chauffeur and others running away at approximately 1.20 a.m. was not the murderer but an accomplice. He dictated nothing concerning his suspicions of Mrs Ennismore Smith. The pages already headed 'Evadne Delamere' and 'Mrs Barrington Braybrook' also remained blank. From now onwards, Roger had decided, he would keep his records impersonal; personalities could be carried in his head. There is such a thing as a law of libel.

When he had finished he looked, but not very expectantly, at Miss Barnett.

This time, however, comment was forthcoming. 'May I ask you a question, Mr Sheringham?'

'You may, Stella. By the way,' added Roger benevolently, 'did you get the shoes and things?'

'Yes, thank you. Here is the bill.'

'Very reasonable,' said Roger, scrutinising it.

'I'm sorry you think so. I intended this to be a lesson to you. What I wanted to ask you was – '

'Oh, before I forget, there are two large parcels waiting for you. I'll tell Meadows to bring them in. I got you the midnight blue frock as well, by the way. Oh, yes, and three hats. Oh, and two lots of unders, one for use and one for the laundry. Yes, and a few oddments as well. You'll know what to do with them; I don't.'

'That was quite unnecessary. I shall only accept what was stipulated in the bet.'

'But I can't wear them myself.'

'That,' said Miss Barnett indifferently, 'is your affair, Mr Sheringham.'

'Hardly any man,' mused Roger, 'wears trousers of Japshan; they may be very pretty, but they don't do for the city. (Wilhelmina Stitch.) And though I'm very keen on effects in triple ninon, without the right perspective they cease to be effective. (ECB) In other words, Stella Barnett, you'll oblige me by taking these useless garments off my hands. You needn't wear them. Take them away and bury them if you like; but rid me of them.'

'Please be serious, Mr Sheringham. I refuse to – '

'That is an order.'

'Oh, very well,' said Miss Barnett impatiently. 'Now perhaps you'll let me put my question. Don't think I wish to interfere in the slightest way with your amusements, but do you intend to follow up these remarkable ideas you've just dictated to me?'

'I do,' said Roger cheerfully.

'You don't, I suppose, intend to tell anyone about them?'

'I'm going round to Scotland Yard to do so this very morning.'

Miss Barnett looked at him quite earnestly. 'Then I really do think it my duty, as your confidential secretary, to ask you to consider seriously whether that is wise.'

'How do you mean?'

'I shouldn't care for you to become the laughing-stock of the police force,' said Miss Barnett primly.

'This is touchingly considerate of you, Stella.'

'Not at all. I mean, it might reflect on me. People will say,' said Miss Barnett calmly, 'that if you take leave of your senses, I should have brought you back to them.'

'Oh! People will say that, will they? Then you don't agree with my ideas?'

'I think they're preposterous, and I consider it my duty to tell you so. Fantastic. Why, you told me yourself yesterday that the police had arrested that man, which they certainly wouldn't have done without a clear case against him. Although I saw nothing about it in the paper this morning.'

'Not arrested,' Roger said, hastily skimming over this piece of thin ice. 'No. I didn't say that. They didn't arrest him, as a matter of fact. Some technical difficulty, I gathered. But they've got him under observation, which is the main thing. They know where he is now, and they can get their hands on him any time they like. The bet, if you remember, was simply concerned with him being in the neighbourhood of Monmouth Mansions that evening. The police can't arrest on a mere cause for suspicion like that. No magistrate would grant a warrant.'

Miss Barnett looked at him a little suspiciously, but to Roger's relief did not pursue the topic. 'Well, anyhow, that isn't the point. Really, Mr Sheringham, I advise you most strongly to leave well alone.'

'But I've been so very ingenious,' pleaded Roger.

'It is always possible to be ingenious, if one is content to be far-fetched.'

Roger bowed his head beneath this crushing aphorism. 'Anyhow, get them typed and I'll decide later. I've got to eat my breakfast now.' He went out of the room, not ill-pleased.

Whatever Stella's opinion of the subject matter may have been, her industry was commendable. By the time Roger had breakfasted and dressed the notes were ready for him.

'Thank you,' he nodded, stuffing the carbon copy into his pocket. 'I shan't want you any more this morning, Stella. I – '

'You're not really going to Scotland Yard?'

'Not immediately,' Roger prevaricated. 'Perhaps not at all. I shall see. This afternoon we'll got to a *matinée*.'

'We?'

'You and I.'

'Mr Sheringham, I came here as your secretary; not – '

'Stella Barnett, for goodness' sake do be quiet. It's extremely rude to take up your employer before he's finished speaking.'

'I beg your pardon.'

'I should think you did. I was going on to explain that you will resume duty at one o'clock, in the vestibule of the Criterion; for lunch. You will have your pad and pencil with you, and we shall obtain further specimens of bright young frog-talk. We shall then proceed to the Sapphic Theatre, where I have reserved two stalls, on duty. I want a précis made of *Sinners Three* there, which I understand is the best farce that has appeared since *The Glad Eye*. You will have your pad, and you will take shorthand notes of the development of the plot, the exits and entrances, and the general structure. This will be extremely useful to me if I ever write a farce. Moreover, as I am rather particular about the appearance of the people I am seen about with, you will be so kind as to wear your midnight blue, and the hat and etceteras which I bought to go with it. And lastly, I didn't care to mention it earlier, but that is the real reason why I bought the extra garments not specified in the bet. I wouldn't mention it now, if you didn't force me to by saying you refuse to accept them. In the course of your duties it is essential that you will have to be seen about with me a good deal in public, and I really can't risk my reputation by being seen with a girl who dresses so shockingly dowdily as you do. I don't think I need labour the point; that hat you were wearing yesterday...; you will understand. You will therefore be good enough to consider the garments in those two boxes as your uniform, to be worn when attending me in public. That is all, I think. Oh, no. You owe me a hundred cigarettes. Make them Sullivans as you suggested, yes.'

'A – a hundred cigarettes?' muttered Miss Barnett, over whose face during this harangue an interesting set of emotions had chased one another.

'Yes. You lost that bet. I never told you you'd won it; I merely asked you what was the latest fashionable material for ladies' shirtings. I admit I allowed you to think you'd won it, but I considered that a more tactful way of gaining my goal than telling you straight out that I simply couldn't be seen dead with you in that hat again. You have, therefore, only yourself to blame, as you can't help seeing. Run home now, please, and array yourself in your – no, in *my* midnight blue. And kindly put a little more powder on your face today; I detest shiny noses at lunch. That's all, I think. Oh, no; here's half-a-crown.'

'Half-a-crown?'

'Yes, to buy you a lipstick. Enter it up to petty cash. One o'clock in the Criterion vestibule, please.'

'For that young woman,' remarked Roger to himself with satisfaction, as he ran down the stairs, 'needs taking down about as badly as any young woman in this town, and it's about time someone did something about it. That young man of hers must be a spineless animal. I think I'll get in touch with him and take him in hand. He's in for a hell of a married life otherwise.'

He hailed a taxi and directed the driver to Monmouth Mansions.

Roger did not find in the courtyard of Monmouth Mansions that which he had come to seek. He had hardly expected to do so. That would really have been too great a stroke of luck.

He drove to Scotland Yard, and asked for Moresby.

'Moresby,' he said abruptly, 'I want to talk to you seriously about this Monmouth Mansions case.'

'Then sit down, Mr Sheringham,' Moresby replied genially. 'You know I'm always ready to hear you talk.'

'Trying to break down Jim Watkins' alibi?' Roger asked sharply.

'It's cast-iron,' Moresby said dolefully. 'So far as we can see at present that Lewes alibi of his is absolutely cast-iron.'

'I see.' Roger was going to mention no names. He had come to Scotland Yard solely because he ought to hand over to Moresby the conclusions he had formed the previous evening, whether they turned out to be right or wrong. But he was going to leave the application of them to the police. If they chose to try to fit them into their contemplated case against Jim Watkins, and waste them in doing so, that was the affair of the police. Not a word was Roger going to say about Mrs Ennismore Smith, or what that unfortunate lady stood for.

'Well, Mr Sheringham, is that all you wanted to ask?'

'No, it certainly isn't.' Roger leaned back in his chair and rested one ankle on the other knee. 'Look here, Moresby, I've been thinking about this case, and I believe I've got something to give you which may prove useful. You may have come to the same conclusions yourself; I don't know. But I'm here to tell you mine.'

'In accordance with your duty as a citizen, sir,' said Moresby smugly.

'In accordance with my duty as a citizen of this benighted country,' Roger agreed, 'which doesn't even leave a man his own private thoughts. But before I tell you my private thoughts, Moresby, in accordance with my duty, I want to test them by one or two questions. Will you answer them?'

'I don't know of anything about this case that I shouldn't tell you, Mr Sheringham,' Moresby replied with caution.

'Excellent. Then tell me this first of all. Had the rope that was hanging from the kitchen window a bit of string tied to its lower end?'

Moresby looked surprised. 'Yes, it had.'

'Ho!' crowed Roger. 'A nice little bit of string tied very tightly round it, with just an inch or two loose beyond the knot?'

'That's just about it.'

Roger looked at the chief inspector with pride. 'I deduced that bit of string, Moresby.'

'Did you, Mr Sheringham? Well, well.' But Moresby was highly interested, Roger could see.

'I did. Now, may I see a copy of the doctor's report after the p.m.?'

'I have it here, I think.'

Moresby produced the document, asked no questions, and sat patiently while Roger ran through it.

The latter nodded now and then, as if finding something that he had expected. He put the document back on Moresby's desk and changed ankles.

'This confirms me, I think. Now, Moresby, I'm going to ask you a question and I want an honest answer: had you considered the possibility of the murder not having taken place at 1.20 a.m. at all, but a good deal earlier?'

For once Moresby omitted to smile tolerantly. 'Earlier than 1.20 a.m.?' he repeated, stroking his chin and looking at

Roger fixedly. 'With the evidence of Mrs Ennismore Smith, and all those people who saw the man running away from the place? No, Mr Sheringham, I can answer that quite honestly; we haven't.'

'Then I propose to put an entirely new view of the crime in front of you.'

'Anything that helps to break down the Kid's alibi will be welcome enough, sir.'

'You still have no doubt that the Kid is responsible, then?' Roger asked, noncommittally.

'Oh, bless my soul, no,' replied Moresby with great heartiness. 'It's the Kid who croaked her all right. The trouble is to fix it on the little scoundrel.' From Moresby's tone one might have gathered that the Kid had been suspected of stealing jam from a cupboard.

'Then listen to me – and don't say afterwards that you thought of it yourself. What about sending for that shorthand man of yours? No? Well, I suppose I shall have to trust you.

'Now, there's not the least doubt, as you point out, that the Ennismore Smiths did hear noises above their heads at approximately 1.20, and there's not the least doubt that a man was seen climbing over the courtyard wall, and subsequently running away, at about that time. Let us take those for granted and put them on one side for a minute. What I want to do first is to point out to you that, apart from these two facts, there is nothing to show definitely that death did not take place a good deal earlier.

'First so far as the body itself is concerned. The doctor said at the time that, according to the external signs, death might have taken place as much as twenty-four hours earlier, so we're safe enough there. Now, in my opinion the doctor's remarks in that report on the condition of the stomach provide definite evidence that death did take place earlier than 1.00 a.m. He says that the stomach was not empty. At 1.00 a.m. it would have been.'

'No sir. She had a cup of tea and a currant bun or two last thing. The dirty cup was by her bed, and there were crumbs in the bed. We've had the crumbs analysed, and they're the same as the currant buns in a tin in her larder.'

'Excellent. Then it all depends on what time she had the tea and buns, doesn't it?'

'I don't see how we can find out that.'

'I have found it out. At least,' amended Roger more truthfully, 'the information was presented to me by the way. I had a talk with Mrs Pilchard a few days ago, and she happened to mention that Miss Barnett, who, like most elderly people, was a woman of fixed habits, always went to bed at nine o'clock when she was alone, and always took a cup of tea and a bun to bed with her, "to warm the stomach" as my informant put it. That is news to you, Moresby?'

'It is, Mr Sheringham,' the chief inspector replied nobly. 'And interesting news too.'

'Well, I suppose one shouldn't blame you,' Roger said unkindly. 'The time of death looked so definite to you, no doubt, that you didn't bother to go into the facts concerning it. The doctor's report puts the time of this little meal as one and a half to two hours before death. You therefore accepted it as somewhere between eleven and half-past?'

'We did. And a very reasonable time it seemed.'

'Oh, yes; quite reasonable; but, just as it happens, incorrect. Well, you see what I mean. I looked up the point last night, and so far as I can make out, if she had had this tea and buns at 9.00 p.m. her stomach and small intestine would normally be empty by 1.00 a.m., with an indistinguishable mush in the large intestine. But the doctor says there is much containing matter and currants in both the small intestine and the stomach. He is therefore justified in putting the meal which left these results at from one and a half to two hours before death. And as we know Miss Barnett was alone that evening, and there is no reason to suppose that she varied her usual habit, we are thoroughly justified, from the evidence of the body itself, in putting the time of death at 10.30 to 11.00 p.m. Aren't we?'

'I must agree with you, sir, that it seems as if we are.'

'Well, don't be so grudging about it.'

'Not at all, Mr Sheringham. I think it's a very smart piece of work on your part,' admitted Moresby handsomely, 'and it certainly does give the case new possibilities. But I'd like to hear how you get over the noises at 1.20 and the man who climbed over the wall.'

Roger thought for a moment. If Moresby had spoken the truth when he said that the police were still convinced that Mr James Watkins was at the bottom of Miss Barnett's death, he was anxious not to disabuse them. It was possible to give Moresby a reconstruction on this basis by ignoring one important point altogether and stretching another – the two main points on which his own case against one of the inhabitants of Monmouth Mansions really depended, namely, that the visitor must have been not only a woman but a woman personally known and liked by Miss Barnett to have been admitted at all at so late an hour, and that the visitor, who must have spent a considerable time in the flat after Miss Barnett's death, could not possibly have got out of the building after the bottom door was shut without either leaving traces of a burglarious exit or summoning Mrs Boyd, neither of which alternatives had occurred.

'Let us, for the sake of argument, and disregarding his alibi, which it's up to you to break down, assume that the murderer of Miss Barnett is your Camberwell Kid. You've already told me what happened before the crime, how he came into the building not long after dark and waited in that cupboard, and Beach told me how he might have got into the flat, by pretending to be from Scotland Yard himself. We'll assume all that, and we'll assume that he did not intend murder at all, but that circumstances arose in which he lost his head and committed murder. You agree to that?'

'That's our reading of the case so far, yes.'

'Well, what happened next? As I told you last time I was here, he set the stage for a struggle and noise, and arranged his rope to make it look as if he had climbed down it after the bottom door was shut. I don't know whether you'll agree to that?'

'For the sake of argument,' said Moresby cautiously. 'But you've changed your ground rather, haven't you, Mr Sheringham? I thought you told me last time you were here that it wasn't the Kid at all, but someone copying the Kid's methods.'

'One must keep an open mind,' Roger replied with dignity. 'I may have thought that then. But at that time I didn't know that the murder had been committed so much earlier. One must be prepared to change one's ideas as fresh evidence appears.'

'Just what I always say myself, sir,' remarked Moresby comfortably, and quite without truth.

'Besides, at present I'm reconstructing the case on your own theory of the murderer's identity. And I may say,' added Roger, in his turn untruthfully, 'that it isn't the murderer's identity that I'm concerned with. It's his method, which I consider far more interesting.'

'Anything connected with this murder interests me, even the murderer's identity. Well, go on, Mr Sheringham. You've left him setting the stage and hanging the rope out of the window. What next?'

'Why, he goes down and escapes through the front door just before it's shut.'

'That's certainly more reasonable than what you said last time,' the chief inspector meditated. 'You said then that he went out through the front door, although we were putting the time so much later then. And that was the flaw in your argument about his not having gone down the rope, because he couldn't have got out through the front door. You evidently didn't know that the lock on that door was out of order, and the door couldn't be opened even from the inside without a key to the big mortice lock.'

Roger did not reply that he knew only too well, and that his information had come from Sergeant Afford himself. He merely said mildly: 'And you didn't consider it advisable to tell me? What a reticent devil you are, Moresby. It's an uphill job trying to give you a hand in a difficult case.'

'I notice you haven't given me a hand yet over the difficulty of the man the chauffeur saw and the noises in the night,' Moresby grinned.

'I'm just coming to them. Now as to this running man, we know he isn't your Camberwell Kid on the evidence of the chauffeur, who got a better look at him than anyone. On the other hand, we're still assuming that the Kid is the real murderer. Well, my suggestion is the only obvious one, that the man the chauffeur saw is an accomplice, or accessory after the fact, or whatever you like to call it. I suggest that the murderer, when he realised what he'd done, sat down and put in a few minutes' hard, cool thinking, of which setting the stage and so on was only one result. The other result was the concoction of an alibi – this alibi that's been worrying you so much, of course.

'What he did, on getting away from the place, was to nip round to the man he could trust best, make a clean breast of what he'd done, and demand help. The help consisted in going to the courtyard of Monmouth Mansions, waiting till the chauffeur returned, and then escaping ostentatiously over the wall and running hard for several hundred yards, so as to attract the attention of as many people as possible.'

'The Kid knowing that there was a chauffeur, that he was out that night, and that he would be coming back?'

'I give the murderer credit for having spied out the conditions to that elementary extent.'

'Yes,' Moresby assented. 'I think we can give him that credit.'

'But that wasn't all the accomplice's job,' Roger continued with gusto. 'The other part of it was actually to produce those noises in Miss Barnett's flat that woke up the Ennismore Smiths.'

'Is that all? And how did he do that, Mr Sheringham?'

'Why, by means of that piece of string of course,' Roger retorted. 'Surely you can see that, Moresby? Why, it's the only possible way he could have done it.'

'So it is, Mr Sheringham,' Moresby agreed heartily. 'So it is, sir. What is the way, though?'

'This. Now listen carefully, Moresby, because this really is rather clever of me. The murderer didn't hang the rope out of the window at all; and *that* explains why nobody saw it. What he did was to hang a length of string from the window, which he either had with him or found in the flat, and then he arranged the rope in such a way that it could be pulled down easily from below by means of the string, the top end of which was tightly tied to the rope. *And*, arranging the rope in coils on various smooth surfaces, he stood some china article or such-like in each coil, which would not

189

impede the rope's progress but would be overturned as it went and go crashing on to the floor straight above the Ennismore Smiths' heads; and no doubt a few heavy pieces of furniture were balanced carefully too, like the old trick of the four-brick trap, with the pendent brick supported on a twig, so that they too would topple over and add to the shindy. That's what the murderer did, Moresby.'

'Well,' said Chief Inspector Moresby, 'fancy that!'

Roger pulled the carbon copy of his notes out of his pocket. 'Here, look through these. I've only given you the bare conclusions. Here are the arguments for them in a little more detail.'

Moresby read through the pages in silence. Then he leaned back in his chair and pulled at his walrus moustache. His eyes twinkled at Roger.

'Mr Sheringham, I'm beginning to feel glad I took you round with us last Tuesday. I'll keep these notes if I may. I fancy the Chief will be interested in them.'

Roger grinned with satisfaction. He knew that this was Moresby's way of saying that he had done a piece of really valuable work.

It amused him to reflect that Moresby had no inkling of the far more valuable piece of work that he was still engaged in doing.

chapter fourteen

Moresby had no information concerning the rosary.

Roger was disappointed, Moresby no less so. Both agreed that the rosary ought to be a most valuable piece of evidence, if only one could understand why the devil it was there at all. Roger put forward his arguments upon it at some length. Moresby listened politely, and gave it as his opinion that the rosary had been left by mistake. Roger was inclined to the opposite view, as more amusing. In the end they had to leave it exactly where it had been before, an enigma.

Roger went off to keep his appointment at the Criterion, Moresby to confer with his Chief – a conference in which, Roger knew, his own name would crop up more than once. Roger was not ill-pleased. Moresby's superintendent was one Green, a large and rotund man but without the bonhomie that should accompany largeness and rotundity. It seemed to Roger that Superintendent Green hated most things in this world, but amateur assistance in the work of his own department most.

Mr Sheringham enjoyed his lunch. Stella arrived, punctual of course to the tick, and looking prettier than ever in the midnight blue. Really, thought Roger, this young woman would be completely charming if only she didn't altogether lack any charm at all; it's a pity. But he certainly found her a stimulating companion.

Not very much conversation from the next table was taken down at lunch. Roger was too occupied in the attempt to draw his companion out upon the subject of her engagement. On this topic, however, Stella proved even more reticent than usual. She refused to part with the slightest atom of information concerning her young man, herself in connection with the young man, or even her views concerning marriage.

On one point only did she condescend to enlighten him, but that was an illuminating one.

'Your engagement must be very recent,' Roger hazarded. 'I see he hasn't had time to get you a ring yet.'

'I don't believe in engagement rings,' replied Miss Barnett briefly.

Roger looked at her wistfully. She could be so useful to him as a novelist if only she would. Lively as his imagination was, it quite failed to picture Stella in the throes of an engagement. Why couldn't she tell him, frankly and analytically, her own reactions to the situation? It was nothing less than her duty to the great British public.

As a last resource, he hinted as much to her.

'You want to use me for one of your books?' she asked, as calmly as ever.

'I do, Stella.'

'Is that why you engaged me?'

Roger looked uncomfortable.

Miss Barnett considered the point. 'Well, it's a novel kind of duty, to be engaged by a novelist in order to have one's character studied, but I think it's fair enough; you pay me a salary, and you make what you like out of me. Yes, I have no objection to the situation. You find me interesting then, Mr Sheringham?'

'I do. Most interesting.'

'Why?'

'Because you're so different from any other girl I've met. Are you annoyed?'

'That you should find me interesting? Not at all. I'm pleased, naturally.'

'Not naturally, by any means,' Roger grumbled. 'With any other girl it would be "naturally," but your reactions are quite unforetellable.'

'How fortunate,' Stella replied serenely. 'Otherwise I suppose I should have been dismissed by now. Well, Mr Sheringham, you haven't told me yet whether you are ashamed to be seen with me today?'

'I'm afraid I was rather frank this morning.'

'Not at all. I much prefer it. And I quite agree about the hat I was wearing yesterday. I put it in the fire when I got back to my rooms this morning.'

'You – put it in the fire?' echoed Roger, dumbfounded.

'Of course. After your candour.'

'But I should have expected you to flaunt it at me every day and all day long, after that same candour.'

Miss Barnett smiled gently. 'You're quite right, Mr Sheringham; you don't seem able to foretell my reactions at all. I really don't know why. This one, I should have thought, was obvious. I saw yesterday afternoon that you had exceptionally good taste in women's clothes; quite a flair for them. This morning you condemned my hat; I respect your judgment, I burnt the hat. Isn't that almost inevitable?'

'Stella,' said Roger, bestowing the highest compliment that man can bestow upon woman, 'you talk exactly like a Man.'

193

'So long as I don't look like one,' replied Miss Barnett, almost demurely. 'Must I ask you again? You seemed to me to shelve the question just now. Are you still ashamed to be seen with me?'

'No, I'm not,' Roger said fervently.

'You consider I do justice to your midnight blue velvet?'

'I consider it was an inspiration to buy it and force you to wear it. You do like compliments then, Stella?'

'When they're sincere, certainly; just as I welcome insults when they're sincere too. No – no more wine, thank you.'

'Dash it, you've only had one glass. You can't leave the whole of the rest of the bottle to me.'

'I said, no more for me, thank you. Perhaps you'll learn soon that I inevitably mean what I say. Is that,' mocked Miss Barnett, 'different from all other women you've ever known?'

Roger looked at her gloomily. He had thought fondly that he had taken this young woman down a peg or two in the morning. Now she was thanking him for insulting her, and apparently with sincerity.

Miss Barnett ate a piece of fresh pear Melba with an abstracted air. 'By the way,' she said, dreamily, 'I suppose you're trying to flirt with me, Mr Sheringham?'

'Now why on earth do you suppose that?'

Roger, who had been flattering himself that he had for once been thrown into the company of a beautiful girl without making the slightest attempt to flirt with her, was more surprised than annoyed.

'When a man tells a girl that she's different from all the other women he's ever met, it invariably means that he is asking her to flirt with him,' pronounced Miss Barnett, glancing coolly at her host from under her long lashes. 'Besides, I take you for the kind of man who invariably tries to flirt with any girl he's left alone with for more than five minutes. Anyhow, if you are asking, my answer is no. So please don't try any more.'

'I wasn't asking you to flirt with me,' said Roger violently, now more annoyed than surprised under this unjust accusation. 'I mean I wasn't trying to flirt with you.'

'No?' said Miss Barnett indifferently, far more interested in her pear Melba than her host.

'Because, if we are to explain our feelings, I consider you at one and the same time the prettiest and quite the least attractive girl I know.'

'Oh!' said Miss Barnett, not at all calmly.

'And it doesn't seem to matter to you,' Roger added unkindly, 'whether you take that as a compliment or an insult, since you welcome them both, because it's quite sincere. Will you have some coffee?'

'No, thank you.'

'Then we'll get along.'

They looked at each other quite stormily for a moment.

Then Miss Barnett uncrossed her new stockings, scrutinised her new hat in the new mirror from her new handbag, applied a touch of the new lipstick (duly entered against petty cash), smoothed down her new frock, picked up her new gloves, and announced herself ready.

Roger followed her to the door, muttering naughtily. Sitting there in his clothes and telling him he was trying to flirt with her; nothing in the world he wanted less than to flirt with her; sooner try to flirt with the North Pole; and why the devil shouldn't he flirt with her if he wanted? and why the devil did this girl always make him feel like a schoolboy? and why had he answered her back so childishly and vulgarly? and why did she invariably make him think, say, and do the wrong thing, remaining infernally cool and collected herself? and why the devil *had* he engaged her at all? and why the devil hadn't she the decency to give notice?

But what annoyed him most of all was the knowledge, since she had pointed it out to him, that most decidedly he *had* been flirting with her; subtly, tentatively, ever so faintly challengingly, but quite undoubtedly flirting.

Damn!

He obtained a cheap revenge by keeping her busy taking useless notes throughout the entire play – and disliked himself heartily for being such a cad.

It was a genuine relief when she refused his half-hearted offer of tea after the show, and stated her intention of going back to the Albany to transcribe her notes at once, in order to be free for 'Ask Mama' the next morning. Roger let her go.

It was not until after she had gone that he realised that in spite of her earnestness of the morning, she had not asked one single question about his decision upon her aunt's death, not even whether he had communicated his ideas to Scotland Yard or not.

'She's not human,' Roger groaned. 'Simply not human. No wonder someone murdered the aunt.'

He walked off in the direction of Wardour Street.

The address at which Mr Ennismore Smith purported to carry on business, of the very nature of which he was doubtful, was already inscribed in Roger's dossier. He now strolled slowly past the house, noting the small brass plate on the lintel, 'Carrol and Smith.' Carrol, he knew, was out of the business years ago, and the premises had shrunk from five rooms to one; moreover, with the ebbing of his fortunes 'Smith' had in self-defence become 'Ennismore Smith'; only the elderly little brass plate had remained unchanged.

Roger had no intention of calling on Mr E Smith in his place of business. He wanted the meeting to look quite accidental. Consulting his watch, he saw that it had just turned half-past five. He glanced up and down the street. The place to meet Mr Ennismore Smith was obvious, almost exactly opposite.

Roger crossed the street, entered the *Peacock*, and asked for a glass of beer.

Anyhow, he reflected, still a little savagely, beer is better than tea any day.

He had not long to wait. Exactly three minutes later Mr Ennismore Smith walked in, with the air of one coming home.

Roger affected great surprise. 'Why, hullo, Ennismore Smith. What are you doing here? What'll you drink?'

Mr Ennismore Smith looked vaguely at him. Quite evidently he did not recognise Roger from Adam. But in matters of this sort he was practical enough. 'Thanks, old boy,' said Mr Ennismore Smith. 'I'll have a sherry and bitters.'

A sherry and bitters was placed before him. The two men exchanged the usual conventional nods and becks and wreathed smiles before committing the liquor to their lips.

Roger was thinking quickly. As the man did not recognise him, which would serve his end best, to remind the other of their last meeting, or to hide his connection with the police? The latter seemed the safer course.

For a quarter of an hour, therefore, they exchanged small talk about racing, rugger, and the deplorable state of the film business, without a word upon anything so unpleasant as murder. The conversation was interrupted constantly by Ennismore Smith's greetings of numerous friends, but Roger had drawn him into the corner of the bar, placed him against the wall with himself on the outer flank, and held him there firmly. Sherry and bitters trickled in a constant stream down Mr E Smith's throat.

'By the way,' Roger casually said at last, when he judged that the time and the men were ripe. 'By the way, you had a murder in the neighbourhood the other day, didn't you? I seem to remember you've got a flat somewhere off the Euston Road.'

Mr Ennismore Smith had long ago accepted the fact that Roger knew his name, his business, his habits, his wife, while he himself did not know even his interlocutor's face; but with characteristic lack of enterprise he had done nothing about it. Roger had banked on this.

Now he drew himself up a little, and threw out his chest a quarter of an inch. 'Same building, old boy,' he said, not without pride. 'Flat exactly above ours.'

'No! Do you live in Monmouth Mansions? Why, of course you do. I remember now. That's funny. I've a very old friend who lives in Monmouth Mansions too. Evadne Delamere. I expect you know her?'

'Know her? Know Evadne? I should think I do. Old boy, she's one of the best. One of the very best.'

'Yes. I ran into her the other day, and we had a chat. She told me all about the police inquiries in the building. She seemed a bit hipped over it.'

'Hipped, old boy?' inquired Mr E Smith solicitously. 'Why?'

'Oh, this matter of accounting for your movements that the police always want. She said nobody could be expected to remember exactly what they'd been doing between certain stated hours a day or two ago. In fact she was quite emphatic about it. I expect you had the same trouble?'

'No,' mused Mr Smith. 'No, I don't remember the police asking us anything like that.'

'Well, I expect it's lucky,' Roger said with a slight sneer.

'Eh?'

'I don't suppose you could have remembered exactly enough to satisfy them, any more than Evadne could.'

'Why not, old boy? I'm perfectly certain I could. Why not?'

'I'll bet you the next drink you couldn't,' said Roger promptly.

'Done, old boy,' retorted Mr Smith, no less promptly.

After that, of course, it was child's play.

Mr Smith's account was certainly straightforward enough. He had reached home last Tuesday evening just before six-thirty. How did he know that? Why, for the simple reason that it was an hour earlier than usual, old boy. He'd had a stroke of luck that day, and went home to collect the missus and take her out to dinner and a theatre. Bit of a treat for the poor girl for a change. Easy enough to remember a day like that in these sanguinary times, eh?

'Oh!' said Roger, much disappointed. 'So you and Mrs Ennismore Smith were out for dinner and a theatre that evening?'

'Why, no, old boy, we weren't,' deprecated Mr Smith. 'The missus is a bit old-fashioned, you know. Still believes in paying bills, and all that sort of thing.'

'Don't tell me you were paying bills all that evening?'

'Certainly I wasn't.' Mr Ennismore Smith repudiated such an out-of-date suggestion with scorn. 'But the missus – well, to tell you the truth, old boy, she snitched the windfall for bills. So we didn't get our theatre after all. You married?'

Roger shook his head.

'Ah, well, there's a lot to be said for marriage,' opined Mr Ennismore Smith, with fine philosophy.

'Then what did you do that evening?'

'Why, sat at home, old boy. The whole blessed time. From half-past six till we went to bed at half-past eleven. I wanted to split the difference and go to the movies, but the missus had brought home some damned frock that had to be altered that evening, from the sh – ' Mr Ennismore Smith checked himself abruptly and glanced at Roger.

The latter gathered that the shop was a sore point in Mr Ennismore Smith's life, and one that he strove to conceal, probably without the least success, from his friends.

'You sat together the whole evening, then?' he said easily. 'Most domestic.'

'The whole evening, old boy. Most domestic, as you say. Have another.'

'This one appears to be on me,' said Roger, and gave the order. 'But your wife wasn't in the room with you all the evening? Come, I believe I've caught you out there.'

'She was, old boy. 'Pon my davy she was. Why, who said she wasn't?'

'Didn't I see something in the papers about her being on the landing round about eleven o'clock, in connection with the inquiry into who was the last person to see Miss Barnett alive?'

'If you did, old boy, it was a mistake,' affirmed Mr Smith earnestly. 'Why, she didn't even leave the room the whole evening; not till we went to bed. I'll take my oath on it. Very busy sewing.'

'Now, that shows you how easy it is to make a slip,' Roger pointed out didactically. 'She must have left the room at least once, when she went to get the evening meal ready.'

'Got that myself,' retorted Mr Smith briefly.

'Oh!' said Roger. There was a little pause. 'Well, the drink seems to be on me.'

'Oh, yes, and by the way,' remarked Mr Smith with manly frankness, 'while we're on the subject, I'm in a damned awkward situation, old boy. Left my pocket book at home, and now I've run out of loose silver. Damned awkward, old boy, you see, because I'm meeting a Man – yes, a Man, and – well, could you oblige me till tomorrow, old boy?'

If he calls me 'old boy' again I shall cry like a child, thought Roger, reaching for his pocket book. 'Of course. How much do you want?'

'Well, a pound *would* see me through,' meditated Mr Smith, glancing at Roger with an evidently practised eye. 'Or two pounds would be safer. Or if you could make it three, old b — '

'Here's a fiver,' said Roger.

chapter fifteen

Mr Ennismore Smith had been speaking the truth; of that Roger was sure. Or, at least, what he was convinced was the truth. And the interview had confirmed another impression: that if Mrs Ennismore Smith really had planned and executed Miss Barnett's murder, the very last thing she would have done as well would be to take her husband into her confidence. No, if she had done it she had successfully deceived him both as to her action and her absence from the sitting-room. At first sight her alibi was complete.

But only at first sight. In reality it was full of holes. Mr Ennismore Smith might believe himself to be speaking the truth, but what was to have prevented him from dozing off for half-an-hour during the evening? What was to have prevented his wife from using the well-worn trick of rigging up a dummy in an armchair which, seen from behind by a somnolent husband, would leave him with the undoubted impression that she was in the room? She might even have staged a quarrel, in order to explain the silence with which any possible observations on the part of the husband would be met. There were half-a-dozen holes in the alibi. And yet this was all the merest speculation.

Roger stopped at the nearest telephone for a few minutes, and then sought the Albany, not knowing what to think.

His conscience smote him as he encountered Stella in his study, still working on her notes taken at the *matinée* although it was now nearly seven o'clock.

'Oh, that's all right,' he said, gruffly, because of the conscience. 'No need for you to finish these tonight.'

'Thank you,' Stella threw over her shoulder, continuing to type briskly. 'I prefer to finish them.'

'You'll spoil my nice dress.'

Stella went on typing.

Roger went into his dining-room and mixed two cocktails.

'No, thank you,' said Stella, typing. 'I don't care for cocktails.'

Roger drank both cocktails, moodily watching his too industrious secretary. She looked so charming, with her bright brown head bent over the machine; and she was not charming at all; it was a great pity.

That unknown young man of hers must be a hero, in his way.

She finished the work, and collected the sheets of paper.

'I've just been talking to Ennismore Smith,' Roger hazarded.

'A waster,' replied Miss Barnett briefly.

'Why do you say that?'

'I can tell a waster when I see him.' She looked at Roger; rather too pointedly, Roger thought.

'Stella,' Roger said impulsively, 'I'd like to meet your fiancé.'

'Indeed? Do you want to study him too?'

'Perhaps. Ask him to lunch with us tomorrow, at the same place.'

Stella hesitated for a moment. 'I'm afraid that's out of the question.'

'Why?'

'He won't be in the neighbourhood.'

'Then ask him to dinner with us. We'll go on to a theatre, where you won't have to take notes.'

'It's very kind of you,' replied Miss Barnett competently, 'but I'm afraid it isn't possible.'

'Why not?'

'Why are you so anxious to meet my fiancé, Mr Sheringham?'

'Why are you so anxious that I shouldn't?'

'I'm not in the least anxious that you shouldn't. It's a matter of complete indifference to me. Why do you want to meet him?'

'Well, we'll say, to see if you're as stern with him as you are with me.'

'How absurd you are.'

'Stella, there's something behind all this. Are you ashamed of your young man? Does he wear his collars back to front, or exist on a nut diet? Why are you ashamed of him?'

'How extremely rude you are. I'm not in the least ashamed of him.'

'That's a curious answer for a young woman nominally in love. You ought to be proud of him.'

'I am proud of him. Extremely.' To Roger's eye Miss Barnett looked more harassed at the moment than proud.

'Then bring him to lunch tomorrow. Otherwise I shall really begin to think there's something odd about this young man of yours,' Roger bantered.

'Oh, very well,' said Miss Barnett, jamming on the new hat quite viciously. 'I'll ask him to meet us at the restaurant tomorrow. It's – exceedingly kind of you.'

'Not at all.'

There was a pause, while Miss Barnett arranged stray bits of hair in their proper places under her hat.

'I went to Scotland Yard this morning,' Roger remarked mildly.

'Oh? I'm sorry to hear it. They laughed at you, I suppose?' But Miss Barnett was plainly far more interested in the set of her hair than in Roger's adventures.

'No, they thanked me.'

'And sniggered after you'd gone, no doubt?' observed Miss Barnett scornfully, to her reflection in the mirror.

'What a sceptical woman you are. I can assure you, Scotland Yard hasn't nearly such a rotten opinion of me as you have. No, they did not snigger after I'd gone. They actually took me quite seriously. They actually thought I'd done a valuable piece of work. They were actually convinced by my puerile reasoning.'

'You don't mean,' said Miss Barnett slowly, no longer quite so interested in her hair, 'you don't really mean to say that they agreed with you about – all those complications?'

'They did,' Roger told her complacently. 'Actually.'

She gazed at him. Roger gazed back.

'What are they going to do, then?'

'Oh, follow it up. Tackle the problem again from that point of view.'

'So that's why they haven't arrested that man? They don't think he's guilty now?' Roger could no longer complain of a lack of interest on Stella's part. She presented a picture of extreme interest as she continued to gaze at him, her hazel eyes a little wider than usual, her pretty (but oh, so unkissable) lips slightly parted.

'Oh, yes. *They* still think he's guilty.'

'Oh!' Stella looked thoughtful. 'Oh, I see. But you don't?'

'I do not.'

Stella continued for a moment to look at him thoughtfully.

'Then you're wrong, Mr Sheringham,' she said with decision. 'Good night.'

Roger looked after her regretfully. She really was a most extraordinary girl, and a most exasperating one; but he wished she were staying to share his dinner-table. For once Roger, who had the heartiest scorn for people who relied solely upon human companionship for their amusement, felt lonely.

He did not enjoy his dinner at all, though Meadows had been as ingenious as usual. He could not help wondering whether Stella was having a nice dinner too – and whether she was having it in the company of the unknown hero.

'Damn it!' he thought, in disgust. 'The girl's becoming a positive obsession with me.'

The girl continued a positive obsession with him. After dinner he settled down seriously to work out the flaw in Mrs Ennismore Smith's alibi. On the evidence he had laid before Moresby that morning, confirmed by the doctor's report, Miss Barnett's death must have occurred between ten-thirty and eleven (though he had not thought it necessary to point this out); had Mrs Ennismore Smith really been in her own sitting-room, sewing a dress, between ten and eleven, and must he give her up once and for all, or was there a way round? Roger settled down in front of his fire for as fruitful an evening as the previous one. Yet all he could think about was the extraordinary behaviour of Miss Barnett. In whatever direction he looked, she was extraordinary. What in the name of goodness, for instance, had made her refuse the legacy that had dropped into her lap so happily? Why, it should have been just the opportunity for her, engaged as she was to be married. What did the unknown hero think about it? Did she really want to go on working? It seemed a shame that she should have to work at all. Certainly she was very much wasted as a mere secretary.

'Go away, Stella,' groaned Roger. 'I want to be brilliant about your aunt again.'

But Stella would not go away.

'Hell!' said Roger finally, as he got up to go to bed.

'I don't like the idea of this engagement at all. He can't possibly be good enough for her. What that girl needs is a...'

But at that point Roger Sheringham remembered himself.

Roger had the opportunity the next day of judging for himself whether the man was good enough for her or not. The revelation which was given him at lunch left him more bewildered than ever.

The morning had been one of real work, in which 'Ask Mama' had been finally grappled with, defeated, and got into the post. Stella had arrived for work in the frock which was not the midnight blue, the confection in jade *peau de soie*, with a little satin hat that exactly matched it; altogether a highly unsuitable outfit for a business-like secretary. She had explained shortly that she had thought it best to wear them, as she was to lunch in his company and had no clothes of her own that would not disgrace him. Roger assented that this had been undoubtedly the best course, but gloomily because of a suspicion that the confection had been designed not so much to save him shame as to gladden the unknown hero.

As they entered the restaurant an unmistakably frog-faced young man rose from a chair in the lounge and said to them accusingly: 'You're late.'

'I'm so sorry, Ralph,' Miss Barnett replied meekly. 'Mr Sheringham particularly wanted to get a manuscript into the post.'

'I detest unpunctuality,' pronounced the frog-faced young man.

'Mr Patterson, Mr Sheringham,' said Miss Barnett, not without confusion.

Wonderingly, Roger shook the frog-faced young man's cold, dank hand.

They went in to lunch.

Roger forced his bewilderment under and tried to play the genial host, but it was in a dream that he asked his guests to choose between grapefruit, smoked salmon, or melon. Somehow he had visualised Stella's fiancé as a hefty, iron-browed man, with a cleft chin and a double-bass voice. That she really could be engaged to this little miserable...

'Smoked salmon, thank you,' replied the little miserable.

'So will I,' said Stella.

'I think you'd better not,' said the little miserable firmly. 'Smoked salmon makes you spotty, Stella. I've noticed that. You'd better have grapefruit.'

Stella said nothing. Roger looked at her inquiringly.

'Oh, yes,' she nodded. 'I'll have grapefruit, please.'

The frog-faced one went on to choose her lunch for her. He allowed her very little of what she apparently wanted to have.

Conversation however was not difficult, because the frog-faced one took charge of that. He spent the first two courses in telling Roger how to write novels. Falling under the spell, Roger listened humbly and promised to try to do better next time.

'But of course,' remarked the young man to his fiancée, 'Sheringham writes for the million, so what can you expect?'

'Have you read any of his books?' asked Stella.

'I've glanced through one or two,' said the young man, with a slight shudder.

'Really, you know,' Stella suggested, almost diffidently, 'I don't think he's *so* bad, Ralph. I mean, considering.'

'My dear girl!' protested her fiancé.

Roger had an odd feeling that he was not there at all.

'And how do you find Stella?' inquired the young man kindly, after the fish had been dealt with.

'Oh, well, I – I think she's most efficient.'

'You want to watch her on details. Stella has no mind for details at all. I mean, look at the way she dresses. Did you ever see anything more ghastly, for instance, than that hat?'

Roger, who had chosen the hat himself with some care to go with the dress, felt that he disliked this young man more than he had ever thought he could dislike anyone.

'This hat?' Stella cried. 'Oh, Ralph, I think it's charming.' Roger noticed gratefully that she had not given him away.

'If it were charming, my dear girl, it wouldn't suit you. I've told you over and over again that charm isn't your style at all. You haven't any. Has she, Sheringham? You've noticed that, of course?'

'Well,' Roger said, and discovered to his annoyance that he was getting puce about the ears.

'Stella has no sex appeal,' pronounced Mr Patterson frankly. 'It's a great pity, really, I think. But she may develop of course; she's crude at present; she needs experience, mellowing. Frankly, I'd hoped you might do something in that line for her, Sheringham, but she tells me not.'

'Ralph!' cried the unfortunate Miss Barnett, and Roger noticed with interest that she too had a distinct shade of puce about the ears. He began to understand why Stella had not been anxious to bring her fiancé to lunch.

Mr Patterson had clear-cut views on other matters besides his fiancée. Inevitably the question of Miss Barnett's death cropped up, and though Stella had plainly not confided to the frog-faced one Roger's peculiar interest in it, Mr Patterson held forth on the subject at some length, roundly condemning the incompetence of the police in not having made the obvious arrest.

'I understand,' Roger said mildly, 'that Miss Barnett is refusing the legacy which comes to her in view of her aunt having died intestate.' It was perhaps an observation not in the best of taste, but Roger was interested to obtain the young man's views on that point.

'Nonsense!' said Mr Patterson, giving them succinctly.

'But, Ralph, I – '

'Nonsense!' repeated Mr Patterson firmly. He turned to Roger. 'Stella has some ridiculous idea of that kind at present, but of course I shan't allow it.'

'Won't you really, Ralph?' wistfully asked Stella. 'I'd much rather.'

'Certainly not. I've already told you I forbid you to do anything of the kind. It's merely an absurd whim, and I don't want to hear any more of it.'

'I expect you know best, dear,' replied Stella meekly.

Roger could hardly believe his ears, or his eyes.

Mr Patterson proceeded to give his views on the lack of sanctity of human life. That old woman, he affirmed, was much better dead. She had been no use to the world alive; why lament her? (Roger gathered that if Miss Barnett had been no use to the community alive, her uses dead were considerable; the community in this latter case being identified with Mr Patterson himself.) Her murderer had performed an act of sheer social amenity in removing her. The police might be, and certainly were, incompetent; but the result of their incompetence was altogether admirable; long might Miss Barnett's murderer retain his freedom.

'As an ardent criminologist,' announced Mr Patterson, 'though hitherto merely an academic one, I salute this public-spirited practitioner of the science.'

'Are you interested in criminology?' Roger asked.

'I dote on it,' replied Mr Patterson simply. 'I know the dates of all the murderers of England, and their executions.'

Rather to Roger's surprise, Stella had appeared distressed at her fiancé's opinions, and had been doing her best to prevent him from giving utterance to them, though without success. Now, with a touch of the old Stella that Roger had thought he knew, she picked up the conversation from under her fiancé's nose and deposited it with a jerk on the safe field of athletics by remarking, with complete irrelevance: 'Are you going to the University Rugger Match this season, Mr Sheringham?'

'Oh, yes,' said Roger, recognising her manoeuvre. 'I usually do.'

'You used to play, yourself?'

'I used to trot about behind the scrum and try to look as if I was doing something. Golf's really my game.'

'Oh, is it? It's Ralph's too. He's plus two.'

Roger, who was plus one, managed to stifle the expression of incredulous amazement that rose of its own accord to his lips, and looked at his frog-faced guest with a new respect.

'Really?' he said.

'Now I'm getting too old for anything really active,' agreed the latter, in the gruff tones of one embarrassingly praised to his face. 'Used to be a hurdler.'

'*Used* to be! Why, Mr Sheringham, only last year Ralph won – '

'Shut *up*, Stella!'

Stella shut up.

The conversation, however, remained, between Roger and Mr Patterson, safely on the athletic topic for the rest of the meal.

Mr Patterson then glanced at his watch, and left them as abruptly as he had greeted them. 'Got to catch a train,' said Mr Patterson, and left.

'Ralph lives in Tunbridge Wells,' observed Stella, as if that explained all.

Roger returned to the Albany with his secretary in a somewhat dazed condition; and the more he tried to think, the greater became his respect for the frog-faced man – the more so as Stella, removed from his influence, rapidly reverted to her other self and snubbed his one or two conversational openings ruthlessly.

'The girl's a positive Jekyll and Hyde,' Roger thought, in bewilderment.

He glanced at her, sitting in a jade attitude, in the corner of the taxi. Was she really in love with that fellow? How could one be in love with such a one? If froggie would a-wooing go, one would have thought that Stella Barnett would have been just about the last person on earth to respond to his advances. And yet…

Why, the girl had been positively *humble*…

How the devil had the fellow established this almost hypnotic ascendancy over her? He had only to crook his little finger and she leapt to obedience, wagging her tail as if she liked it – and no piece of sugar ever offered as a reward. It was uncanny.

'Treat, 'em rough,' sighed Roger. 'But, good Lord, who ever would have thought that Stella would have fallen for the mental caveman stuff? Blast that frog!'

Mr Sheringham was not pleased.

chapter sixteen

Roger dismissed his secretary early, after an afternoon spent in struggling desperately with the first chapter of a new novel. By tea-time he had given up in despair the attempt to dictate. With so many things jostling in his brain, the requisite concentration on such an uncongenial task was for once lacking. He ate a moody tea under Stella's eye, now as accusing again as ever, and then almost literally forced the girl out of the flat. He wanted to think.

Settled down in solitary peace, he thrust with an effort all frog-faced young men out of his mind and concentrated on the important job.

It would not be quite true to say that at this stage Roger had finally exonerated Mrs Ennismore Smith. The alibi that her husband gave her was, as he had shown, not without holes; she still stood out as the suspect *par excellence* of Monmouth Mansions; there was still no doubt that both mentally and physically the bare possibility remained that she might have murdered Miss Barnett. But it was really no more than a bare possibility, and indeed never had been. Roger knew that well enough.

Besides, certain inquiries he had caused to be made since his conversation with Ennismore Smith tended if anything to exonerate her; certainly they did nothing to incriminate her.

His telephone call on leaving the *Peacock* had been to an inquiry agent whom he knew as reliable. He had asked for urgent information concerning the Ennismore Smiths' financial position, and whether it had shown any signs of improving during the last week. The report had reached Roger just before tea-time. The Ennismore Smiths, as he had guessed, were in a bad way: they owed money to every tradesman in their neighbourhood, and no one who knew them would give them further credit; so far from improving during the last week their position had grown worse; several writs were out against them, and a judgment summons had been served, and they had been unable to meet it; they might expect to be sold up at any moment.

Roger argued that though the state of affairs was certainly bad enough to warrant, in the opinion of a proud and desperate woman, almost any steps to remedy it, if the steps had been taken the position would almost certainly have been improved, particularly as Miss Barnett's money had been mainly in one-pound and ten-shilling notes and therefore untraceable; and the position had not been improved. Not unthankfully Roger decided that Miss Barnett's murderer must be looked for elsewhere.

There were, he knew, a number of loose ends sticking up still from the case, though he was not sure what they were. Perhaps one of these might give a pointer in a fresh direction. He took up a pencil and notepad and began to make a list of them, jotting them down as they came into his mind.

POINTS AS YET UNEXPLAINED
(Relevancy or the reverse not known)

Half-empty whisky bottle and glass on sitting-room table
– This fits in very well with the police theory of the Kid, but

not with mine. It may, however, be said to fit in with mine as a part of the general stage-setting; but this is not altogether satisfactory, because I have already decided that the criminal is a woman, and there is such a decidedly male touch about this whisky bottle considered merely as a property whisky bottle. Would it not be simpler to consider it not as part of the setting at all but just due to a natural desire on the criminal's part for stimulant after such a nerve-racking experience? This fits it credibly enough into my reading of the crime and has the merit of simplicity; but it does not seem to help in any way.

The candle – This too really fits better into the police theory than mine. If the murderer's whole object was to make it appear that Miss Barnett died much later than she really did, why be afraid of using the electric light? The police say the Kid used a candle because he always does use candles. I can only say that the murderess used a candle because she did not want the electric light to be seen by Mrs Pilchard, who might think her friend was still up and knock. The candle again is not of any help that I can see.

The false teeth – This is a point I had completely forgotten, that Miss Barnett's false teeth were in her mouth although she had gone to bed. The police attached no significance to it. Naturally she would put her false teeth in before talking to a strange man. (Curious that they did not notice that it would be equally and indeed far more natural that she should put on a dressing-gown at the same time.) The same remark applies no doubt to my own theory: naturally she would put in her false teeth before talking to a woman whom she knew, but not intimately. It is not, however, nearly so natural. Many women are as reticent before their own sex as before the opposite, but certainly not most; certainly not Miss Barnett. Would she really bother to have done that? But of course she would not have known before she opened the door who was outside. Which brings one straight back to the dressing-gown. Why the dickens is there this absence of dressing-gown? It was not even among the scattered clothes on the floor. The presence of the false teeth may have no particular significance, but I cannot get it out of my head that the absence of the dressing-gown has.

Absence of vest – While we are on the subject of clothes I may as well make a note of this point, though I can't see that it has any importance compared with the dressing-gown. Moresby said, *à propos* of her slovenliness: 'Well, she wasn't as bad as she might have been. She did undress at any rate. In my experience most women of this type only half-undress, and put their nightgowns on over the rest.' The fact that Miss Barnett did not do this is therefore, according to Moresby, out of character; and anything out of character is worth noting.

And so far as Roger could see, those were the only points in the case that had hitherto received no examination; that they had now done so seemed to add nothing further to its enlightenment.

He reviewed briefly some of the old points. The various anomalies connected with the running man had now all fallen into place, on the assumption of his being the murderer's accomplice. The bundle which the chauffeur had seen him retrieve was, of course, the light coat in which some of the other witnesses had seen him, and which apparently had been discarded further on in his progress. His hat would have been alternately on his head and in his pocket, further to confuse the issue, as appeared to have been his object in these quick-changes. The question of his identity had as yet received no illumination.

Roger realised that he had been neglecting this question. Satisfied with having pinned the man down as accomplice instead of principal, he had scarcely thought about identifying him. Yet such an identification was scarcely less important than that of the chief personage. Besides, with any luck it should be a strong pointer towards the latter, possibly even an inevitable one. How to narrow down this seemingly illimitable field? That was an interesting speculation.

But that was what Roger, without more knowledge of the inhabitants of Monmouth Mansions, found himself unable to do. All he could see was that the man must be the most intimate friend of the inhabitant who had committed the murder. Which inhabitant had such an intimate friend, who could be relied on for support even to the extent of murder? Well, there was only one way to obtain information on that head, and that was to go round to Monmouth Mansions and try to find out.

Roger went.

On the way he checked up such knowledge as he considered he already had in this connection. The most intimate friend of Evadne Delamere was undoubtedly John Barrington Braybrook. But she was ruled out from the role of murderess for reasons already adjudged amply sufficient, while he had an unbreakable alibi. On neither of those two flats need he waste time. Augustus Weller and the Kincrosses had been exonerated even from suspicion, and Roger saw no reason to alter his mind concerning them. Two more flats out of it. Who then remained? Mrs Pilchard, and the Ennismore Smiths. And they too...

'Dash it,' said Roger aloud, in the darkness of his taxi, 'I'm going to examine *someone* tonight. Let it be Mrs Ennismore Smith.'

But the Ennismore Smith flat was not his first call after all. Glancing up at the building as he paid off his taxi, Roger distinctly saw a light in the flat of the late Miss Barnett. It was only just past nine o'clock and the bottom door was not closed. He ran straight up the stairs, and rang the bell of No. 8. There was no reply. He rang again, for a very long time. The door was thrown open. 'Well?' said a voice, not at all a welcoming voice, proceeding from a face indistinctly seen in the twilight from the landing.

'Good evening, Stella,' Roger replied pleasantly. 'May I come in?'

'Really, Mr Sheringham. Is this a business call?'

'Certainly not; it's a friendly one. I take it that we can be personal friends as well as business acquaintances?'

'Oh, no doubt. But in that case I'm afraid you can't come in. I don't receive male friends in my flat at this hour.'

'Good gracious, Stella,' Roger scoffed, 'I had no idea you were so conventional.'

'I'm not conventional in the least,' coldly returned Stella, who was still young enough to rise to this ancient fly.

'Oh!' Roger suddenly realised that he was probably being extremely tactless. 'Do you know – I beg your pardon, Stella; for the moment I'd quite forgotten.'

'What?'

'Why, that you're engaged.'

To Roger's astonishment Miss Barnett elected at this point to blush violently. 'I'm not concealing my fiancé here, if that's what you mean, Mr Sheringham.'

'But I didn't… I mean, why shouldn't you?'

'If you don't believe me, you'd better come inside,' said Stella, almost violently.

'But I do believe you.'

'Come inside!'

Roger went in.

Indubitably there was no fiancé in Stella's sitting-room; or if there was, he was remarkably well-concealed.

'By Jove,' Roger approved, 'You've done marvels with this place, Stella. If it wasn't for those lustres on the mantelpiece I should hardly know it.'

'Will you have some whisky? And a cigarette?'

'I thought you neither smoked nor drank spirits?'

'Both the whisky and cigarettes belonged to my aunt,' Stella explained coldly, proffering a box of Player's.

Roger took one. 'Thank you, but I won't have a drink, thanks. You're right, Stella. I am here partly on business. Seeing a light, I came up, because I should rather like to have another look round, if you don't mind.'

'Are you still worrying over your absurd theories, Mr Sheringham?'

'I am. And they're by no means so absurd as you imagine, young woman. I may look round then?'

'If you really want to,' Stella replied indifferently. 'I'm afraid you'll find the bedroom in rather a muddle. I haven't finished unpacking yet.'

'Unpacking? Have you moved in here yourself, then?'

'Yes. Yesterday.'

'You never told me.'

'I really didn't see the faintest need.'

This being unanswerable, Roger strolled off to the kitchen.

Whatever vague hopes of fresh inspirations or discoveries he had entertained were, however, soon dispelled. Under Stella's strong if shapely right arm the flat had taken on an utterly different appearance. Gone was the squalor. Most of the furniture had been changed. Moreover, any chance of meditative reconstruction was completely spoilt by Stella, who waited for him in grim silence in the doorway of every room he entered, as if suspicious that he would make off with a spoon or a coverlet if not watched.

She was, moreover, so unresponsive to his attempts at light conversation, and so evidently anxious for his absence, that Roger, hard-hided though he could be when he felt the occasion required it, could not think that this occasion did. He took a somewhat subdued departure.

He did not, however, go directly to the Ennismore Smiths'. He went all the way downstairs, to the flat of Mr Augustus Weller. The excellent beer that Mr Weller kept was not his main inducement; he had a favour to ask of that exuberant young man.

Mr Weller was in. His welcome, however, was not nearly so exuberant as before. He seemed subdued, crestfallen. Roger could not help feeling that his invitation to come in lacked heartiness. The reason was obvious (but not plain) on Mr Weller's sofa, rather confusedly patting her hair.

'Mr Sheringham, Miss Peavy,' said Mr Weller despondently.

'Good evening,' said Roger. 'I came,' he said to his host, 'to ask if you could tell me the number of the Kincrosses' flat. I've forgotten it.'

'You wanted the Kincrosses?' asked Mr Weller, brightening. 'I do.'

'You want to go up and see them?' Mr Weller's face was growing lighter every second.

'I do.'

'Rotten,' said Mr Weller, with now false gloom. 'I was hoping you could stay on a bit here. I'll take you up.'

On the stairs Roger took Mr Weller's elbow. 'The *Miss* Peavies don't wear wedding rings, you know; and the best thing to have said when you opened the door would have been, "Mr Weller is not at home," and shut it again firmly.'

'Thanks terribly,' said Mr Weller thoughtfully, 'I'll remember that.'

'And I'll forget it, on one condition. I'm not going to the Kincrosses'. I'm going to the Ennismore Smiths'. But I don't want him there. Detach him for me, so that I can go in five minutes later and not find him there, and have him detached for twenty minutes. Otherwise I'll go back to your flat.'

'Sheringham,' said Mr Weller earnestly, 'detached the blighter shall be. And I agree with you; she's a charming woman.'

'I merely,' said Roger coldly, 'wish to ask her a few question about – '

'You can ask questions about the Aga Khan's grandparents,' interrupted Mr Weller with great cheerfulness, 'so long as you do it in the Ennismore Smiths' flat and not mine. I'll tip him the wink that our Evadne wants him. That'll charm the wart.'

Roger marvelled gently that Mr Weller should be so cognisant of what its principals seemed to regard as a guilty secret.

He waited five draughty minutes on the top landing, noting with approval the sounds from the floor below that indicated the successful detachment of Mr E Smith, and hoped that for all their sakes Mr Barrington Braybrook was not already in occupation of Flat No. 5. Then he went down and rang the Ennismore Smiths' bell.

Mrs Ennismore Smith opened the door to him, after a short wait. The smart, authoritative manageress of the dress shop was only dimly recognisable in the drooping figure, obviously dead tired, who leaned against the edge of the door she had opened.

'Yes?' she asked in a dispirited voice.

'I'm sorry to bother you at this time of the night, Mrs Ennismore Smith,' Roger said briskly, 'but I find I have to ask you a few questions.'

Mrs Smith peered at him in the dim light. 'You are...'

'I think you will remember me. I was present at the first interview you had with Chief Inspector Moresby, in the flat above, last Wednesday.'

'Oh, yes, of course. I thought I recognised you. Please come in. I didn't realise at first that you were from Scotland Yard.'

Roger followed her into the sitting-room. She sat down, and invited Roger to do the same.

Over the back of a chair a dress had been hanging, which she picked up before seating herself. 'Will you excuse me?' she murmured, the moment they were seated, taking up her needle. 'I have some sewing which is rather urgent.'

'Of course. Do you sew every night?'

'Usually.'

Roger nodded sympathetically. She would earn a few more shillings by bringing home the garments that required altering. Probably she would have to conceal carefully from her assistant, in the interest of dignity and discipline, the fact that she carried out the alterations herself.

'You were sewing in this room during the whole evening when the crime was committed, were you not?'

'I expect so,' said Mrs Ennismore Smith wearily. 'I mean, yes, I was. One of your officers asked me that this afternoon.'

'Sergeant Afford?'

'Yes, I think that is his name.'

'He came to see you in Shaftesbury Avenue, didn't he?' asked Roger, pleased to be getting this light on Moresby's activities.

'Yes.'

'To ask you,' Roger pursued, taking a chance, 'whether you heard any noises in the flat above before you went to bed that night – between, perhaps, ten and ten-thirty?'

'Yes.'

'Exactly. And I've come to bother you on the same point, to ask if you can add anything at all to what you told him this afternoon.'

'I'm afraid I can't.'

'No? Let me see, you told the sergeant...?'

'That I heard, so far as I remember, nothing at all. As you know, my husband told him the same thing, when he went to see him at his office afterwards. My husband and I have talked it over together since then, and we're quite sure that neither of us heard anything at all unusual that evening.'

'Yes, but what does that mean – unusual? Does it mean that you heard absolutely nothing at all, or simply the sounds you usually did hear?'

'It's difficult to remember so long afterwards, but my impression is that we heard nothing at all,' Mrs Ennismore Smith replied, looking up a moment from her work. 'Is the point an important one?'

'Possibly. I suppose you can hear noises in the flat above if they're sufficiently loud?'

'They don't need to be particularly loud,' Mrs Smith replied dryly. 'Listen now.'

Roger listened. In the silence the footsteps of Stella on the creaking floorboards were clearly audible above their heads. They ceased, to be followed by a very faint scrape.

'What was that?'

'Miss Barnett's niece. I believe she moved in yesterday.'

'I mean the scrape?'

'She was striking a match.'

'Good gracious, can you hear a match being struck?'

'These ceilings can't be much thicker than paper.'

'Then you must have been able to hear almost everything Miss Barnett did?'

'No doubt, if we cared to listen.'

'I mean, anyone crossing her sitting-room, even on tiptoe?'

'I imagine so. One heard the boards creak.'

'And yet you heard nothing that evening?'

'No. But that wasn't unusual. We very seldom did hear anything in the evening. I think Miss Barnett used to go to bed quite early.'

'Yes, of course.'

Roger was puzzled. Almost certainly the intruder must have been at work between ten and half-past. All those preparations could not have been made noiselessly. At the very least the footsteps of someone moving about the flat must have been plainly discernible. And yet the Ennismore Smiths had heard nothing. Or had they simply forgotten?

'You say Miss Barnett generally went to bed quite early. Would you have considered it unusual, then, if you had heard her moving about her flat as late as ten-thirty?'

Mrs Ennismore Smith paused in her sewing to consider this point. 'Without hearing voices at the same time, to indicate that Mrs Pilchard was with her, yes, I think I should.'

'Unusual enough to remember?'

'At this distance of time, probably not; but certainly the next day.'

'And yet you didn't remember anything of the sort the next day?'

'No, I can say that quite definitely; I didn't.'

'I see.'

But Roger did not see at all. This was most perplexing.

'You're sure you were still up yourselves at that time, ten-thirty? You hadn't gone to bed earlier?'

'Perfectly. I verified that point for your sergeant by looking up our books. I found I had taken a certain dress home for alteration, from the shop in which I work,' replied Mrs Ennismore Smith bravely, 'and I remembered doing it quite well. It kept me up a good deal later than half-past ten.'

'And I understand that you were in this room the whole evening without leaving it once?'

'I could not possibly swear to that.'

'That is your husband's impression.'

Mrs Ennismore Smith smiled ever so faintly. 'My husband is often inclined to be a little more positive than I should care to be myself.'

'You think you may have left the room during the evening then?'

'I should think it quite probable. In fact I distinctly remember doing so once at least. I went into the kitchen to put a kettle on to boil, soon after my husband came in.'

Roger nodded perfunctorily. 'Quite early, yes. But after that? You had your meal in here?'

'Such as it was, yes. But really I can't tell you whether I remained glued to my chair for the whole of the rest of the evening or not. Surely it can't be of any great importance?'

'No.' Roger stroked his chin. 'In any case, during the whole evening you heard, so far as you can remember, nothing at all from the flat above – not even Miss Barnett going to bed?'

'Not even that.' Mrs Ennismore Smith looked up again. 'And perhaps one might call that unusual. It was generally quite obvious when Miss Barnett was going to bed. She had

225

a habit of appearing to drop things on the floor in the process.'

'Her clothes?'

'Perhaps. It used to sound more like a succession of boots. We usually heard her quite plainly from this room, although it isn't directly under her bedroom.'

'And yet you heard nothing that night?'

'No. I may have been too absorbed in my work to notice it, of course, but I seem to have a distinct impression that Miss Barnett had not gone to bed when we did.'

'Humph!' Roger felt more puzzled than ever. Things were not working out at all as they should have done. He made up his mind to confide in his hostess a little more fully, in the hope that her memory might be stimulated.

'Mrs Ennismore Smith, I know you don't understand why I'm asking you all these questions about the evening. I'm going to tell you. There's a suspicion that Miss Barnett may have met her death considerably earlier than we first thought – at between ten and half-past instead of after one o'clock. That's why I'm so anxious to find out whether you heard any unusual sounds during that part of the evening.'

There was no mistaking Mrs Ennismore Smith's surprise. 'But I heard the man upstairs – both of us heard him, after one o'clock.'

'Yes, but we think there may be a different explanation of that. Anyhow, now that you understand what's in my mind, I want you to examine your memory more closely still to ascertain whether you can dig up anything unusual that you noticed that evening, however trivial. Please!'

But Mrs Ennismore Smith, after wrinkling her brow for a minute, had to shake her head. 'Nothing, I'm afraid, except the absence of Miss Barnett's bedtime sounds.'

'Did you hear anyone on the stairs – any surreptitious footsteps outside?'

'I don't remember any.'

Roger looked at her in despair. She ought to have the key to the whole puzzle in her hands, and all she could do was to make it more baffling than before.

'Is there anything I can suggest to jog your memory? Any point of time during the evening that might have a vague connection in your mind? When your husband nodded in his chair – when you finished the sleeves of the frock and began on the waist – just after you pricked your finger?'

Mrs Ennismore Smith smiled her faint smile. 'None of those. In fact the only unusual trifle I can remember during the whole evening is a piece of string blowing in for a second at the kitchen window and then out again.'

Roger jumped in his chair. '*What?* Say that again, please.'

Mrs Ennismore Smith, not without surprise, said it again.

'When was that?' Roger demanded excitedly.

'When I opened the kitchen window for a minute, after putting the kettle on. There was such a draught that I closed it again at once; but in the interval a piece of string blew in and straight out again.'

'The end of a piece of string?'

'No, it looked like the middle of a piece.'

Roger beamed at her. Then his beam changed by slow stages into a stare of something approaching incredulity. 'But – you said you put the kettle on soon after your husband came in?'

'Yes. Towards seven o'clock, so far as I can say.'

'And a piece of string blew in at your kitchen window *before seven o'clock*?'

'Certainly it did. Why, is there any reason why it should not have done?'

There was, apparently, every reason; but Roger did not tell her that. Instead he sat gazing at her like a stuffed owl, till Mrs Ennismore Smith grew quite alarmed. Her visitor was doing a piece of extremely concentrated thinking, but Mrs Ennismore Smith did not know that.

'There's nothing else you can tell me?' Roger said finally, in a somewhat stifled voice. 'Well, I'll get along then. Thank you very much, Mrs Ennismore Smith. Thank you.' He rose as in a dream, and walked to the door like a sleepwalker.

Mrs Ennismore Smith tried to show him out, but he was simply unconscious of her presence. He was trying to reconstruct, all at once, every single idea he had had about Miss Barnett's murder, and the effort demanded concentration.

For the moment his notions were still jumbled. Only one fact stood out blindingly bright: the contents of Miss Barnett's interior were not her bedtime bun and cup of tea at all, they were her tea-time bun and tea.

In other words, Miss Barnett had been murdered not at half-past ten, but at six o'clock.

Every single alibi that the case had provided went west at a stroke.

chapter seventeen

Roger was still thinking rapidly as he descended the stairs. Obviously before he left the building an interview with Mrs Boyd was required. She had been on the watch round about six o'clock. He rang her bell.

The door was opened not by Mrs Boyd but by a short, thick-set man who wore no collar and had plainly not shaved that morning. He looked at Roger inquiringly.

'Can I speak to Mrs Boyd a moment, please?'

'Em!' called the unshaven one shortly, over his shoulder. 'Genelman wants you.' He turned on a carpet-slippered heel and vanished without a word.

Mrs Boyd made her appearance, resplendent in an enormous carbuncle brooch on the large bosom of her black dress, the effect of which was somewhat marred by a dirty apron she wore below it.

'Oh, it's you,' she said, regarding Roger without favour. The implication was that the unshaven one had misled her as regards the character of her caller.

'Your husband?' asked Roger pleasantly.

'My own lawful wedded 'usband,' replied Mrs Boyd with truculence. 'And any objection, young man?'

'Not at all,' Roger said hastily, as Mrs Boyd wafted a spirituous cloud towards him with her words. 'I just wanted to ask you one or two questions, Mrs Boyd. Now can you tell me – '

'No, I can *not*,' retorted Mrs Boyd shrilly. 'And what's more, I will not neither. Coming pestering folks with your questions at this time o' night. I'm sick of you pleece, and that's a fact. Seem to think decent people 'aven't nothing to do but answer silly questions all day long and day out. I tell you flat, I'll answer nothing more today, so take it or leave it.' Mrs Boyd added point to her words by shutting the door heavily in her would-be interrogator's face, and vanished in a miasma of gin.

Not unthoughtfully Roger accepted the rebuff, and took himself back to his rooms. It was impossible to do anything further that night.

With this new discovery the case had become undoubtedly neater. Two or three loose ends were now folded back into place. Once more ensconced in front of his own fireside, Roger reconstructed the crime anew.

The murderess (he still inclined to this sex for the criminal) must have entered Miss Barnett's flat some time between half-past five and six. There was no need to vary the means of gaining entrance. As Mrs Boyd had good reason to know, Miss Barnett had been extremely particular whom she admitted. The vast probability still favoured someone known and respected by her (or of course an unknown, whose mere position demanded respect on sight, but that was most unlikely). Deliberate murder was almost certainly intended, and all arrangements would have been made with the accomplice in advance, so that there would be no need to waste time. That put the likelihood of entrance close to the hour of six.

Having killed the old woman, the whole object of the criminal would then be to leave the appearance of a later hour. With this object the body would be undressed and put into the nightgown. Roger was pleased to notice that two small points which had occurred to him only a couple of hours earlier now made themselves remarkable as two slips on the criminal's part: the false teeth had been left in the mouth, and the body had not been put into a dressing-gown. Moresby's comment on the absence of the underclothes fitted in here too.

As against these, other small facts had played into the criminal's hands. The partaking by Miss Barnett of buns and tea twice within five hours was the most notable of these; but it was by no means outside probability to suggest that this was no piece of blind luck but within the criminal's knowledge, and adroitly used. Then there was the cup of tea by the bedside and the crumbs, so painstakingly analysed by Moresby's orders, in the bed. It was, of course, possible that both these were deliberate plants, but Roger was more inclined to the opinion that they were two bits of luck. He was led to this opinion by the appearance of the bed. Nothing is more difficult than to tumble a made bed so as to give it a convincing appearance of having been slept in; but Miss Barnett's bed had been unquestioned in its convincingness. In other words, Miss Barnett's bed probably had been slept in, and never made; in which case the old crumbs would have remained in it, and why not also the dirty cup on the chair by it? Miss Barnett's slovenly habits made any such things more than likely.

The criminal would then have time to set the stage and make her escape before Mrs Ennismore Smith's return to the flat below, with the consequence that no noises would be heard. The exit must have been effected before six-thirty. Well, a quarter of an hour would be ample for everything – say 5.55 to 6.10. Alibis must therefore be checked for that period, and Mrs Boyd questioned (when sober) as to callers or leavers observed round about those times.

In the meantime, was Moresby to be informed of this vital development, or not?

Roger went to bed on that question.

To bed, but not to sleep…

Mr Barrington Braybrook had not left his office on Tuesday, October 25th, until nearly seven o'clock. Assiduous inquiry at Harridge's Stores, lasting nearly the whole day and necessitating the taking of a clerk in the wine department out to lunch, at last brought Roger this information, backed by the unimpeachable evidence of ledgers.

He cursed the wasted day, and got back to his rooms just after five, tea-less and cross, to find his secretary waiting for him, at her typewriter, in an attitude of patient resignation. Roger rang the bell.

'Meadows is out,' Stella told him.

'Then he'll be sacked when he comes in.'

'He told me it's his half-day.'

'I don't care. I'll sack him. He shouldn't have half-days. I'll sack everyone. I'll sack you, Stella.'

'Have you had your tea?'

'No.'

'I thought not. I'll get you some.' She whisked off with brisk efficiency.

Roger sank into an armchair and began to toast his toes. Really, it wasn't at all a bad thing to have a woman about the place. At least, for some things.

The woman came back, bearing tea and crumpets. She poured out for him. Roger ate his way through three crumpets, and their buttery placidity soothed him. He felt better.

'Why, Stella,' he asked, 'does it take such an infernally long time to find out what a certain person was doing at a certain time on a certain day?'

'Does it, Mr Sheringham? I can't say I've ever tried. I don't see why it should.'

'Nor do I. And yet that's just exactly the thing that nobody seems ever able to remember. If I were to ask a man what he was doing at six o'clock last Tuesday week, as I propose to do shortly, he simply won't have the faintest idea.'

'Then ask a woman.'

'I propose to do that too – and she'll have still less.'

'I don't believe it.'

'It's a fact, my dear girl. It's one of the things that just can't be remembered. Why, even you, with all your infernal efficiency, would fall down over that.'

'How exceedingly dogmatic you are. Is this another bet? I should have thought you'd have learned better.'

'I'll certainly back my contention. What article of attire are you short of at the moment?'

'Never mind that. I'll bet you a level half-crown.'

'My dear Stella, I like to make my bets worthwhile. How about three pairs of – '

'I said, a level half-crown.'

'Oh, very well. A snivelling half-crown it is. Well, win it!' Roger smothered a yawn and inserted the last piece of crumpet into the cavity.

Stella began to do calculations on her fingers. 'At that particular time on that particular day I was sitting in the Coliseum, watching – I think it was a troupe of comedy bicyclists just about then.'

'Stella Barnett, a large sum of money is at stake. You can't expect me to accept your bare word.'

'I'm afraid you'll have to,' Stella said coolly. 'Half-a-crown, please.'

'You must prove it first.'

'How can I possibly prove it? Unless – I wonder if I've still got the counterfoils in my bag?' She got up and fetched it, and rummaged in its interior. 'There you are,' she exclaimed triumphantly, producing two pieces of yellow paper. '"Second house, October 25th." I'm not quite so unmethodical as you imagined, you see.'

Roger handed over half-a-crown. 'I see there are two counterfoils,' he remarked mildly. 'You weren't alone, then?'

'Even I haven't come down to going to the Coliseum alone yet,' Stella retorted.

'What time does the second house at the Coliseum begin? A quarter-past five? If I were engaged to a charming girl,' Roger meditated, 'I shouldn't take her to a place of entertainment at such an unpleasant hour. I should take her at a reasonable one, and give her some dinner first.'

'Mr Patterson – Ralph doesn't live in London,' said Stella, flushing slightly. 'It isn't very convenient for him to be late.'

'If I were engaged to a charming girl,' Roger mused, 'I should study her pleasure, not my own convenience.'

Stella's flush deepened. 'Mr Sheringham, aren't you being rather impertinent?'

'I expect so,' Roger smiled. 'But to tell you the truth, I've had such a tedious day that I feel impertinent. No, you needn't bridle, Stella. I'm not going to make love to you. Not because it's against my principles to make love to another's, but because you're so uninspiring.'

'I suppose,' said Stella very coldly, 'it is part of my duty, as a character for study, to allow you to discuss me in this offensive way?'

'Undoubtedly,' Roger agreed. 'And talking of that, I'd like to meet that young man of yours again.'

'Why?'

'I want to ask him what the devil it is that he sees in you.'

Stella jumped abruptly to her feet, almost upsetting the tea table.

'I must go and call on him, I think,' Roger said lazily. 'Will he be in this evening?'

'I'm afraid I can't tell you.' Stella was jamming on her hat, quite viciously. 'He lives in Tunbridge Wells.'

'So I understand. It's a long way, but I think it's worth it. Because I really believe he'd tell me. What's his address?'

Stella made no answer.

'Temper, temper,' said Roger, maddeningly.

There was a silence.

'What are his hobbies?'

More silence.

'I shall ring him up.'

'You don't know his number.'

'Oh, he is on the telephone? Thanks. Inquiries will get me the number.' Roger got up from his chair.

'Mr Sheringham,' said Stella furiously, 'I forbid you to ring up.'

Roger stared at her. 'Well, of all the infernal cheek. Why?'

'He won't be there. He – lives with his parents. You'll annoy them.'

'Indeed I shall do nothing of the sort. I just want to leave a message for him.'

'What message?'

Roger smiled. 'Well – to ask him to write and let me know why he takes his fiancée to such an impossible thing as a five o'clock music-hall performance, let us say.'

Stella actually stamped her foot. 'Mr Sheringham, you're impossible. You're not to ring Ralph up!'

'But why not?'

'Because – well, because it's so absurd. As it happens, it wasn't him with me that evening at all.'

'Oh!'

They measured each other. The situation, which a moment ago had been farcical, seemed to have changed into something like drama. The room was agog with unvoiced challenge.

Roger dropped back into his chair. 'Oh, very well. But I wouldn't have given you away. I just thought he'd like to run up on his motor-bicycle to have some dinner with me. I suppose he takes you about pillion?'

'No, he doesn't; because he hasn't got a motor-bicycle; he's got a car,' Stella snapped, and then stared. 'What made you think he had a motor-bicycle?'

'I didn't,' Roger returned equably. 'I was making conversation. By the way, Stella, there's something I've been meaning to ask you. I've got to go to an infernal fancy-dress dance next week. Where can I get a fancy dress?'

'I really haven't the least idea.'

'Well, where do you hire yours?'

'I make my own, when I need them.'

'But I can't do that,' Roger said with pathos. 'I'm so unhandy with my needle. Will you make one for me one day, instead of typing?'

'What kind do you want?' Stella asked grudgingly, applying the finishing touches to her coat collar.

'I thought of going as a monk. That's a good idea, don't you think?'

'Why a monk?'

'Oh, well, we're both compulsory celibates, aren't we? Oh, are you going, Stella?'

'Unless there is any work you wish me to do?' queried Miss Barnett, more than coldly.

'No,' said Roger, 'I think you've done it all for me. Good night.'

'Good night,' Stella replied icily.

'Usual time tomorrow morning?' Roger called towards the closing door.

'Naturally.'

For a long time after Stella had left him Roger sat in his study, wearing a frown which gradually deepened. It was, as he knew, Meadows' evening of absence, and on such occasions he dined out. This evening, however, he made no move till his usual dinner-time was long past. For the last time (as he vowed) the case of Miss Barnett's murder held him absorbed.

When at last he rose it was with a feeling of disgust. He was sick of the case, that was the truth. He wished he had never begun on it; he wished he was not the kind of person who is compelled to bring to a finish what has been once begun; he wished he had not solved it. For having done so, he did not know what to do with the result.

It was that question which had kept him in his chair for the last two hours. There had been no fumbling around the solution; that had come to him, full-grown, in a flash of inspiration much earlier. In one instant's illumination he had seen the truth, with every detail neatly fitted round it, even the cake of mud. The rosary, of course, had been the key, as he had felt all along that it would be. How absurdly obvious everything was, now that one's eyes were opened.

But what to do about it? That had been the problem since. The words of Stella's frog-faced young man had recurred to him, and Roger could not but agree with them: Miss Barnett had been of no use to anyone alive, dead she was. On the other hand, her death had been due to a peculiarly callous, premeditated murder. One cannot let such things pass with a mild reprimand. On the other hand again...

In the end Roger had decided his own action. He would give Moresby exactly the same data as had enabled himself to see that truth; if Moresby remained blind, that would be Moresby's fault. And whether Moresby did remain blind or whether he did not, Roger would convey tactfully to the owners of the secret that the latter was a monopoly no longer.

He took up the telephone and asked for Scotland Yard.

Moresby had left, and Roger was put through to his flat in Battersea.

'Hullo?' came Moresby's voice. 'Oh, Mr Sheringham, is it? Well, sir, what can I do for you?'

'This Euston Murder. Have you got your man yet?'

'Not exactly. We're still up against one or two difficulties, Mr Sheringham, and that's a fact. But we've got things well in hand. You can expect to hear of an arrest at any time now.'

'I see.' Roger's tone was dubious; Moresby was an optimistic man. 'On the same evidence as when we discussed things last?'

'The same, yes.'

'Nothing new come to light at all?'

'No, Mr Sheringham, sir, I don't think so.'

'Well, I've been thinking things over, and I'm ringing up to give you three points that have occurred to me, and a piece of evidence that I found out for myself.'

'Indeed, sir?' If Roger's tone had been dubious, Moresby's was no less so. It was plain that Chief Inspector Moresby was sceptical regarding the importance of fresh evidence unearthed by Mr Sheringham.

'Yes, and after that I'm through. The case is quite obvious now, and I'm going to forget it from now on. Tomorrow I begin a new book, and you know what that means. This is the piece of evidence – or, rather, the conclusion from it: Miss Barnett was murdered not at ten-thirty but at six o'clock.'

There was a silence at the other end of the line.

'Did you say something about evidence, Mr Sheringham?' Moresby asked with care.

'I did.' Roger passed on the two items of evidence which proved his statement.

'I see,' said Moresby, very thoughtfully.

'And these are the three points I want to bring to your attention.' Roger mentioned the first.

'Oh, well, we knew *that*, sir, of course.'

'You did? Good. But did you know this? My second point: Miss Barnett smoked Player's cigarettes.'

'She did, sir. I saw the box. But I don't...'

'And here is the third point: nuns hunt in couples.'

'What!'

'Think it over,' advised Roger, and rang off.

He glanced at his watch. It was a quarter past eight.

He took up the receiver again and asked for another number; that of the reliable inquiry agent. Though assurance may be sure, there is no harm in making it doubly so.

chapter eighteen

Roger broke off the conversation about the Coliseum.

'I'll dictate,' he said, and took up a dictating position on the hearthrug.

Stella looked up. 'Am I to take down in shorthand, or on the typewriter?'

'The typewriter. Head the page "Synopsis".'

'Is this for the novel you began the day before yesterday, or something new?'

'Something quite new. Don't be surprised,' Roger said with a faint smile, 'if you recognise some of the people. I told you I was studying types for a new book. I'm going to put it down in synopsis while it's fresh in my mind.'

Stella nodded.

'Miss Barnstaple is an elderly woman, living alone in a top flat in a block of mansions,' Roger began, in measured phrases. 'She is a recluse, with no friend but another elderly woman occupying the other flat on the same floor, a Mrs Roach. Miss Barnstaple has a private income of comfortable dimensions. She is also a miser, and keeps a large sum of money in a box under her bed, a fact which is rumoured freely among the other inhabitants of the building and in the neighbourhood generally.'

Stella's eyebrows rose a little as her hands darted among the keys. It was plain that she considered this opening not altogether in the best of taste.

'Miss Barnstaple – call her Mrs B for short,' Roger went on, 'is slovenly in her habits, dirty, and careless. Her friend, Mrs Roach, is in many ways a pale edition of her, but far more likeable. She too had a comfortable income, but by unwise speculation has recently lost large sums. Her financial position is at the moment not secure – By the way, this is pure fiction, you understand.'

'Of course,' Stella said briefly.

'Also in a difficult position financially are the Pevensey Joneses, a middle-aged couple who live in a flat below Miss B. He is vaguely connected with the theatrical business, she manages a small hat shop in Wardour Street for a firm of Jews. Characters: PJ, weak, genial, a charming sponger, would be shady if he had the nerve; Mrs PJ, proud, plucky, dead honest to the last farthing – Got that?'

'Yes.'

'The caretaker of the building is a Mrs Floyd, truculent, unobliging, quarrelsome, but efficient; inclined to drink when cash is free. Her husband much the same; by trade, I think, a jobbing plumber. We won't bother for the time being about the other inhabitants of the Mansions.

'One day, at about – Oh, I was forgetting. Cross that out. New paragraph. Miss Barnstaple has a niece, Ella Barnstaple, a pretty, athletic girl. (This is the heroine, of course. Purely fiction.) By a curious family history which we need not dwell on at the moment, Miss B has never seen her niece; but that does not appear to worry niece or aunt. This niece, I should say, is engaged to be married to an intelligent young man and ex-hurdler, Randolph Pickering (hero), who lives at Sevenoaks (a town quite near another place called Tunbridge Wells, in Kent, you may remember). Got that?'

Stella nodded.

Her eyebrows rose again as Roger proceeded.

'One afternoon Miss Barnstaple is found murdered. She is lying, in her nightdress, in the bedroom. The bed is rumpled, as if she had been in it when roused to open the door to her murderer. The doctors cannot put the time of death more definitely than that it must have taken place more than twelve hours previously and less than twenty-four. The flat is in a state of considerable upheaval, and a vigorous search has evidently taken place. The box under her bed in which Miss B kept her money is empty. The whole crime bears evidence of a certain professional criminal whose methods are known to the police, and for whom an official hue-and-cry is at once raised. This is what the murderer intended, though I cannot think that the fact of the crime being attributed at once to a particular individual was foreseen; that was just a stroke of luck. Got that?'

'Yes, but...' Stella hesitated. 'You don't surely intend to write a novel on these lines, Mr Sheringham?'

'Why not? I've got an excellent plot out of that affair. It may strike you at first sight as a little fantastic, but I can defend it. Ready?

'The crime was actually carried out in a most ingenious way. The problem before the murderer was to obtain entrance to and exit from the building with no possibility of recognition, or subsequent identification. Some kind of disguise was necessary. It must, moreover, be a disguise which would in itself afford an excellent excuse for ringing Miss Barnstaple's bell, with the object, of course, of ascertaining whether she were alone or not; and if the former for getting inside the flat. Moreover, it must be a disguise which would cause no remark. In the end the disguise chosen was the really excellent one of a nun, or Sister of Mercy, collecting charitable subscriptions – a common sight in London, as of course you know. So meticulously was the part played that a call was actually made on the housekeeper, Mrs Floyd, as in the ordinary way of course it would be; the object of this would be to avert suspicion from the nun should anyone else see her inside the building. Indeed, only one mistake was made here, namely, forgetfulness of the fact that nuns invariably go about in pairs; either they don't trust each other, or they don't trust the male inhabitants of London, but see them singly one never does.

'The successful adoption of this disguise (and for a long time it was completely successful) gives us one facet of the criminal's character, ability to act a part. If, therefore, we have among the same set of characters one with ability to act a part we have a valuable pointer towards the criminal's identity, haven't we?'

'Are you addressing an argument to me, Mr Sheringham, or dictating a synopsis?' asked Stella coolly.

'Perhaps a little of both,' Roger admitted. 'Anyhow, take it down exactly as I speak it. Am I going too fast?'

'Not in the least.'

'Very well. Another facet of the same character is afforded by the carefully staged appearance of Miss Barnstaple's flat after the murder. It was quite obvious that it had been prepared by somebody thoroughly conversant with the method of detection used so much by Scotland Yard, the *modus operandi*. Everything was carefully arranged to give the appearance of the work of a professional criminal; rope, candle, gloves, dirtied whisky glass, everything. This could only be done by somebody sufficiently interested in criminology to have read with close attention descriptions of the appearance of other similar flats or houses as the police see them after a murder.'

Roger paused, but Stella neither spoke nor looked at him. To all appearances she was quite indifferent to this remarkable synopsis, if not actually bored.

'The murder, I should have said, took place a few minutes after six o'clock. The stage was set by the murderer, therefore, with two objects: one to make it look like the work of a professional, the other to make it appear that Miss Barnstaple had been killed seven whole hours later. The murderer, of course, had found out enough about his victim's habits to be practically certain that no one would call on her in the interim; and if anyone did, refusal to answer the bell would not be in the least out of character. To effect this deception, therefore the body was undressed and put into a nightgown. Some crumbs in the bed, and a dirty tea cup on the chair by it, left there from the night before, were two lucky accidents to bear out this deception, but a mistake was made in not removing the false teeth from the mouth. Also the body was *too* undressed. A woman of that description would retain at least her vest, and probably her stocking too – Did you say anything?'

'You really want me to go on taking this down?' Stella asked with some asperity.

'Why not?'

'It seems so totally unnecessary.'

'It's not unnecessary in the least, I promise you. Where were we? Oh, yes. Well, we needn't bother to put down the accomplice's part in pulling the rope through the window and causing the noises that were heard in the flat below. You can add that later from the notes in the dossier. We'll get on to the interesting part, about the heroine.

'I'm going,' said Roger, with slow deliberation, 'in this story to make the heroine the murderess. You don't mind, Stella, do you?'

They stared at each other.

Stella's face went first very pale and then very flushed. 'Why should I?' she asked, in a voice that was low but just as controlled as ever.

'Why indeed?' Roger said briskly. 'Then I'll tell you how it was done. In my story, of course.

'The niece had taken two tickets for the second house at the Coliseum, which begins at 5.15 p.m. She was not accompanied, however, by her fiancé, who was at home for dinner that night, which means that he must have left London quite by six o'clock. As a matter of fact, I happen to know that he was home before seven, so that he must have caught a train not later than half-past five.'

'How do you know that?' Stella interposed quietly.

'I took the trouble to find out – in my story of course. I consulted an inquiry agent before I went to the Coliseum last night. His report came through by midnight; it was an easy job. But about that niece. She admits that she went alone to the Coliseum because at the last moment her girlfriend could not come with her. Probably she put her coat over the vacant seat; however, we needn't go into that. The important thing is that she wasn't present during the whole performance. She missed, for instance, both the sketch "Turkish Cigarettes" and "The Melody Three," both of which were in the bill last week. Moreover, as far as I could reckon, both would have occurred between a quarter to and a quarter past six. Yes?'

Stella was staring at him. 'Is this your idea of being funny, Mr Sheringham? I remembered them both perfectly, as soon as you described them. I – '

'Yes; well, never mind. This is merely fiction, remember. In my story, what the niece does is to heave her coat and things on the seats and absent herself for half-an-hour or so. Either with her, or deposited in some convenient place, she would have a nun's habit, so easy to slip on in a few seconds over ordinary clothes; the long skirts would hide even her high-heeled shoes. It could be done on a tube stairs, or a public lavatory – anywhere.

'Then she goes to Monmouth Mansions. Her business there does not take all told more than a quarter of an hour, because she is an efficient girl and she has rehearsed it all very thoroughly. By twenty minutes past six she is back in her seat in the Coliseum, with six hundred pounds or more in her attaché case, and her part of the job is done with. She retains, of course, the counterfoils of her tickets instead of throwing them away in the usual way. And she is very ready, subsequently, to volunteer information of where she was at that particular time.

'Apart from the others I mentioned, the only slip she has made is the depositing of the piece of mud on the kitchen linoleum; but that isn't really her fault because it was given her to deposit and she was only carrying out orders. The slip lies in the fact that it is a distinctive kind of mud. As it happened, the police identified it as coming from the Bracingham district. But Tunbridge Wells – I mean, Sevenoaks is only six miles from Bracingham, isn't it?

'Well, that's finished her part. At eleven o'clock that same night her fiancé goes to bed. That's in evidence. What is not in evidence is that at eleven-thirty he must have got out of the house, taken out his car, and come back to London – there to play his part, as set out in those notes you took down for me the other day. And the only slip *he* made was also one he couldn't very well help, namely, in having a face like a frog's. The chauffeur (whose evidence you may remember) mentioned to me that the man he saw climbing, *or hurdling*, over that wall seemed to be grinning to himself. I think that's a very good description of the hurdling grimace of an already frog-faced young man, don't you?

'Did I say the niece made no other slips? Well, I don't know whether you can call it a slip to use the rosary at her waist for the weapon of strangulation; because if you think long enough, rosaries do suggest nuns. But you certainly have to think a very long time before the connection occurs.

'It was an odd coincidence that the niece should have obtained a post afterwards as secretary to a novelist who happened to be interested in the detection of crime in general, and of her own in particular. I don't know whether it wouldn't have been better if she hadn't been quite so crushing over the really ingenious discoveries he made, or had evinced a little more of the interest she must have been feeling in them; because her indifference certainly did strike him as a bit overdone, in the circumstances. But her first indignant refusal of the legacy was clever, and of course it was so easy to come round afterwards on her fiancé's advice. (By the way, Miss Barnstaple would have left a will, of course: the niece found and destroyed it.) She was just a shade too anxious to get on with the cleaning of her aunt's flat, and eliminate any traces which the police might have overlooked. But on the whole she played her part all through just as well as she played it that afternoon in the Shaftesbury Avenue shop.

'That's how my story goes, Stella.'

Stella had not made any pretence of taking down Roger's last speeches. She had been sitting humped in her chair and gazing at him with a suffused face and teeth clenched into lower lip.

For an appreciable interval now she did not speak. At last she managed to utter, in a stifled voice: 'Mr Sheringham, I-I-I-' Then her astonishing self-control gave way. She plunged her face into her hands and her body shook.

Roger looked at her with embarrassment. Had he been wise to tell her so straightly? He had meant to wrap it up more. He had committed himself much more deeply than he had intended. Matters could not possibly be left now as he had meant to leave them. Idiot that he was, he should have hinted only, keeping up the guise of fiction, not having blurted the whole thing straight out. This was going to be the very devil...

The telephone bell rang, and he went across mechanically to answer it.

'Mr Sheringham?' said Moresby's voice. Roger thought it sounded more genial than ever. 'Thought you'd like to know, sir, that it's all over bar the shouting.'

'Eh?' said Roger.

'Acting on the hint you gave me yesterday, I got busy last night and pulled Lil in – the Kid's girl, you remember. I'd tried before, but she wouldn't talk. Last night I got her to. How? Oh, well, the Kid's pretty serious about this other girl in Lewes, and Lil didn't know that. He'd told her he was just making up to her, to make sure of the alibi. We tipped Lil the wink that that was all my hat; and when she'd properly got it into her head she opened her mouth all right. Nothing like jealousy to make 'em talk.

'Well, I congratulate you, Mr Sheringham. It all happened just as you said. You mentioned, in your first point, that a place of public entertainment wasn't a good alibi. Well, we knew that, though we thought the times didn't fit. Of course I was suspicious about that alibi from the first. He volunteered it all so pat. Anyhow, they had a box at the cinema, and the Kid put on his nun's rig-out there. He told Lil he'd be back in half-an-hour, but it was over an hour before he got back, in a frightful stew. He told her all about it, and showed her the cash. He'd never meant to commit murder, of course. But he'd kept his head, and arranged things just like you said he did, and emptied an ashtray into that cupboard on his way down. He wanted Lil to go and pull the rope down that night, but she jibbed. The idea of the man running and being seen came from her.

'In the end the Kid went round to a pal of his, Charley Davies, and told him of the hole he was in. Charley agreed to pull the rope and run away, for half the doings. We know Charley all right. We pulled him in an hour ago, and he's come across. Both he and Lil are accessories after the fact of course. We shall charge him, but we let Lil turn King's Evidence; it was worth it to us. I've just been on the telephone to Lewes. The Kid's there all right (he's never been out of observation of course), and they're going to make the arrest for us.

'And I must say, Mr Sheringham, in fairness, that it's really due to you that we're able to get him so soon.'

'Yes,' said Roger mechanically.

'We'd have got him in the end all right by ourselves of course; we always do; but you saw just a few yards ahead of us all the time.'

'Yes,' said Roger.

'The Chief's mighty pleased, I can promise you. He'll be on the line himself in a few minutes to tell you. Thought you might like to hear from me first.'

'Thank you, Moresby,' said Roger, automatically, and hung up the receiver as one in a dream.

He looked at Stella. She was still rolling about in her chair, a handkerchief to her mouth. Roger had seldom seen a girl so overcome by laughter.

It is in moments of great crisis that the real man shows himself. Roger was at one of the great crises of his life. If he did not grasp the situation firmly this girl would go on bursting into hysterical merriment at the mere mention of his name as long as she lived. Probably she would turn over in her grave for a snigger from time to time when Roger Sheringham got on to the psychical ether.

Somehow he produced a smile. 'I was hoping, Stella,' he said, 'that I'd frightened you. It was a pretty good case I managed to put up against you. Perhaps I oughtn't to have pulled your leg like that, but – '

'You meant it!' Stella choked. 'You really thought – ooooohuh-huh-huh-huh-HUH!'

'My dear girl,' said Roger, pained. He really was pained. Dash it, the girl should believe him.

But Stella very obviously did not believe him. Roger might have reflected that it was nice to see Stella being human at last, but he did not.

She continued to give way to her mirth. The tears poured down from her pretty eyes over her pretty cheeks and into her pretty open mouth, but Roger found no joy at all in this prettiness.

The telephone bell rang again.

It was Sir Arthur Macfarlane, the Assistant Commissioner, and he had some very complimentary things indeed to say to Roger. Roger listened to them with one ear only; the other ear was busy attending to the sounds, now more stifled, that still issued from Stella.

Then an idea occurred to him; a really great idea, worthy of the man. 'Sir Arthur,' he said, 'do you mind repeating the gist of that to my secretary? She's a most sceptical young woman, and refuses to believe that I've helped you one little bit.'

Sir Arthur intimated his readiness to see that such mere justice was done.

Roger handed the receiver to Stella. 'Control yourself, woman, for goodness' sake. The Assistant Commissioner for the Criminal Investigation Department wants to speak to you.'

Stella took the receiver and listened. Gradually her face changed. From mirth it registered incredulity, from incredulity belief, from belief to penitence, from penitence respect, from respect admiration. Roger remarked these changes with satisfaction.

She hung up the receiver. 'You really were pulling my leg, then?' she asked, in quite a humble voice.

'I told you so,' Roger replied airily. 'Apparently I did it better than I expected. I'm sorry I had to take the name of your fiancé in vain to be so successful.'

Stella began to repair the ravages of her merriment. 'You needn't bother about that,' she said, busy with powder-puff and mirror. 'One good leg-pull deserves another. After that I'd better confess too. I'm not engaged. I never have been.'

'What! But you distinctly told me...'

'Yes, because I thought I'd be safer,' Stella said frankly. 'You look to me like the sort of man who'd make love to any unengaged secretary, and all that nonsense; so I invented a fiancé. Then when you insisted on meeting him I had to ask Ralph Patterson to take the post for a lunch-hour. The Pattersons are my oldest friends. Ralph and I were practically brought up together.'

'But why tell me now?'

'Oh, I couldn't have kept it up much longer. My acting works best in curtain-raisers, not five-act dramas. Besides, you'd detect it.'

'Then you're not engaged at all.'

'That,' said Stella gently, 'is rather the idea.'

Roger took a deep breath. 'Stella, will you marry me?'

'No,' said Stella.

'Thank God,' said Roger.

ANTHONY BERKELEY

DEATH IN THE HOUSE

When Lord Wellacombe, the secretary of state for India, collapses in the House of Commons and dies, everyone suspects a stroke. His death causes political waves as a successor is sought and there is the question of a bill to be put through. But then tests show Wellacombe to have been poisoned and not by any conventional method – a thorn covered in South American poison is discovered under the dead man's coat collar. Is this the work of an international terrorist or someone closer to home?

'Anthony Berkeley is the supreme master not of the "twist" but of the "double-twist"!' – *The Sunday Times*

JUMPING JENNY

A Roger Sheringham case.

Gentleman sleuth Roger Sheringham is at a fancy-dress party where the theme is murderers and victims. The fun takes a sinister turn however when a real victim is discovered hanging on the roof. Is it suicide – or a perfect murder?

Anthony Berkeley

The Layton Court Mystery

A Roger Sheringham case.

Mr Victor Stanworth, an apparently carefree sixty-year-old, is entertaining a party of friends at his summer residence, Layton Court. When one morning he is found shot dead in the library it is hard to believe it is either suicide or murder. As one of the country-house guests, gentleman sleuth Roger Sheringham resolves to solve the murder. As he pursues the truth he does not conceal any of the evidence, and the reader is able to follow his detection work to the conclusion of this original mystery story.

Murder in the Basement

A Roger Sheringham case.

'Don't come down, Molly. There – there's something pretty beastly here. I must get a policeman.'

When Reginald and Molly Dane return from their honeymoon to a new house, they are curious to explore the cellar. Reginald notices a corner where the bricks have been inexpertly put back to cover a hole dug in the floor. Convinced he will find treasure he takes a pickaxe to it – but discovers a body of a woman in a shallow grave, not treasure in a chest. Chief Inspector Moresby and gentleman sleuth Roger Sheringham are soon on the case. What was the victim's identity? Why was she shot through the back of the head and why was she buried naked except for a pair of gloves?

ANTHONY BERKELEY

THE POISONED CHOCOLATES CASE

Roger Sheringham's most famous case.

In this, the best-known of Anthony Berkeley's novels, amateur detective Roger Sheringham investigates his most famous case. When Joan Bendix makes a bet with her husband for a box of chocolates, no one imagines that winning will cost her her life. The seven she eats poison her, and the two her husband eats nearly kill him. The Sheringham Crime Circle find the unusual case baffling, but eventually come up with some very interesting theories – which they then proceed to disprove one by one. Due to a series of false clues the identity – and motive – of the killer appears to be out of reach...

THE SILK STOCKING MURDERS

A Roger Sheringham case.

Gentleman sleuth and novelist Roger Sheringham would not have ordinarily been curious about the suicide of chorus girl Miss Unity Ransome. However when he receives a cry for help from a country parson attempting to trace his missing daughter Janet in London he finds himself involved. And when three other young women are found hanged dead by silk stockings, Sheringham realises that what he is investigating is actually murder.

OTHER TITLES BY ANTHONY BERKELEY AVAILABLE DIRECT FROM HOUSE OF STRATUS

Quantity		£	$(US)	$(CAN)	€
	DEATH IN THE HOUSE	6.99	12.95	19.95	13.50
	JUMPING JENNY	6.99	12.95	19.95	13.50
	THE LAYTON COURT MYSTERY	6.99	12.95	19.95	13.50
	MURDER IN THE BASEMENT	6.99	12.95	19.95	13.50
	NOT TO BE TAKEN	6.99	12.95	19.95	13.50
	PANIC PARTY	6.99	12.95	19.95	13.50
	THE PICCADILLY MURDER	6.99	12.95	19.95	13.50
	THE POISONED CHOCOLATES CASE	6.99	12.95	19.95	13.50
	ROGER SHERINGHAM AND THE				
	VANE MYSTERY	6.99	12.95	19.95	13.50
	THE SECOND SHOT	6.99	12.95	19.95	13.50
	THE SILK STOCKING MURDERS	6.99	12.95	19.95	13.50
	TRIAL AND ERROR	6.99	12.95	19.95	13.50

ALL HOUSE OF STRATUS BOOKS ARE AVAILABLE FROM GOOD BOOKSHOPS
OR DIRECT FROM THE PUBLISHER:

Internet: **www.houseofstratus.com** including synopses and features.

Email: **sales@houseofstratus.com**
info@houseofstratus.com
(please quote author, title and credit card details.)

Tel: **Order Line**
0800 169 1780 (UK)
International
+44 (0) 1845 527700 (UK)

Fax: **+44 (0) 1845 527711 (UK)**
(please quote author, title and credit card details.)

Send to: **House of Stratus Sales Department**
Thirsk Industrial Park
York Road, Thirsk
North Yorkshire, YO7 3BX
UK

PAYMENT

Please tick currency you wish to use:

☐ £ (Sterling)   ☐ $ (US)   ☐ $ (CAN)   ☐ € (Euros)

Allow for shipping costs charged per order plus an amount per book as set out in the tables below:

CURRENCY/DESTINATION

	£(Sterling)	$(US)	$(CAN)	€ (Euros)
Cost per order				
UK	1.50	2.25	3.50	2.50
Europe	3.00	4.50	6.75	5.00
North America	3.00	3.50	5.25	5.00
Rest of World	3.00	4.50	6.75	5.00
Additional cost per book				
UK	0.50	0.75	1.15	0.85
Europe	1.00	1.50	2.25	1.70
North America	1.00	1.00	1.50	1.70
Rest of World	1.50	2.25	3.50	3.00

PLEASE SEND CHEQUE OR INTERNATIONAL MONEY ORDER
payable to: HOUSE OF STRATUS LTD or card payment as indicated

STERLING EXAMPLE

Cost of book(s):. . . . . Example: 3 x books at £6.99 each: £20.97
Cost of order:. . . . . Example: £1.50 (Delivery to UK address)
Additional cost per book:. . . . . Example: 3 x £0.50: £1.50
Order total including shipping:. . . . . Example: £23.97

VISA, MASTERCARD, SWITCH, AMEX:

☐ ☐ ☐ ☐ ☐ ☐ ☐ ☐ ☐ ☐ ☐ ☐ ☐ ☐ ☐ ☐ ☐ ☐ ☐

Issue number (Switch only):

☐ ☐ ☐

Start Date: Expiry Date:

☐ ☐ / ☐ ☐   ☐ ☐ / ☐ ☐

Signature: _____

NAME: _____

ADDRESS: _____

COUNTRY: _____

ZIP/POSTCODE: _____

Please allow 28 days for delivery. Despatch normally within 48 hours.

Prices subject to change without notice.
Please tick box if you do not wish to receive any additional information. ☐

House of Stratus publishes many other titles in this genre; please check our website (**www.houseofstratus.com**) for more details.